ALSO BY FRANK LENTRICCHIA

Johnny Critelli

AND

The Knifemen

TWO NOVELS BY

FRANK LENTRICCHIA

SCRIBNER

SCRIBNER
1230 Avenue of the Americas
New York, NY 10020

Text set in Garamond No. 3

DESIGNED BY ERICH HOBBING

Manufactured in the United States of America

1   3   5   7   9   10   8   6   4   2

Library of Congress Cataloging-in-Publication Data
Lentricchia, Frank.
[Johnny Critelli]
Johnny Critelli; and, The knifemen: two novels/by Frank Lentricchia.
p. cm.
I. Lentricchia, Frank. Knifemen. II. Title. III. Title. Knifemen.
PS3562.E4937J64   1996b
813'.54—dc20   96–11133   CIP

ISBN 0-684-81408-0

AUTHOR'S NOTE

Utica—a classic American ethnic town, of about seventy thousand, and since the late 1950s in slow decline of population—is located in the center of New York State, 233 miles north by northwest of New York City, by way of the New York State Thruway: a well-kept toll road.

Johnny Critelli

To My Mother
Ann Iacovella Lentricchia
and to My Father
Frank John Lentricchia

Fabled by the daughters of memory.
And yet it was in some way if not
as memory fabled it.

JAMES JOYCE, *Ulysses*

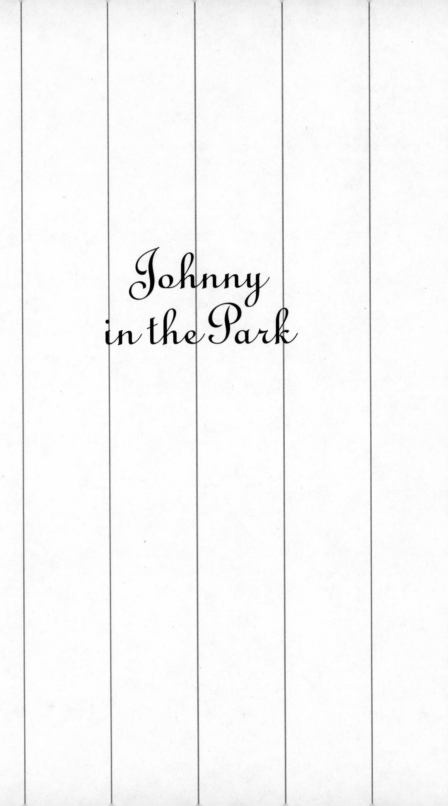

Johnny
in the Park

$\mathcal{N}$aturally, at the time, he was bored, and he saw nothing. Lefty? People had trouble remembering his name. It was the summer of 1956 and he was sixteen, with a red-hot driver's license, so what the heck was he doing standing around with his hands jammed down into his pockets, with her, of all people, in this public park which runs for a thousand rolling acres of great elms, and a creek where it was said that trout ran in the springtime, horribly named Starch Factory Creek. This vast green along Utica's eastern border, haven for the fifty thousand Italians of the east side. And maybe about a quarter of a mile from where he stood, perched up and sparkling on rising ground in the park's southern section, the Little League field, best in town, and site of his triumphs four years earlier, but now already passing from his memory, good riddance, already he desired deliverance from his past. Forget everything. Forget these boring Italians. This green place was most of all *their* domain. The domain especially of all these darn old Italian ladies. Hers, yes, his grandmother's, Natalina Mattia Iacovella, who just couldn't wait to make the traditional demand upon him, now that he had acquired the magical license, to take her to the park so that she could pick free dandelion salads by the bushel, all summer long grandmothers in the park bending all the way over, never kneeling, cutting into the earth, and their newly licensed grandsons so sullen and so bored, peering into the future, absent. "Frankie," she had said in heavily accented English. So that must be his actual name, because that's what she said. Then in Italian: "Bring me to the park. Do this favor for me and I will make a beautiful rum cake just for you."

Naturally, thirty-seven years later, at fifty-four, he believed that he had gained sudden and inexplicable access to the past, to that very moment of his boredom in the park, standing around like a jerk with his grandmother who was picking luscious dandelions, wearing Hollywood shades (he! not the grandmother! she doesn't wear shades!), on a partially cloudy day in July of 1956, rocked back a little on his heels, wanting to be cool.

He thought he was remembering. How marvelous this hungry sweep of memory. He insisted on the word: *memory*. He loved dandelion salads. There was no limit to how much he could eat. This is what he saw, looking through the boredom: she, Natalina, a five-footer, tipping the scales at one hundred and fifty pounds, multiplied everywhere in his vision, all over the park, so many Natalinas at so many angles to his vision. Over there, just a great rounded ass. Here, frontally, massive and pendulous, the endless breasts. And such variety of side views, of the curving bodies emerged and fixed in his field of vision, out of the earth emerging and curving up and around and then back down in, where you belong, cutting in, earth-attached at the feet and hands, so many Natalinas, in a green field where she erodes a little, where she blackens in the weather.

16

In the spring of 1952, a group of Italian-American busi-
nessmen decided to build an extraordinary Little League
ball field, like a yearning for a major league stadium, in the
park on Utica's east side, complete with press box and spiffy
concession stands, you should have seen the dugouts: a gift
to the male children of the children of the immigrants, who
would play ball, go to college (first in the family to do so),
and leave Utica for good. "Little League," 1952, the words
were a romantic call to athletic greatness to preteen males,
in this year of Mickey Mantle's sophomore season with the
New York Yankees, a team whose lineup was studded with
Italian-American names.

The Mick was not (apparently) Italian. He was just twenty
and many of the twelve-year-old Little Leaguers on Utica's
east side identified with him. "Worship" is a better word. An
eight-year difference in age. What was that? They would be
teammates in eight years. The Mick and me! And hadn't so
many of the players' fathers already transformed him into
one of us? Mantle? Who were Mickey's parents trying to
kid? We knew. *Mandolino* he was called on the Italian east
side. *Mickey Mandolino*, this blond bruiser from Oklahoma
was actually the secret son of the great DiMaggio. He had
to be, to play ball that well, to replace DiMaggio, who was
the father. How do you replace the father?

Many of the males of the third generation between the
Little League age limits of eight and twelve would try out,
in this, the second year of Little League existence. The ball
field had even been given a name: Rufus P. Cavallo Stadium.
Uniforms like the big leagues. The scoreboard, the adver-
tisements covering the outfield fence, the smell of the hot

dogs, the typewriters clicking away in the press box behind home plate, the public-address system booming out the names, you could hear it a mile away, at least. *And pitching tonight for the St. Anthony Dodgers, Lefty Lentricchia*, who had, at the time, at most, two inches on his *nonna*, Natalina Mattia Iacovella, on that night in July of 1952, when Lefty's father Frank, Frank Senior, sat in the exact middle of the bleachers between home and third base, and opposite, in the bleachers between home and first base, in the top row at the far corner, in mirrored sunglasses, a man who had been more or less on the road, working, since the summer of 1935, home now for three weeks, and drawn there to this game as much by the conflicting accounts in the sports pages as by the sport itself: *Who was this kid? Dom, Bill, Frank, Lefty, Len Lentricchia, they called him. Whose kid was he?* The man in the mirrored glasses had grown up intimately with the Lentricchia brothers, *Dom, Bill, Frank*, and then lost touch. Seventeen years ago—1935. Whose son was this lefty hurler, who threw the ball too fast for his size and age, and whose name they kept changing? The man in the mirrored glasses was Johnny Critelli. The light that night was just right, so that you could see the image of the field reflected sharply in Johnny's glasses. You could see images of the players, his focus steady on Lefty. The eyes of Johnny C. Yourself as the image of yourself with Johnny looking right through you.

Tonight the kid was good. Faster than ever and wild enough to scare the opposing hitters. He had made one of the little tykes literally crap his pants. And even the fearsome Nick LeoGrande was tonight being held at bay. Through four innings: no hits, no runs, no walks, no errors, eight strikeouts. And even LeoGrande he had somehow

18

struck out, but not before Big Nick had hit two balls just barely foul and so darn far that people in the stands started the scandalous rumor that LeoGrande was illegal, he was actually seventeen years old. The parents of the St. Anthony players wanted an investigation. This LeoGrande was the sweetest kid, but he was too strong for Little League. Lefty had fooled him once, but it was doubtful, they said, no, it was impossible, they said, that he could be fooled again.

There were two opinions of Johnny's looks: some said he was a handsome man; others couldn't remember, they found him nondescript. For seventeen years Johnny had been a traveling man, an extremely persuasive union organizer, who had been all over the country for so long that his tone, accent, and even rhythm had become alien. Wherever he was, people believed he was from somewhere else. Where, exactly, no one could say. Johnny Critelli was the center of many speculations, many secret images. The man's papers were not in order.

On the face of the Dodgers' pitcher, staring concentration, reflecting the father, origin of staring concentration, sitting in the third base bleachers. The father still as a statue. Tonight nothing was being given away by the faces. Except the kid's body wouldn't obey the face. With each strikeout the kid would do a little uncontrolled hop, little body spasms were taking place out there in full view of twenty-five hundred people. As if something were trying to jump up out of the body, which is what Johnny sees, too much inside, trying to jump outside. The father is perfectly stiff. Johnny believes that the kid needs to be rescued, whose ever kid he is. The help of his teammates who play flawlessly behind him will not suffice: the brilliant Tantillo will not suffice; Salerno (who consumes one hot dog between each inning) will not suffice; no, not even Tranquille, who chants rhythmically behind Lefty, *hum hum hum babe!* will suffice.

Johnny has no family, neither immediate nor distant. Only the union. Johnny has but the dimmest memory of parents. His key memories are of the brothers Lentricchia: *Frank, Bill, Dom.* And their father, *Augusto*, most of all of their formidable father. He remembers that the three brothers had three names each. Sometimes he couldn't keep them straight. He remembers the grooved intensity of their father. Whose kid was this who the papers call Len, Dom, Bill, Lefty, Frank, and, last week, Joe? Who the heck is Joe? The shortstop Tantillo is liquid smooth, floating in Johnny's glasses.

Through five innings now: no hits, no runs, no walks, no errors, nine strikeouts. One inning away from glory, baseball perfection. The Dodgers have racked up nine runs. The kid himself has hit safely twice, each time running and hopping to first base in a spasm dance. And Johnny now is beginning to react to the kid's spasms, in tiny sympathetic spasms of the shoulders, Johnny is reacting.

In the sixth and final inning Johnny Critelli feels himself urged by a cause unknown to float out and rush down upon the kid in gentle breezy force, this is the urge, to rush out of himself and soar down upon him, the boy of the spasms, and to lift him up and out, even as Lefty works hard on Big LeoGrande, one out from perfection, Johnny feeling himself leave himself, this man of ambiguous face and voice has witnessed enough of turbulence and intensity and mania, *it is time*, Johnny's hour has come round, and the kid, working hard on Big Nick, feels the floating and this is very good, this exit, this assumption, floating up from the body high above the field, this is very very good, and the father's gaze lifted up now high above the field, the father at long last drained of something too much, the father's face at long last full and sensuous, not witnessing the event unfolding right there on the field itself—the son becoming imperfect as Big Nick LeoGrande touches him harshly for the one hit that Lefty will give up that night, a high deep drive, how beautiful it is, the most beautiful thing in the world, sailing far beyond the centerfield fence: St. Anthony's 9, Ventura's Restaurant 1.

✳   ✳   ✳

My father told me: "Johnny Critelli was for the working man. He died in a head-on collision out west, in 1952. I think it was in August. They never sent the body back. They said there was nobody to send it to." My father said: "Johnny Critelli had a terrible death."

I

Fathers

I have to tell you something. My father and I, we're tremendous together. We tremble in each other's vicinity. Five months ago, in January of '93, I turned over to my Italian-American agent the manuscript of a so-called confessional work, *The Edge of Night*, then immediately broke down. The tongue, the autonomous tongue. When I was a child they said "canker sores." Now I'm all grown up, now they say "lesions," the word applied to the tumor discovered in my father's colon. You, my father, who art not yet in heaven. Impossible to speak for six days. Language lesions directly from God. The tongue seeks catatonia, and this is how it begins again. This concerns the origin of new writing, in dreams of a flexible and endless tongue, in thoughts of my father, nothing left now but my father, so I summon him, Frank Senior, Big Frank, who's saying "*Madon*', Frank, it was the worst one I ever heard," and he's doing that Italian gesture with the hand swiveling up and down with such ease, as if the wrist had been lubricated, and my father smiles small to himself, he diverts his glance to the floor, oh how my father loves the floor when he talks to me! glancing many times, diverted, the hand now shaking and shuddering, the

25

hand is remembering the worst one, like a special scene in a movie, and he enjoys it more the second time, his remembrance is better, "Frank, you can't imagine how bad," proud of his firstborn, even in this proud, his hand trembles, because as far as he's concerned it's in the category of the straight A's in college except for those two B's in freshman English from the professor who you revered, that Jewish one, *Madon'*! the standards on that Jew who you revered, did he die yet? this screaming, this hollering, this yelling at the top of the lungs, in the middle of the night (naturally), like the one-hitter I threw on the one night in forty thousand that he didn't have to work for a change, Little League 1952, there he is, we hardly see each other, home at last is my diverted father, *Madon'*! Ulysses Lentricchia home from the swing shift, drinking his cold beer with pepperoni and the sharpest provolone he could locate in late morning expeditions that he undertook by himself, and those enormous American crackers brought back from Anglo regions unknown, for private feasts at 1 A.M., what could have been better than when it started, what possibly? the murder scene (naturally, what did you expect? the murder scene) in the opera going full blast down the hall in the bedroom just off the kitchen, when it started, when the killer started in on the killing full blast out of the blue as he sat there in the kitchen, my diverted father was actually eating. "MY ARM! MY ARM! MY ARM!" So he looks up from the sports page, so he glances in the direction of the bedroom of the screams, but he does not get up immediately, because he needs to take it in, because he needs to savor it with the pepperoni and the provolone, my father is so happy. I was unconscious, but I think that I was doing it for him, I was entertaining Big Frank. I think that I was screaming for my daddy.

She, the mother, who else? she had her own perspective, naturally. This is the mother who said during a recent three-way conversation, which was quite a nice conversation, with me and my father, I'm forced to inform you that it was relaxed and happy, and I mentioned that my older daughter would be dropping by in a little while, and guess what my mother says in response, in the context of three faces overtaken by tranquillity, and all of a sudden she comes out with, matter-of-factly: "Good, then I'll have someone to talk to." My daughter arrives, the two of them go off into another room, I won't say *where they belong*, and I don't have to tell you that we had no desire to follow, because we're not stupid. My father said to me (this is an exact quotation): "I don't like to be a third person when two women, you know?" The morning after my arm! my arm! she says, "Too bad you can't hear yourself, you don't know how much you scared me with that goddamn voice of yours, you don't know what it does to me," one-quarter horrified as she remembers, re-running it, worse the second time, the face back in the moment, and three-quarters furious, *La Mamma Furioso*, "Somebody should scare *you* like that, then you would know," that this, of all things, has to be done, yet again, no escape for as long as I live there, again and again: "Too bad your atheist professors in Utica College who I should call on the phone can't hear you in the middle of the night," says the mother. "Stop making believe you're an atheist," she says.

I forget their birthdays almost every year, I don't understand why. I try every year to remember, then I usually fail. I think that I don't want them to have birthdays. For example, God doesn't have a birthday—I don't mean Jesus, I mean God. Jesus is not God, Jesus is merely the son. God the Father and God the Mother, I remember them the next morning when the reviews of my performance are stated, when the reviews themselves become a performance, which I re-run now, back in the theater of my mind, where it's better, happy like my father. Remembrance is better, even when it's worse it's better, this remembrance of things that never were as I remember them. I'm trying not to say "fiction," because I'm trying hard not to make it up. Have you ever heard of a fictional character dying outside the text? My father will die outside this text, as will yours, if he's not already dead. I realize that I didn't say "my mother." I do not wish to denigrate the deaths of mothers.

Off of your pajamas, right off, "Frank, you clawed it right off in your sleep, from the shoulder down, and what gets me is you were a fanatic on keeping your nails short, so it's a mystery how you got the whole sleeve so fast. It must have been bad, *Madon*'!" My father loves me. MY ARM! MY ARM! MY ARM! Our fathers love us, the sons. Of course, they love the daughters, this we already know, but us too, it must be true. The father must be the one who says to the son, "Come, I will give you rest."

My mother, at long last, now in her mid-seventies, is beginning to vocalize to her very own murder scene in the middle of the night, providing the commentary, becoming a screamer she is, and she's doing something to my father that I wish I could do. She's scaring him. My mother and I, we're midnight opera stars. I wonder what they're like? His I'm referring to. He must have them, he's got to, but it's not possible for me to imagine a scream coming out of him. A son doesn't want to imagine that. My father must be afraid of something, even though he's not supposed to be, because the father has to be the one who says to the son, "Be not afraid, I go before you always."

28

Beautifully he hides it, a thing of fascination forever, perfectly hidden except once, and this comes to me from his
close friend, Joe Fiore, Joe Flowers, as my father used to call
him, who told me, with sweat on his forehead, "Your father
looked like he had no blood. Your father went white like
that wall, and then this party, this is a relative on your
father's side of the family who all of a sudden learned something about your father the hard way. This is a party you
yourself can't stand, Frank, I can't say his name because it
wouldn't be right. After that, this particular party was good
to your father, even though he doesn't go to confession, but
neither does your old man, as far as that goes. God forgive
me, I would say your old man doesn't really need to. This
particular rotten party is a better person now, that's the
main point. More people who know your father should
know your father better. One of these days I'm going to get
the nerve up to ask you when was the last time *you* went to
confession, but not today. No blood, Frankie, I was afraid
even though I wasn't the one he looked at with that face,"
said the man my father called his best friend.

I believe that my father believed he could actually do it,
you know what I'm referring to. Make somebody holler at
the top of the lungs. You would never guess from looking at
him. This must be his fear: that he's perfect for the role, that
you couldn't be ready for him. All of a sudden he turns you
into a screamer, your body is actually flying through the air
and you're so surprised that you almost forget to scream.
You never had a chance, you never knew that a judgment
was being made. The process of judgment was never displayed, the sentence was not announced. Suddenly it's the
act of execution. Who would have believed it, because from
looking at him and being in his company you couldn't

know. But this gentle man knew. My gentle father can kill your father. He could maybe imagine the pleasure, even as I do now. My father can kill all the other fathers. Because there must only be one. One man's family. It must be true.

In fact, my father said the words "You clawed it right off in your sleep" only two weeks ago, in the middle of May, at the dinner table, at my sister's, in Prospect, New York, just twenty minutes north of my hometown, Utica, where "My son who is a professor at Duke University is going to give a graduation speech." In Prospect, my father revealed my mother's sudden ascent to the level of the operatic. In a strong falsetto he imitates her: "HELP ME! HELP ME! HELP ME!" We all laugh. He said he thought someone was killing her. We all laugh. He thought someone was killing his wife. The wife laughs. My sister's older daughter says, "Grandma, who was killing you?" Grandma says, "Someone was choking me." Who? Someone. I think of my mother being killed in the opera, the leading soprano, *la prima donna assoluta*, dead, *La Mamma è morta*! and I laugh. We're all happy.

It's my birthday in ten days (which they never forget) and we're celebrating tonight, in Prospect, because I'll be home on the actual day, and I want another slice of cake, no I don't want another slice, I want a slab of that rum cake with the cannoli filling, which you can't buy in North Carolina. I could put away the entire cake with the cannoli filling. You think I'm exaggerating? Before I die, I want to put away an entire rum cake with the cannoli filling, in one sitting, with my parents watching. That's our son. They're pushing eighty and I'm pushing the middle fifties. Is this what this is all about? The applause of the primal audience? Pleasing them before it's too late? Kill the entire cake, for their entertainment, and now they're putting another rum cake on the table and I'm still hungry, so bring on the rum cakes, and bring on the old Utica friend who says, "They manipulate my prostate every six months, so they don't have to operate, they treat me digitally, but eventually they operate," and bring on the mother who says, "My bowels are killing me," bring on Julio, the uncle, who says, "You still got that picture we took in the boat?" Julio, the Sicilian uncle, who says, out of nowhere, "I don't understand why, I can't say," knowing that I will supply the proper context, I know the grievous reference which we will never discuss, and Rocky D, quick, bring him on, the godfather who makes dollhouses in his cellar, with that black discoloration on his forehead, now the size of a half-dollar, I can't take my eyes off it. Christ, I'm hungry. *Eat them with these sentences. They die while you write the book, while you're writing. Eat these sentences, these are their bodies. The last supper is a supper of sentences. The only supper.* "*Madon'*! what an appetite," my father never said, the hand definitely trembling.

With those I care about, it is good to meet not too frequently for conversation. To converse and to eat. Better to do it here, in my writing room, trying to eat them, in conversation with the dead and the about to be dead, who are called the living.

When I was a child, my mother said, If you say bad words I'll make this sewing needle get hot on the stove and sew your tongue to your lips. I'm going to put a nail through your tongue. She was trying to stifle a smile. I was trying to stifle a giggle. Frank, she says, stifling nothing this time, not smiling, Good, write about your father and yourself. It will take a lot of imagination. You know what they say? They say it's not over until the fat lady sings. Frank,

31

I'm putting a lot of weight on lately. I'm still alive, in case you haven't noticed in that room of yours, locked up night and day. Wake up! You have a nice Wal-Mart not too far from your house. A person with your type of mind should go over there once a week. Just to walk around in Wal-Mart. Just so you don't go crazy. Unless that's what you want, Frank. Is that what you want? Because you think it's good for the writing?

*   *   *

The tongue in January, then the flu in February, for which antihistamines are indicated, this doctor says "indicated" for my flu, but this doctor's indication must be ignored, because I know what they will say the next morning when they discover the partially clad body and the vial of indications, minus one. Because it only takes one. Do not accept the coroner's report. Naturally, after the autopsy, they say, we know what they say. They interview my associates and my students, not my scattered friends, and my associates and my students say they are not surprised. You think they're gentle in there? I'm talking about the morgue. They use big electric saws in there, they plunge knives in, *plunge*, they're getting off on it, they stab, they slice open the intestines and spot the diverticuli in my amused intestines, and they look into the stomach and see the tremendous sensitivity, the shyness, the touchiness of the Catholic stomach. The evidence is incontrovertible, the last ecstasy by my own hand, but not by "I," because somebody walks into the Duke Hospital Emergency Room, which they changed the name of to the Trauma Center, somebody walks in with a long brown bag, and what do you suppose is contained in the long brown bag but a long bread knife, sawtooth edge

32

honed tremendously, and then this particular party walks into a cubicle where they're working on a gut-shot teenager, who screams, over and over, "Oh Daddy Jesus Oh Daddy," and this particular party says, Ladies and gentlemen, this is a test of your skills, this is only a test, and he whips out the long bread knife, tremendously honed, and saws it viciously across his own throat in the vicinity of the jugular, which goes from normal to beyond repair in one second, even for these medical persons in white clothes of high emergency skills, in the Trauma Center itself! beyond repair, and as the blood shoots to the nine-foot ceiling, someone says, I was just kidding, this is not a test. Someone lies and says, This is not a test, this is Frank. This is only Frank. Someone is telling lies. This particular party has my exact looks, my exact dental etcetera, but this party is not Frank, I don't care what they say, because this rush of this desire, this wave of this rush, this totally tremendous possession, I was growing fur on my hands, for Christ's sake! Goddamn you, stop calling me Frank! This sweep of this need to do big damage, self-slaughter against which the Everlasting has fixed his canon. Against my will, my will is done. Somebody loved the wave. I heard a beautiful voice say: Jump off this Catholic cliff and God the Father who is your Father will save you, because your tremendous Father loves you so much.

The rush will not come if I sit up all night, and the rush comes only at night, because the devil cannot bear the light. The worst rush comes at her house in February '93, the home of the companion, who respects the word "devil," who's caring for me on an emergency basis, as I sit up all night in the spare bedroom, after ten seconds of lying down in the spare room where she keeps the pictures of her

33

familiar dead, the brother and the father, in the room of the so-called dead. Only the dead may use this bed. The companion believes. The morning after, I say to the companion, "the room." I say, "The pictures in the room wanted me to become a picture in the room." After I become a picture in your death room, after you add me to your beloved gallery, will you spray me on a regular basis with Windex? Will you, as it is your wont, forget to dust the top ledge? Kindly do me these kindnesses and I shall give you good voice, as you lie beneath me, in this bed of the dead, in the room of your beloved dead.

*   *   *

Henry DiSpirito, Johnny Critelli, Joe Fiore, Rocky DeCrisci, Julio Mutolo, Bill and Dom Lentricchia, Frank Senior, the names of real men who live, or who have lived in, Utica, New York. Some are dead, some are getting close, and some others still have moved to Florida, where they continue to get close. Those of you who live, please understand that I'm writing as fast as I can. My father and mother have moved to Florida.

Often, I'd drift in at one, one-thirty in the morning, and catch him in his peace, going to town on the pepperoni and the provolone. Then it was just him and me, our respective solitudes preserved at the kitchen table, the illuminated theater of our calm, in our quiet dark house. "He hit another one today. A tremendous blast." The hair stands up on my forearms. His reference is to Mickey Mantle, whose name he doesn't have to say. He, him. My father is happy to give me the news. He knows what Mickey means to me. He retrieves another small plate from the cupboard and begins to feed me. I could slice my own pepperoni and provolone, but I don't. I want him to do it. He likes to do it, because it's for me, but mainly because he likes to do it. The way he holds the knife, the fine concentration of his gaze on the work before him. The way he shuffles some more of those high-class American crackers on the plate for crackers only, making them land in a design. Pepperoni, provolone, and American crackers; knife, hands, and arms. The position of the head—that, too: slightly cocked. Lips a tiny bit pursed. The greatest pleasure of all would be to peep at him through a hole in the wall, he in his self-delight, myself unseen. To watch him from the dark in his illuminated space, the two of us in maximum happiness. You ought to see him handle his paintbrush on a blank dumb wall: disappearing into his ecstasy, eyes filled to the brim and even over the brim by the surfaces of what eyes may behold, rocking so easily to the rhythms of his craft, you, my father, we are the rhythm.

I'm flying through the air with the greatest of ease, my father is making my five-year-old body fly through the air with the greatest of ease. He won't kill me because he's in control of himself. I must have been driving him crazy that night at Uncle Bill's, when Uncle Bill was living on Bleecker Street with the wife he loved the most, Angie Bombace, who was the one he called to say he still loved Aunt Angie when he had two months to go from the cancer that started in the colon, jumped to the liver, then spread everywhere. "That goddamn cancer," my mother says, "that's all you hear about anymore." I love Aunt Angie. I wonder if she's still alive. I had to be driving my father nuts that night playing my favorite game all by myself with the grown-ups watching. I was a good cowboy caught in an ambush with seven crooks. I made the sound of every

35

bullet. Loud. POW POW POW POW!! The battle raged on a long time. Then I got killed. Then I came back to life. Then they killed me again. Etcetera. How many times was he supposed to listen to this? How many? This intrusive kid messing up the grown-ups' evening. There was a limit. I remember Uncle Bill that night who had two young daughters who didn't live with him, you know why, and who didn't come to his funeral, and no son, either, to grieve the father's death. What a kick he was getting out of my game! I think Uncle Bill was very proud of me. "Holy Jeez," he would say. He loved it, especially when the final hail of bullets takes me out and I hit the floor with total realism. "Holy Jeez! Did he hurt his head?" I'm flying from one room to another. Catch me, Uncle Bill! I fly through the doorway and onto a bed and I don't even scream or cry. Would you call further attention to your little ball-breaking self in that situation? I must have been one tough kid. My mother blows her stack. Uncle Bill laughs and says to my father, Jeezus, Hank, to my father, who was born *Francisco*, signed things *Frank*, which was what he was mainly called, *Frank*, but sometimes, *Hank*. Two times when I was a kid one of my relatives called *me* Hank. Do you realize how thrilling that was? Hank Junior, that's me. Did he send me flying into a refrigerator? Did he try to smash me through a wall, for Christ's sake? Did I land on the floor or on the middle of the bed? Your father never did anything that scared the piss out of you? Maybe you just don't want to remember. I'm remembering this: "Try some of this, this is excellent. You want a beer? *Madon'*, Frank, what a blast he hit today!" Nights like that, going to bed with the hair on our forearms standing up, even when the Mick hadn't delivered that day. I'm forgetting the body that flew through the air

36

with the greatest of ease. I'm remembering my real father, the father in his craft, rocking in his rhythms, and I'm not forgetting my reason for believing that Bill wanted to be my daddy.

Here's the picture: my father, Bill, and this particular long-misled friend of Bill's, standing around in the parking lot of a funeral home in the early sixties. Three cigars in the twilight. The friend says something to Bill about how's that son of yours at Duke? My father, the most obscure of the Lentricchia brothers, matter-of-factly makes a claim on his paternity, right then and there. I'm having trouble imagining those three men in that parking lot talking. I can see them but I can't hear them. This is a true story. The friend leaves, his head in chaos. Bill says to my father, with a plaintive touch, and without a trace of embarrassment (this I can't imagine), Bill says: "Why did you let on, Hank? Why did you have to let on?"

I was very young, at the kitchen sink getting a drink, when I turned quickly to look over my shoulder at the door directly behind me leading to the front porch and the street. The door with a small window at the height of a man like Bill. I turned and saw the head, not even a neck, just the severed head, and a serious face, staring at me. Bill was trying to love me when he thought I couldn't see him. Through the window, standing outside, when it was hard to see him, at dusk, in the dark.

*   *   *

Johnny Critelli sucks me in. He may have sucked Bill in. My father sucks me in. Bill? He sucked everybody in. This was the secret of Bill: he made you want to feel safe with him, even as he tore your face off. Christ, how he poured out his

37

innerness when he came into the room. This is my self: *mangia! mangia!* Who was eating who? Bill was essentially a writer and he came all over you. You were the paper. He leaned hard into the language, he was hard, he opened up its hole, making words that became standard in our family. We repeated his inventions casually, as if they were in the dictionary, sometimes in the presence of strangers. We forgot that they weren't real words. I once said one of his crazy words to a teacher of mine in college who didn't understand. A word half Italian, half English, signifying "big"; "big killer" (male); "wonderful." I was speaking Bill Lentricchia, I was the medium. I am the medium.

He was looking for something he didn't have and thought he deserved, son of a bitch he had been robbed. He wasn't born with original sin. He had suffered, instead, Original Theft. There was a period in the 1960s when he thought that he had been robbed of me. It wasn't me, he was wrong.

Listen again to his plaintive tone: "Why did you have to let on, Hank?" I was his fiction; my father had spoiled the story. My father did not say, "He's my only begotten story. For stealing my story, I sentence you to death." But Bill had it ass-backward. How insane to substitute the so-called need of the son for the need of the father. It would have done him no good to get it straight. Sooner or later he would have learned that he couldn't get through to our fathers who art in heaven and earth and hell. We say to them, Father, I am not worthy. And what do they say? Do they contradict us in loving thunder? Son, they don't say, you are worth more to me than my life. Because this is what the ridiculous son wants them to say. They say, instead, Turn around while I watch you for three seconds through the

38

window. Don't look back, don't even think about it. No eye contact, because eye contact embarrasses me. I am the unseen father and you must be the son of perfect faith, who does not ask about his worthiness, a question of no interest to me. Son, "son" means the pathetic male who has faith in the father. "Son" means, my son, the weak word maker. You know what I need? Can you imagine that I have need? I'll tell you what I need. I need to come in. I need to stand at the kitchen sink. *You* go outside. Bring a chair with you because you're too short. You'll always be too short. Stand on it. Look at me through the window, look at me, you loveless little fucker. Now make believe you love me, and I'll make believe you're not looking at me. I promise not to turn around. Let's put on a big act for one another before one of us goes over the edge. You be the author for a change. You want to kill somebody? Sonny?

Bill died in Clearwater, Florida. They shipped the body up north. To Utica, "under all that snow," my mother says, even though they buried him in August. Why did Hank have to let on? Because I, in my confusion of fathers, don't have a problem with what Bill did.

*   *   *

Venice, March. Eight days. With the companion. And, in a sense, with Bill. Venice made it worse. I carried bad desire to write, secretly to Venice. And to Venice I carried something else, which I would not reveal to the companion: a vague image of an incident—a seed of adventure, a touch of obsession. I'm not sure of the difference. I'd heard about this incident in childhood, then heard the story a number of times over the years, though my memory of the incident rests entirely now on a recent retelling, sometime around 1985 or 1986, Christmas Eve, or Christmas Day, two or three years after one of the two known participants, my father's brother, the one who called himself *Bill*, signed official papers *William*, was christened *Guerrino* during World War I, *Guerrino*, little war, dead for two or three years when I heard the telling I'm remembering now. I wanted my bad writing desire to marry my emerging image in Venice. I like the word *emerging*, it's so hopeful. I wanted my secret image to become a story, but I was brooding upon a frozen frame. I needed to run the tape backward and forward. I was hoping that my Venetian brooding was the key to the story that ran through it, if there was a story, but I couldn't get out of the locked room of the image. Guerrino was in the room with a special friend. The special friend was Johnny Critelli. If only I could put time in. If only I could say that they, Guerrino and his special friend, were somewhere else, in the first place, before which there was no other place. Then they had to go to the place of the room. Something happened and then they left and went to a different place, because they had to, which was the wonderful place they wanted to be all along, Guerrino and his friend. Narrative. How do you achieve a thing like that?

I saw much of Tintoretto in Venice and quickly became jealous of what I conceived to be his good luck. He had what I wanted, but only because he was born at the right time, it was a gift, this lucky man who had a father he never feared, or maybe he was scared to death of his father. One of the two, I can't decide which. Tintoretto's images of Christ have time in them. His images bear time, and give birth to more time. Then they destroy it, they destroy everything. World-shattering narrative embedded in the image. He didn't have to make the story up and impose it upon his culture. That bastard. The people who commissioned those pictures, the people who looked at them with pleasure, we who look. The knowing in advance is part of the pleasure. The story of Christ came before, they knew the names, and they leaned, they were supported in a community of story. They leaned. This is what I have to believe about them. It helps me to feel heroic. Give us this day our daily bread of story. I can't lean, but I want to lean. In another glance, I take in one of those portraits Tintoretto did of some nobody, some rich contemporary, and I say, Who's that? And then I say, Who cares? I approach and read a forgotten name, *Paolo Stronzo*, that's right, you got it: *Paul Turd*, and I understand that this is what I traffic in, names nobody knows, or maybe even wants to know, I traffic in shit, I'm involved in incidents of obscure import, and "obscure import" is my most hopeful phrase, isn't it? I lust for Tintoretto's situation. A story in advance. A new book, written before it's written. I want to cheat. Give me your story or I'll break your legs. I just need to disappear into a story, that's all it is.

Eight days in Venice. Just in time I recover from the tongue and the flu. Have I told you that the companion is female? Have you forgotten? Already? In our cultural context it is so easy to forget. There is tremendous pressure. In our cultural context, "the companion" signifies that I am a homosexual, attended to in his final hours by his longtime companion. To the best of my knowledge, I am not a homosexual. To thine own chaos be true. In our cultural context, there is such pressure to know who we are. Thou shalt not covet thy neighbor's sexual preference. This is a female companion of Celtic extraction, who says, "I will not dry the infernal silverware." Venice in the middle of March, where she claims I give my greatest performance. With a loincloth.

41

In Venice, the companion coins a word: "Tinterotic." She says: "Tinteroticism." My mother does not approve of the Venice trip so soon after the tongue and the flu. I tell the mother about the Celtic companion, who she hadn't known about. Suddenly the mother approves. The mother says (this is an exact quotation): "Now you've got the full prescription." Imagine this ethnically broad-minded mother of Italian extraction, who says, thinking of the son in Venice: "You're relaxing when you're seeing beautiful things that you like."

Every night in Venice, late, drifting toward sleep, I concentrate on the incident that was said to have occurred in Utica, New York, sometime in the middle thirties, hoping that I would see through the image and find the narrative flow beneath, but in the dark nothing jumps up to hug me. Instead, I find a little detail, a bit of color here and there. This tale passed down in my family shouldn't be honored with the word tale. It was the context of the telling, usually at the dinner table, that's where all the fun was. The last telling I can remember was during a shocking holiday feast at my father's brother's house in Clearwater, Florida, 1985 or 1986, at the home of the one who calls himself *Dick*, his brother *Dom*, christened *Dominick*, and called, but not since he was a kid, to his face, by my father and by Bill he was called *Doom*. *Doom-Dom*, *Dom-Doom*, alternating phrases in rapid succession. The holiday table warped with the weight of the food that Uncle Doom, in his greatness, put forth that day. Five pounds of baked ham, nine pounds of roast beef, sixteen pounds of grouper, a twenty-two-pound turkey. Such tremendous poundage did not engulf the table, because this table was the size they put in a castle in the movies. I can't begin to specify the side dishes, so numerous we accidentally struck two skidding and sputtering to the floor without undue concern, the damage swept away as the coffee perked. Think of this man, the great Doom, who would put forth that kind of poundage, this is who he was, eventually he'll become clear, or maybe not, he may never become clear, this was a man who regularly put outrageous amounts on the table, even if he was eating by himself, think of this man's main dish poundage and an extravagant dessert caused by him, Doom, to be placed for his pleasure in the very moment of the grouper and so on, a twenty-eight-egg *cassata*, so that he could partake at will of a sweet with his meat, think of this food I've specified and you'll easily figure out the side dishes without my help. You may be imagining thirty, thirty-five adult guests, forget the little ones who eat like birds. You would be a normal person if you imagined that number. We were fourteen adults who had to do the job. But we were confident, because we had Doom on our side, Mr. Wonderful, this big man who looked like a movie star, they all jumped into his bed. Six feet is tall for an Italian of southern origin. My mother said, "He loved them all." She said, "I'm not exaggerating."

Somebody said, in the middle of the all-out assault on what Uncle Doom had provided, I'm pretty sure it was me, I'm positive it was me, who said: What did Uncle Bill say Johnny Critelli did in that saloon? Doom suddenly looks like he's going to get sick. My father, who's always a little shy, appears to approve of the question. He shakes his head a little, side to side, as he glances down into his plate with his small smile. I know he's happy. He likes me, even though it's difficult for him to show it. It's not his fault that it's difficult. It's hard for my father to talk. The younger generation and the new in-laws require initiation to tradition. The women who know the story, including Doom's wife (his sixth or seventh, a couple of years my junior) and my mother, protest. Not now, they say, it's not right while we're eating. Somebody, it must have been me, tells it: One night, in a saloon, Uncle Bill said a drunk walked in and threw up on the floor. He must have just eaten because you could see little pieces of meat and carrot. It was a nice stew, Uncle Bill said. And Johnny Critelli said, For five bucks I'll take two slices of bread and make a sandwich. I'll mop it up. Somebody put up the five bucks and Johnny Critelli took two slices of bread and mopped it up, he made a soggy sandwich, the stuff is hanging and dripping out, like long strings of white snot, and he eats it all. That's it. Not much to go on in Venice, city of heavenly cuisine.

✳   ✳   ✳

Middle of the night, the stunned companion locates me at the far end of this elegant Venetian room with a view, backed up against the door. She says I said: "I can't breathe! I'm in the nude!" Johnny Critelli was not standing in that saloon, he was posing, and the Italian word he used to describe his pose was a word he had learned from a neighbor, who was also a sculptor, and whose actual name sounds like my obvious invention, because his actual name is DiSpirito. I have one of his pieces in my house: a moth that looks to me like a vagina.

When this sculptor, who still lives, required a model of the male gender, he called upon Johnny. Most of the time, Mr. DiSpirito stayed off of Michelangelo's turf, most of the time he tried for small animals and insects, forms struggling to emerge, but maybe not struggling that hard, maybe trying for a while, then giving up. It's too hard to live, fuck it. Domination of stone, a lyric art of failure. In moments when he rescues his life-denying theme for the light, Mr. Henry DiSpirito knows extreme delight, he smiles, and, for once, he can bear himself. For his modeling time, he gives Johnny what Johnny requests: pieces of cloth of various sizes and colors, stacked neatly in a clean small cardboard box, all of it more expensive than Johnny knows, or cares.

This is Johnny in the saloon: leaning forward a few degrees over the perpendicular, left foot planked a few inches ahead, the brunt of the weight securely anchored there, right heel perhaps half an inch off the floor: an effect of urgent potential, a man on the verge of lift and motion.

Mr. DiSpirito had shown Johnny the word in an amply illustrated book about Michelangelo, on the page opposite the *David*. Mr. DiSpirito explained. Mr. DiSpirito even let Johnny hold his beautiful book, a thing not easy for Mr. DiSpirito to do. Johnny pointed to a detail of the *David*, a close-up of the face as the sculptor himself would have seen it, and Johnny said, "like a woman." Yes. When he saw the detail of the face of the Virgin in the Rome *Pietà*, he said: "This is David's mother." Yes, said Mr. DiSpirito.

Johnny is posing for us *contrapposto*. That's the word. His left arm fully extended, angled a little downward, toward the meal on the floor, palm open to the ceiling, a gesture at once referential and supplicatory. Three-quarter profile, displaying the beautifully blemished left side of his face.

*   *   *

Bonnie Johnny wears an overcoat of heavy wool, tan-colored, with a jagged rip midback, a dark stain bordering the rip (yes, traces of bloody melodrama), both pockets torn off: one replaced, the left side, with multicolored patchwork in silky-looking material, the style of the harlequin.

Into this beautiful pocket, on a late Sunday afternoon, Johnny stuffs several slices of white American bread. Badly frayed open-toed slippers show us crusted and swollen feet. Under the coat, buttoned so as to reveal only the throat and a flash of chest, briefs. The collar, rakishly pulled up, frames Johnny's straight long brown hair, swept back, going blond, and the pockmarked face, one side only, a brush with ravishment, is enhancing his good looks. Johnny's stink, it would sicken a seasoned garbage collector, is virtually covered by the cologne (not cheap) that Bill sprinkles liberally on the coat, starting high above the head with long strokes of the arm and a single snap of the wrist, in late afternoon, like an abbot blessing the monks at the close of day, shaking holy water from the dipped palm branch, as the light falls at the last canonical hour, the cologne falls on my Holy Fool. The once-fine coat is a gift pulled from a man's body after a frightening struggle, pulled by Bill, who was also called *Goody*, or just *Goods*, who would years later open a barbecue stand in a rural area west of Utica, almost calling it Johnny C's, but at the last minute changing it to Goody's, and he made a small fortune. It was Johnny who sewed together diversely colored pieces of silky-looking material and made the beautiful pocket for the left side. Johnny loved to sew. Johnny had no other loves. Not even Bill. The saloon is dark, making it difficult for us to see the customers at the bar and those occupying the twelve tables. Johnny is self-illuminated, he emits light, an inner radiance of Johnny, causing some of him to glow and some of him to stand in lustrous shadow. Under the eyes, much of the right side, a visible darkness. The left side is brilliant.

In Venice, as I thought about the names nobody knows, as I worried about trafficking in the trivial, I schemed. Steal

Tintoretto's story, sneak the narrative of Christ underneath my image. Find Johnny's mother and bring her to the saloon. Make Johnny say: Woman, behold thy son! At the end, make Bill say: It is accomplished! Johnny will need to drink something. Johnny will need to say, I thirst. Ridiculous. I am disgusted by the coincidence of Johnny's initials. My materials are making an ass of me. Nevertheless, a few weeks back from Venice, I plunge into the gospels. I bring my Catholic Bible with me to Hanover, New Hampshire, where I'm lecturing at Dartmouth, and where, on Easter Sunday, instead of going to mass, I watch again Martin Scorsese's *The Last Temptation of Christ*. The next night I write the first sentence of a monologue for Christ.

✳ ✳ ✳

April Fools' Day. The House of Joyce buys *The Edge of Night*. A few days later, in the middle of the night, I awake with, "Eternal Father, help me to reach into their bowels, that I might rescue their courage, they would shit it forth daily." This is the voice of Christ, who else? in the middle of the night, at Gethsemane. His companions, twelve minus one, are asleep. Jesus in the middle of the night is imagining what's going to happen. I decide on a title for a new book: *Jesus, Mary, and Joseph*. Jesus needs the company of his close friends who are all men. Try not to extract sexual implications and I'll be grateful. The proximity of males is necessary for males. The vicinity, the shelter of males. To the best of my knowledge, my Jesus is not praying for fist-fucking powers of unparalleled reach. Maleness. You think maleness is funny? Maybe it is. She's holding it up, a big hot needle. My mother is holding up a nail and a hammer.

May Day. New York City to see my new editor, who tells

me right off that he used to work in a morgue. I do not necessarily believe that he used the saws. I think he did interviews with the recently bereft. The man had access. You don't need medical training for the saws, for the plunging. The stabbing and the cleavers do not require finesse because, in there, cosmetic considerations do not pertain. I myself could hack away with the cleavers and plunge the big knives into the formerly living meat. I have technique. Didn't I work in a slaughterhouse as a tender teenager? I tell my new editor about the slaughterhouse because our male relationship needs a balance of power. I say, I am the writer from the slaughterhouse. We are brothers. I'm jealous, you saw Joey Gallo's brains. In the morgue one also puts it in the cooler, but one is not supposed to ship it out so that it can be sold and eaten in poor neighborhoods, where they can't afford normal meat. Eat the human dead with your syntax, if you command an extremely flexible syntax you are permitted to partake of morgue meat. Work harder on the syntax. Sharpen it. Tongue the dead. People look at you and the first word that comes out of their mouths is *linguicity*. Let me say the whole truth about the electric saws. Those saws are lighter and sleeker versions of the ones they use to cut down trees. They're *chain* saws, because they have to work quickly in there, where cosmetic considerations do not pertain, and in our cultural context we have female morgue doctors who resemble the women closest to me and who require the lighter and sleeker version, the lady chain saw, not labeled as such in our gender-sensitive period.

At 3 A.M., my editor arises, dresses, takes the key he's kept all these years, takes his cello, and then takes the subway to Brooklyn, to the morgue, his body heavy with weeping. He enters a cold room of many slabs after all these years to meditate once again on the so-called corpses, so many hath death undone, oh God so many. One by one the sheets, delicately lifted and folded back to reveal the faces, how beautiful they are. He wants to forget the profit and the loss, God help me to forget, help me to forget everything. He commences to play, bowing the grand theme of the Hebrew Chorus from Verdi's *Nabucco*: *Va, pensiero*, mournfully he sways and he bows, healing the terrific wounds of autopsy, and now, yes, they arise, swaying lyrically all about him, *va*, as he forgets the profit and the loss, *pensiero*, drawn deep he is into the current so happy, they move about him in a ring of absolution, so happy. The cellist believes in Verdi, the Father Almighty, and the Father grants him forgetfulness.

*   *   *

Eternal Father, help me to reach into their bowels, that I might rescue their courage, they would shit it forth daily. So that I might speak their expelled courage, so that their courage, afloat upon my breath, might return to them, aromatic and redeemed, so that they might inhale the courage of their courage and assume me here in this place of stones and long weeds, help me, First Father, to devour all that they would expel. If from this cup of crucifixion I am forced to drink, if it is your will, awake them now and cause them to want to walk with me up the Hill of Skulls. In this hour of my weakness, make them desire to be me, Father, dear Father, and forgive me, because you understand that I require their presence now more than I have ever required your Sufficient Love. In this chilled darkness, let them press roughly against me, cause them to devour my loneliness, make them greedy for the meal. Reach into me now, stop

up my mouth with yours, my Father in Heaven, then speak
my expelled courage, speak it aromatic and redeemed.

A grown-up man, afraid, begging the father, vomiting at
Gethsemane.

Johnny Critelli of the secret image is stealing himself
underneath the Christ story. Tintoretto from the grave
envies my freedom. Tintoretto brooding from the grave is
overwhelmed by nostalgia for the future. He has the opinion that it would be liberating to become a man without a
story.

*   *   *

I miss him. Then I find him at the center of my secret
image, halfway back into its spatial field, there's my Johnny,
my godly man of rags. To Johnny's far right, a little behind
him, almost to the edge of what we can see, in a half-light
belied by the color of his—what else can we call it?—by the
color of his *costume*: there's Bill himself in a one-piece suit
worn by automobile mechanics, in this suit no automobile
mechanic would ever wear. Clean, crisply pressed, that
washed-out blue you see in a hot summer sky, haze filtered
and delicate, barely blue. This is unmanly, this nineteen-
year-old in a saloon, dressed like that, with his face in
gleaming golden tan, hands jammed down hard into the
pockets, weight rocked back, five nine, one hundred and
sixty pounds, filling up that costume, pouring it out, he's
flaunting his cockiness. You would not have concluded, just
from looking at his picture, that this is a dangerously charis-
matic man. Nose too wide, subtle curvature of the serpent.
Eyes too small, narrowing to slits, almost disappearing
when he smiles, as he does now, so tough on his heels, and

the tightly curled dark hair, shaved close over the ears, then jutting out as we rise to the crown. Of the head itself, you would say that it looks powerful. You might say cruel. You would not say irresistible until you were in his actual presence, talking to him, for thirty seconds. He had more than Doom, and Doom had all there was to have. The men and the women loved Goody forever, no matter how badly he treated them. Let him make the most minimal of efforts, they forgave everything. Goody, shine your light down upon us, or we shall die. Oh Goody Goody. Only of Johnny was he in awe.

When he must have been called *Guerrino*, and nothing else, he wore a dress. Guerrino at two and a half years old, the little Doomster, pushing five, Frank, the first son, a little over six, in a picture like a magnet hanging in my dining room, circa 1920. To the viewer's left, little Doom. My father to the right. In the center, standing on a chair and holding a doll at chest level, in a long white dress, there's little war himself. Doom's left hand grasps the back of the chair, as does Hank's right; Doom's free arm relaxes at his side, while Hank's other hand is drawn up to the chest. Doom: dead on to the camera, a face of transparent sweetness. He likes you. Never, says the face, will there ever ever be anything to forgive. Goody is also dead on to the camera. It is too soon to say the word *resentful*, but not much too soon. And my father, the senior male of the group, in theory the dominant male, but his eyes are running from the camera's gaze, their desire is to divert, to run to his left, outside the frame itself. The hand is pulled up to the chest. The senior male of the group is too young to do what he would come to do so beautifully: hide his vulnerability. Too young for manliness. He fears nothing in the room, not the photographer, not the father and mother, Augusto and Paolina, who stand, apparently destitute of emotion, behind the photographer. It is something which he will never be able to name. At five years old, moving to the interior. At five years old, wanting to be my father.

He could not have known the stories, not at that age, circulating daily in Utica's Italian immigrant neighborhoods, of the paesans in New Orleans, eleven of them lynched. Or the ones in Colorado, slaughtered over some labor disturbance. What he would have heard, at home, was the silence, a double-barreled blast of it from Augusto and Paolina, who talked little, and when they did, just above a whisper. They would not have thought it necessary to talk about the air they were required to breathe. Certainly not in front of *le carte bianche*, the white papers. It's possible he picked up a stray phrase now and then when Augusto's fellow poet and radical, the voluble Silverio Alteri, stopped by. The phrase would have been: "like a melon burst." Maybe he heard a complete sentence: "Eat this, Mr. Policeman." He would have had no context for these words. What could he have understood at that age, even with the proper context supplied?

To this day, I do not believe that my father has heard the story of Johnny's mother, the Critelli woman, as she was referred to after her amazing act. My father, who has considered much, has yet to consider the impact of her pronunciation of Shakespeare's name upon his most impressionable years. The Critelli woman stood a shade under five feet and was a legend for her views of the Holy Family. She was said to have said that Mary was a young woman of nineteen years, having figs and having thoughts, and doing what a normal person does at that age, when the angel came flying

52

through the window, and then the finger she was plunging deeply into her vagina grew longer, and thicker, much thicker, and very hard, and then it exploded at the tip in a beautiful pain, and the semen of God rushed forth to make his only begotten Son in Mary's virgin womb. You see what happens, she said, when you get caught in the act by the angel who has to make his big announcement (*la grande Annunciazione*), flying through the window with his hair on fire? It could happen to me, she said. The next time, the Eternal Father will choose a man to give birth to his only begotten Daughter, and it will be virginal, but also very sexual (*tanto sessuale*). She said that Mary had a yearning to make love with a soft-bearded man, always sucking on her nipples as he moves in her, and she got her wish, many times, with Joseph, who stuttered so badly that he did but rarely speak. The Critelli woman said Mary told Joseph that she knew a cure for his tongue, and Joseph tried the cure, many times. It did not work, but the good Joseph kept trying, many times. The Critelli woman, who possessed delicate cheekbones of breathtaking prominence, said that Joseph did not attend the crucifixion of Jesus Christ Almighty because he, Joseph, was a human being, not a dog. She said, of the three of them, Joseph was the best one, that the Son of God had treated his mother publicly like a piece of shit (*pezzo di merda*), and when she, Mary, let him get away with that, she brought the true shame upon herself. Mary, she said, did not scream every minute of the crucifixion, and now you know why, and who can blame her after what the Son of God did to her in public? For what he did to his mother in public, the Eternal Father saw to it that when he asked for something to drink on the cross, they wanted to give water, they thought they were giving water, because the Romans were not dogs either, no matter what they say, but the Eternal Father turned the water into vinegar in order to teach Jesus Christ Almighty a good lesson for treating his mother like that in public. The Critelli woman, who was not too skinny, was respected for the purity and constancy of her devotions to the Church, and for the awesome generosity that she displayed with the truly destitute—she, the Critelli woman, who did not herself have a pot to piss in. Silverio Alteri was said to have said of her, though not to his best friend, Augusto, that she was more gentle even than that saint on earth, Paolina Lentricchia. So it came as a total surprise and, at the same time, no surprise whatsoever, that she did what she did on August 3, 1918, at approximately 7:08 A.M., outside the gate of the textile mill where she worked, seventy-five years, minus three days, from the writing of these sentences.

No one ever said that she was a Communist or anarchist. Italian immigrant women of her generation had no politics. She associated politics with Augusto Lentricchia, that cucumber, who was always losing his jobs with all those kids to feed, because he, who was so quiet at home, couldn't keep his big mouth shut on the job, where he became a socialist troublemaker, and with of course Silverio Alteri, whose eloquence she feared, and now Jesus Christ all of a sudden her husband catches this malady, who has become too close to those two fanatics, but especially with Lentricchia, who is telling her own husband, who could barely read Italian, that he should learn to read Shakespeare in English, "because it tastes better." The Critelli woman told Silverio's wife, Rose, who went everywhere with a rosary in her hands, even to the toilet, that Lentricchia was deranged (*un gran pazzo*), that his obsessions would send him over the edge—he should throw up poison!—and that all his sons, and one male grandchild, would one day have to pay a very dear price.

She and five other Italian women, who worked in the mill, were fed up to here with the American foreman who patted their asses, and believe me, he did worse than that, too, which they would never specify. Naturally, they never considered telling their husbands, because only two things could come of that, both bad. Either the foreman would be assassinated, or, worse, their clever husbands would put two and two together in a hurry, and then assassinate *them*. So they went to the manager, who would not see them. But his secretary caught the gist of their badly broken English, and the next day, the guard at the gate, six two, two hundred fifty pounds, an American, which is a word the paesans like to rhyme in Italian with dog shit (*merd' di can'*), told them they had been fired. They didn't understand. So he said loud: "*You losa you jobba!*" They understood. The Critelli woman stepped back, but her five friends waded in cursing, endlessly, he not getting a word of it, of course, and then one of them spat on his shirt, because she was too short to spit in his face. He restrained himself admirably, pointed his club at the street, and told them, quietly, "Go home or suck my Swedish sausage," language far over their heads. One of them turns her back on him, bends over, and farts. Loud. He kicks her to the pavement. The five friends have had enough, they're withdrawing, at which moment the Critelli woman, heretofore silent, walks up to this American giant, looks up at him as she grabs her own genitals, as if she had a dick herself, you know what I'm saying, she cups her hand a little, and she says in Italian what one Italian male might say to another if he intended insult. She says, "Eat this, Mr. Policeman." The first thing he does is take a swipe at her, hard, with his free hand, which bears a tremendous pointed ring, and he opens up a gusher of blood from her head that goes into his face and all over his shirt. He looks like he's bleeding to death. The second thing he does is bring the club down on her skull with everything he's got. You drop a ripe watermelon to the pavement from the fourth story. Brain tissue on the sidewalk, like a melon burst. She did not die, what a shame.

This legendary incident of the Critelli woman occurred when my father was a little over four, Doom almost three, Goody a little under a year, and her son, Johnny, seven months. A year later, they took the Critelli woman, a staring vegetable, to the insane asylum, because the family had no resources. The guard was fined eight dollars, a lot of money in those days, for disturbing the peace. Four years later, Mr. Critelli, whose literary passions, after the incident, had become as extreme as those of Augusto Lentricchia, announced to Lentricchia, in bombastic tones, "O what a rogue and peasant slave am I!" and the smiling Lentricchia, naturally, had agreed. And then he, Mr. Critelli, disappeared, never to be heard from again. Johnny, about five, was taken over by the neighborhood. Twenty-two families agreed to care for him for three weeks at a time, for as long as it took. At sixteen he met Bill; at eighteen he moved into a large toolshed on a lot, bought for a song by seven paesans, who used it to grow all the vegetables that their families would need for the year. Johnny Critelli had almost become himself.

The vultures of explanation glide high, in big easy circles, but they will not descend. They are beautiful, and one of them is mine.

*   *   *

It was two years after Johnny's mother was brained, it was on the night before the photo in question was to be taken, the brothers Lentricchia supposedly asleep, when the ebullient Silverio Alteri paid his customary Thursday visit. This good man, who would never lose his job, came bearing a large wooden crate of loose spaghetti and the latest number of *Il Martello*, the radical weekly he could afford to subscribe to and upon which Augusto Lentricchia, each Thursday without fail, for the amusement of his best friend, would cast remarks in his best dour manner. Four months later, on a subzero afternoon, Paolina Lentricchia was smashing up for her kitchen stove one of the numerous crates brought by big Silverio when a sharp-pointed splinter flew up ("by intention," as her husband would say it in one of his ascetic lyrics), in order to blind her in the left eye.

> My wife's eye bleeds,
> And my sons greet a new mother.
> And I? I write the poem.

On this night before the photo was to be taken, the fully sighted Paolina was making bread, as she did every other night of the week, listening to these two men whose political intensity made her giggle. In the midst of one of their denunciations of capital—Alteri, big voiced, a little hysterical, Lentricchia, quiet, in frightening monotone—she would say, Oh, you two cause me to laugh, and then she would touch her face in embarrassment, as if her brassiere were showing. Had she taken her bloomers off the clothesline before Alteri arrived? Then these two men, these two mountebanks, would sip their espresso and start to speak of the miserable weather of upstate New York, feeling vaguely foolish, worrying that maybe they were total buffoons incapable of living in this world with these children and these wives. But on this particular night, in late October of 1920, there would be no politics and (for a while) no moody self-reflection. Tonight they were celebrating a literary success, Augusto's first published poem, in Il Martello no less, and there it was alongside the words of the awesome Carlo Tresca, who had advised them both, a few years back, as he toured the Northeast making angry speeches to pacifist Italian immigrants on the honorable evasion of the draft.

Silverio and his literary superior sit within easy sight and hearing of Paolina, in the little parlor, perhaps a foot apart, together holding and reading *Il Martello*, open to the page of Augusto's poem, centered and boxed in the midst of Tresca's fury! Silverio and Augusto lean toward one another, so as to take the poem head-on; their bodies curve slightly from the shoulders, toward one another their bodies curve. Tremendous grins. Their heads arch over to each other and almost touch, a quarter of an inch, at most, separates the heads, which form the top of the archway. And this is what he sees—my father, of course, who was spying on these grown-ups. He sees two things that he has never seen before.

Silverio puts his arm over my father's father's shoulders; Silverio is happy for his friend. My father is scared a little. He has never seen his father grin. That is the first thing. Little smiles, of course. But never this. Who is this happy man? My father standing in a long red shirt, in the doorway leading from the kitchen to the boys' bedroom, in full view, only Paolina spotting him, who will not give him away, saying nothing as she watches her transfixed son, who is watching the men, who watch nothing, lost in this poem concerning the incident of the Critelli woman, this poem so darkly satiric, elegiac, and surprisingly funny, too, whose title, "*Shakesospira*," was an homage to the Critelli woman: Shake-a-so-SPEE-ra! that's how she had flung the bard's name at her ridiculous husband, who had become entranced by Augusto's masked presence, this Critelli woman who punned on the bard's very name, *sospira*, in Italian, signifying great sighing; in some usages, the long melancholy sigh just before death. Augusto the tight-lipped had kept his title a secret and now Alteri is beside himself, saying the title out loud, many times. Did she pun or did she mishear? Do we care?

My father walks slowly and invisibly through the full glare of the kitchen. He stands hidden behind his mother, peeking around her at the men, who arise now and inform Paolina that they will perform Shake-a-so-SPEE-ra! for her delight. Her husband says, I shall play the heroic black moor. Alteri says, *Ed io sono Desdemona*! And I am Desdemona! Alteri says to Paolina, You have stolen my handkerchief and my honor, you vile man. Her husband, restraining Alteri, says, But before we can permit you the pleasures of our tragic theater, *cara*, you must agree to speak one line of Shake-a-so-SPEE-ra, in English. Paolina says to her husband, softly, Augu, you are a true fanatic. Augu responds, softly: Yes, certainly. And it must be so. There is no other way. Now say this: "Life is but a walking shadow." Alteri bows deeply, then kisses Paolina's hand. My father can't stand it any longer. He runs out into the glare, jumping, shouting Shake-a-so-SPEE-ra! Life is walking! So-SPEE-ra! I am black, Papa! ME ME ME! My father is jumping in the glare, so happy, he is jumping in the sudden silence, the gaiety of adults all gone from this room. My father's jumping is collapsing. It's a little hop now. Then stillness. A formal feeling. Alteri tries to laugh. Paolina climbs onto the kitchen table. She, who has no English, is trying to say "Life is but a walking shadow." Augusto smiles a little, as loneliness flashes across his face. He smiles a little, and he says, You are supposed to be sleeping. Come with me. Say good night. Give Silverio a kiss. My grandfather looks serious, but it's only vacancy. It's only the onset of nothingness. My grandfather was fully there, in the room, for a change. But now he's normal. I am a father. When he becomes old enough to be my friend, it will be too late for friendship. *Desdemona, è tardi.* Alteri, your garrulous love is not enough. My grandmother: still on the table, frozen, hand on face.

The first thing was the grin. The second thing my father saw was more important than the first. He saw himself some place else. My father had jumped out of himself. This was real, Shake-a-so-SPEE-ra. He wanted to be in and under something, between the two men reading, in there, where he saw a nice small space. It would be his space, but they would be there, like walls and a roof. Feelings without thoughts or words, he would never have the thoughts or the words, which is why the feelings became eternal, and which is why the feelings of the second thing became my father's death.

And the next day he walked with his parents to the studio of Mr. Rotundo, having his first real memory, which becomes, naturally, the only memory, of the good thing as it is being lost, the jumping collapsing into the silence. Soon the good thing will lose all specific content and become vague and evil, like a prison, as it sucks present and future into the past. My father was remembering his future in the silence and the glare. He was beginning to die a little as he walked with his parents to the studio of Mr. Rotundo, where a surprise awaited him that would give partial, but lifelong, relief.

*   *   *

What wonder awaits my father in Mr. Rotundo's studio? Behind Johnny C, do not forget Johnny C, there is a bar, behind the bar a large mirror, in the mirror some sort of smudge, at the deep spatial end of my secret image of Johnny C there is a smudge in a mirror which turns out to be, upon closer inspection, another image, of a person entering my secret image through the entrance of the saloon. The person is carrying something dangerous in his hand. The person is my father, and what he is carrying is a tennis racket. Does the name Big Bill Tilden ring any bells? Because that's who awaited my six-year-old father in Mr. Rotundo's studio, Big Bill, not in the flesh, because Big Bill never came to Utica, who just six weeks before had won his first U.S. Open Singles Tennis Championship, and in so doing had inaugurated the most dominant (male) reign in the history of the game, to that point, 1920, and since. It wasn't Babe Ruth who was the Mickey Mantle of my father's youth, it was Big Bill Tilden.

In the room where the brothers Lentricchia are having their picture taken, on my father's left, my father's eyes are trying to run left away from the camera's gaze, he's trying not to be obvious, his parents are watching, to the wall his eyes want to run where he glimpses what Mr. Rotundo had mounted, and what he catches causes him to pull his hand up to his chest—there, in photographic transubstantiation, the life-sized Big Bill Tilden in the act, plastered on the wall by a smitten Mr. R, devotee of sporting magazines, who had never seen a tennis match in his life, and never would, pressing his photographic blowup know-how to the limit, because strictly speaking this is not possible, Mr. R's equipment was inadequate to go to the life-sized length he wanted it to go, but Mr. R refused to be inadequate to the levy of his desire. There's Big Bill, slim, six feet four inches—do you realize how tall that looks to a six-year-old used to looking at short Italian immigrants? Big Bill in flowing white slacks and a flowing long-sleeved white shirt, white shoes, in the act, at the top of his delivery of a monstrous overhead smash, Big Bill standing tiptoe, the narrowest black belt loving his waist, frozen in his splendid grace and violence, this flowing killer, this heavy-jawed angel whose hair is lifting off as he rises, his hair lifting into the glow, going white. Big Bill has an aura and Big Bill is an aura. Everything rushing upward, everything, then turning at the top, this is what my father sees, all force poised at the stillness of the top, poised to rush smashing downward in the grace of his violence. Big Bill was a thing of beauty and he would become, for my father, a joy forever.

Since the night before of Shakesospira, my father has been locked in memory, falling through newfound innerness, exiting the present in free fall of memory, possibly endless, then arrested by this abrupt brilliance of interior sun discovered just to his left. Now, at the origin of obsession, focus, and this six-year-old becoming a little mysterious, getting himself some self. The vision of Big Bill gives my father a little more life than death. My father enters into his long and happy subjugation, his fearful longing for the sublime.

*   *   *

We've known for a while, haven't we? that Doom is there too, because where else could he have been? with Johnny almost ready to do it as Goody rocks back and my father enters, slim, five nine, one hundred and eighteen pounds ("I was one hundred and eighteen pounds when I got married," much too light for the role), racket in hand, and more than slim—frail, hollow cheeked, that darkness about the eyes, our hero, the handsome consumptive, with those little flicks of the wrist of the racket hand he enters, such sweet sexual steel of my father's racket hand wrist, the wrist of Michelangelo's *David*, you know the one I mean, the seductive right one, that's my father's, it's the same one, and all of a sudden we spot him sitting at one of the twelve tables, the overwhelming Doom, they all jump into his bed, with a young woman of non-Italian extraction, a white American of rare intelligence, who has spent three years in college and who twelve years from this night will become the second or third Mrs. Doom, I can't remember exactly, let her be called Roxanne Clark, there she is, Roxanne Clark, and what is it that she's doing there, good Christ in heaven, Roxanne! who said you could do a thing like that at the table with the long tablecloth reaching almost to the floor and the sawdust on the floor where men sometimes spit great clams into it? Did she crawl under that table with the long tablecloth in this dimly lit place, getting her nice dress all sawdusty and shitty? Doom would not have permitted it, Doom, being a little prudish, would not have suffered that which you and I jumped to the conclusion concerning Roxanne, she, Roxanne, not there under the table, who had never done that to a man anywhere, much less under a table, letting herself imagine it in college reading Flaubert, *to suck a man's cock to termination*, and reading James T. Farrell implying that Studs, the Irish kid Studs Lonigan, *with that wet name Studs wanting to fuck his sister fucking me so quickly in that book, draining him dry, not a drop must fall,* she who would become Doom's tidiest housekeeper, *yes, suck them into screaming and crying like big babies, which is what they all are, to terminally suck,* as she believed Molly Bloom had made millions scream and cry, our Roxanne, reading and imagining introducing Mrs. Bloom herself to the dago dick, because she was convinced that Molly's millions did not include even one of those, *Molly sucking hard like tits those dago dicks oh Molly those dago mothermen terminate the brutes* you, Roxanne, who two years into your Mrs. Doomhood wrote three pages of fiction (*lubricated friction*) that would have made James Joyce nod and wink and James T. Farrell drop his head in shame, which is what he deserved, anyway, and who was she going to share those pages with in that family, tell us, oh Christ! with the exception of course of Augusto Lentricchia himself, which is out of the question of course, what an insane idea, he, Augusto, would have given her his beat-up copy of Walt Whitman in all comey Italian (a redundancy) which he knows she can't read, but why should that be any hindrance? so what? Augusto himself was out of the question, and who (Roxanne I'm referring to now) who at a major family picnic on the Fourth of July, in a private moment with my father, that shyest of killers, says to him out of the blue, "I want to lick your wrist," and he, "Not even my wife," and she, "In honor of America," and he, silent, and she, "I want to recognize you." Roxanne herself was totally out of the question.

Roxanne Clark initiated nothing that night, she was small-town 1930s female normal (despite those goddamn novels). She had some thoughts, though, which put her on the verge (*volcanoes in our mouths, yes, your mouth and mine*). It was Doom's idea, naturally. He was so hot he had to do something, so this is what he did, simply and almost discreetly. They're sitting close together. He pulls the long tablecloth up and over their laps. He places her unresisting hand on the real thing. Has she not read the modern books of men, so ridiculous and so beautiful? She's not fazed. He gets the zipper down, which is almost impossible to do in a discreet and unridiculous manner from a sitting position. She holds back her laughter as his body goes into a crazy motion that cannot be described. He finally gets it out, he extracts it, and she takes it into her hand, without too much eagerness and without his prompting. She had never felt one of these before. She likes it. She would like to do many things. In fact, in her lifetime, she will do very few things. She stifles a large laugh, and this stifling causes pain. Roxanne desires to say the word that she had made just yesterday in her notebook, *cunderwear*, Roxanne is thinking of the ridiculous words that she saw in a dirty book, *your blood-engorged member*, and she wants to say all those words (and so much more) all flying over his head, that head of his more beautiful than Adonis, those curls, this happy happy man, Dominick Lentricchia. Cock in hand, she stifles herself, as the drunk throws up in the middle of the floor, exactly where the spotlight hits the floor of Johnny's theater, pieces of meat and carrot etcetera, and the Rox we all love withdraws her hand and Doom, seeing what the drunk has done, begins to lose the luster and the glow, the charisma is beginning to go but it's too late, some things there are that can't be called back, Doom's cock loses nothing tented under there in the darkness, and suddenly Johnny making his announcement and Doom going white while his cock rages against the dark, *son of a bitch it's claustrophobic under here,* and now Johnny makes his descent into the spotlighted area of the saloon floor and Doom all white may himself add something Italian-American to the floor, but his cock is unconcerned, the cock is bobbing and weaving under there like a slow-footed heavyweight champion, looking for an opening, wanting to deliver the crusher someplace, anyplace, it doesn't give a shit where, *this darkness, this claustrophobia, this smell under here*, and Johnny's there at last and Doom suddenly stands and the twelve o'clock cock poles up the tablecloth with the fully ascended Doom and the tender tablecloth thanks to the subtle assistance of the skillful Roxanne slides off at last *I'm free, free at last to be who I am in the open air.* Not Doom, no, never, but Doom's cock comes magnificently in the open air. My father stands over the crouched Johnny, racket overhead, poised to rush smashing downward. Bill the Judas, the great facilitator, pivots, back to scene, hands to knees, ass in the air. Roxanne, our memoirist, with pen from purse, wants to rewrite on a frayed napkin the words Johnny will now speak. With pen poised she desires. Roxanne of the twinkling eyes, the memoirist who needs to rewrite the scene.

The table is set and all the principal players have arrived. The principal players have hit their marks.

II

Companions

J sit here in this spare room, in Clearwater, Florida, and I have questions on my mind. Who told my son to put our real names in a book? What am I supposed to do? Sue my own son? First he wrote nine books nobody could understand in the family, not even my nephew Tommy, who went to college. You want to know what I did with those nine books? I lined them up on top of the television. I took the pictures of his children off. I took the picture off of the first one he married whose father was a Jew. I took the second wife off who was a Lebanese. I took off my fiftieth wedding anniversary. The first two wives call me for the holidays, but my husband won't talk to them. After I talk to them he won't talk to me. Then I won't talk to him. This goes on for a couple of days. And now when we're practically in our eighties and my husband has diabetes on top of everything else he suddenly has to write a real book that normal people might read. You know what he should do with this *Edge of Night*? Do I have to spell it out? Sideways! And if it doesn't fit up there, I'll borrow my husband's ball peen hammer. What's wrong with an Italian girl that he never likes one? And now this new one he's with now, she claims she's Catholic. I think she's supposed to be Irish. I'm going to take a picture of this tall Irish girl. I'm going to tell her I can't put it on top of the television because there's no more room. I'll tell her even though he's my son I'm warning you, wise up fast before he puts you in a book too. He'll murder you just like everybody else. I don't talk the way he makes me talk. Does anybody? There's no more room for anybody on top of the television except himself and one nice little knickknack. Maybe he'll die first, God forbid, because if he doesn't he's going to throw our dead bodies in the city dump, then put all his television books inside the coffins instead of us. He'll ship the coffins up to Utica. He'll make them write on the stone, Buried here are my wonderful parents, my wonderful children, my wonderful wives, and if you don't believe it just dig up the coffins and look inside and you'll see my whole family who I love so much, including the wonderful Irish girlfriend, may they all be nice to one another. After he kills me in his book he expects me to love him for what he did. I'll tell you one thing. I saw his penis when he was a kid plenty of times. Naturally, I'm his mother. I was never that impressed. He'll never be the man his father was. If his father were younger he'd sweep this Irish one right off of her feet, in no time she'd go for him. I went for my husband, didn't I? Oh, my husband will defend Frank, because that's what men do, but they have no love for one another. How can they? Have you ever heard of Johnny Critelli? I heard of him once. He died a long time ago. But I never heard of his mother. He made her up. He told me on my birthday that I was based on Critelli's mother. I said to him, Who the hell is Critelli's mother? What do you mean based? He said back, She doesn't exist, Ma, that's why I based you on her. Can you understand

70

that? Is he saying I don't exist? He claims in this *Edge of Night* that he's black! He claims he's an Italian Negro. I thank God for one thing, that I don't have to be the Irish girlfriend. I exist. I don't tell people I'm black. The Lentricchia men and their friends play cards together, they go fishing together, they watch ball games together, day and night on television. Now they even watch that goddamn golf together. How quiet they are when they watch! They have to watch constantly because they're afraid of each other. They're pathetic and I think my son finally realizes it. I got my own television now in here so to hell with them, they don't faze me. I never met the mother of the Irish one, I don't even know her name and what is she doing already who barely knows my son? She's sending my son shirts. She'll send the shirts. Then one of these days after he gets four or five shirts in the mail from UPS he'll send her one of his books for the top of the television and she'll put it up there. Because what choice does she have? Did I, the real mother, have a choice? In your eighties, which I'm almost in, you want to look at nice memories on top of your television. You want to look at a little happiness. This skinny little book he just wrote, you don't want to see that thing. [*She pauses.*] I hope he loves me. The Irish girlfriend, she's going to have to tell him she likes this book. [*She pauses.*] I better wash this bathrobe more, if you wear a bathrobe as much as I do you better wash it once a week. At least I still go to the toilet by myself. Will somebody do a person like me a favor and tell me who is my son? I think at this age I have a right to know. You lose a name here and there, you lose your mind. His book reminds me that even the good things I remember hurt me now, and this is what I see when I watch television alone in this spare room.

*　　　*　　　*

My friend didn't take to calling me the companion until after he had written the word here, in this the most recent evidence of the illness. Give him this day his daily companion. I believe he means to devour us. And now he promises that he won't utter my real name publicly on paper, in moods of love or otherwise, and he gives repeated assurances in moments manic and depressive (his, not mine) that he'll resist all temptations to write the name of my tragic father, the foundering father, looming and deceased, or those of my hovering brothers, deceased and living, or the name of the mother for whom no word summoned by me could be adequate. He informs me that our sole duty lies in resurrecting our familiar dead with gestures of the flesh, crazy faces, crazy works of words. He says the living are dead and that we must imagine them too. I admit affection for that notion. He says he says, In the presence of each other we imagine each other and ourselves, he says. To leave ourselves, last call, departing from shit at gate twenty in twenty minutes, no carry-ons permitted on board. Invite the living and the dead to visitations of our bodies and minds. Madam Director, my actors say, without irony, lift our shit to heaven. He says he says, Christ save me from he says. I have no desire to spend myself quoting Frank. The woman in Florida, I note, is asked to quote very little. But I'm not jealous. Let the body snatcher leave me a little unvisited flesh. I too exist. Let him translate us all but let him not violate our actual names. Without us, his imaginary intimates, this autobiographer so called, this imagining nobody, much-altering, much-altered lover who eats us, his daily bread. Does he love? I'll tell you what I know and what he does not. That we have desire to tell stories all over his pages he'll not be able to read. This is what we want. To be free within his pages, to shape stories like great arches whose breadth and height and substance we, the so-called intimates, cannot discern and do not wish to discern, clinging to our faith in unseen narrative. We believe in the unseen narrative, making shapes in the dark. He can't believe. How shapely is our shape? He can't say, but you can say. We would be without anxiety in the dark, making unseen shapes. Dump it all, a load of shitty anxiety on the lover's head. This is my rehearsal space. Does it please you? This dingy room of broken chairs at Duke University, without heat, without a telephone, where my young actors come to me to be transported. Guide us to heaven, transform us, Madam Transformer. I don't want a phone, remove the furniture. Contemplate the dirty chipping paint and leave the fecal matter discovered in the far corner by my assistant director, another Italian, who suspects a human origin. The size is suspicious, she says. Theater is made from shit. Here I insulate myself as best I can. He came to me here first, a yearning actor, who once pissed in that very corner because he would not leave, though he wasn't to be called for fifty minutes. He pissed and he stared. How happy he was! He said, You cast me, now I'll cast off all responsibility. We have the assistant director, Miss Cardinale. We have, thanks to his grotesque mimicry, the ever-present Mr. Pacino. We have Mr. Lentricchia in his own so-called person and we have Mr. Lentricchia's family. Madam Director is enwopped. Why should we let him pull our strings, who pretends he hasn't rigged the show? We'll subvert him. We'll rile him. Then perhaps he'll know a happiness he's never dreamed. We'll take him over.

Not that long after we got married, this was in 1936, there
was a woman in the summertime while he sat on the grass
eating his lunch with his friends where he worked. She sat
on the grass ten feet in front of him, without underwear on.
She let her dress go over her knees. She raised her knees
opening up looking into the sun in front of my husband
who was eating with the sun on his back, looking into her.
She wanted my husband and now she was doing this just in
case he didn't know, because now he would know, now he'll
get hard eating his lunch that I made, looking into her so
wide open. I'll tell you what happened. He never got hard.
She told someone, who told my husband's friend, who told
my husband that he must have ice water in his veins. I have
to say something. We don't look like we used to, we almost
have no shapes anymore. In my opinion we look like ugly
blobs. Maybe I should let them cremate me, but I don't
want to burn even when I'm dead. Naturally he got hard. I
admit it. We may not look it now but we had plenty. The
things he did were wonderful. Ice water my ass! My husband's friend said she said that my husband stared at her
vagina like he was a statue, except she didn't say vagina.
When I heard she stated that he stared, then I knew everything. I know what staring means. You should have seen my
husband's father, who my son is looking like more every
day. Naturally he started to get hard, a healthy man in his
twenties. He saw it and she was a beautiful woman. But
when she opened up wide in the grass, he was thinking
about something else, that's why he was staring, because I
saw him staring a million times and I used to ask about it.
Are you bored with me, honey? Do you want me to kiss

your neck? He was in his mind playing tennis, for God sakes! in his mind tennis on his lunch hour, that's what staring used to mean in those days, and it still does. She was ignorant of tennis, that was her big problem. When we were young he worked from eight to six loading things too heavy for him on boxcars all day long without complaining. He was like a rail. He came home exhausted, but not too exhausted. At five forty-five sharp the next morning every morning my husband's friend who was his boss picked him up so they could play. They had to play. My husband didn't learn to drive until he was in his late thirties. When did he have the time? Eight until six on the boxcars. Weekends helping out all day at Rachel's store. From six in the morning until almost eight he and his boss played tennis, plus late Sunday afternoons they had to do it too. They always had to do it. They even did it in the winter when there wasn't too much snow. I made his lunch the night before: six sandwiches, I'm telling you the truth, a piece of fruit, a thermos of coffee and two cookies, but who can put on weight or learn to drive doing what he did? A pound of macaroni just for him, he practically ate us into the poorhouse in the Depression. Oh he got hard, in the sunlight she glistened all over because she wanted my husband to put it in, he saw himself coming on a strange woman before it actually got in, his semen jumping out all over her belly and bush, then he finished jamming it hard all the way in as far as he could, jamming it. He wanted to split that wide-open bitch wide open! He saw this when he was playing tennis on the grass in his mind eating my lunch. But she was ignorant, that was her only problem. Before he came in his pants, the tennis came first. My husband thought he was that famous tennis player he bombasted me about during

75

supper, who turned out to be a homosexual. I said to him when it all came out, Did you read the front page yet? He got arrested! He's a big queer! My husband said to me, What's that got to do with it? Are you jealous of Big Bill? Are you thinking something you're afraid to say? Now I'll tell *you* something! My boss and I are pretty evenly matched, but I beat him almost every time and he never takes it out on me on the job. That's what tennis is, he said. What do you know? I don't care if he sucks his own cock off, because what's that got to do with tennis? Then he threw a box of macaroni against the wall as hard as he could. Macaroni flying all over the kitchen! I was scared because my husband never uses bad words. When he looked between her legs the tennis in his mind definitely started to lose, then it started to win, then it won. And it was the best tennis he ever played, looking into that bag. Ice water? My husband was tempted, but he kept eating my sandwich and he kept playing, and then that's all he was doing, playing like the tall handsome queer. That beautiful bag wanted him, but she didn't understand Big Bill. He loved Big Bill. I think it helped that he was eating my sandwich, he likes what I make him eat. With me and Big Bill my husband has everything he needs. As far as my son goes, he can write this down, but he didn't tell this story. I didn't tell it either, as far as that goes, my husband told it. I just made the sandwiches. Tell me something. What does my son do? Because why should he get the credit?

*   *   *

It's true, this past March we spent time in Venice, I threw time away in Venice. We like to say in Venice. He's convinced he remembers his birth. I'm also convinced. Like incantation, in Venice. I came up from the bottom of the ocean and there he was, just as he says, naked against the far wall. The room was an oven. The room and I were on even terms. There is no reason to doubt it, my friend was suffocating, but in the moment of his crisis he was winning his freedom, he was sliding over into glee. Acting up. Feeling the onset of new writing. He depends upon me, or should I say he depends from me? He's so pleased when I tell him to shut up. Soon the rehearsal will begin and they will expect me to be ruthlessly critical and made speechless by their talent, erring slightly on the side of admiration. All criticism to vanish after the final dress. They're deranged. They need to fear me and it doesn't matter who they are, these wonderful student actors or Mr. Pacino himself. They hand me the power to make them happier than they've ever been. They make me a monster and I accept the role. This is the key: frighten them badly, then love them fifteen minutes later, then frighten them again, but not as badly as the first time. And so on. It is thus that I build a foundation for their concentration. They feel that they must give themselves to me. So I offer them the hint of a female Hitler. Just a hint. My relations with actors are in fact exemplary. We wipe their behinds if necessary, and if the request is sufficiently pathetic. My friend, of course, cultivates his fear of me. It makes him happy to do so. It improves, he says, the quality and duration of his erections. Mr. Maniac asked me to put on thirty pounds. Understand, I am a full-bodied woman. Once, during breakfast: Stop eating. When are you going to tie me up? Then the giggles, so pleased with ourselves. We get on very well. He says it is quite miraculous for a man to like a woman, in addition to love, in addition to fuck. I'm in the nude! I'm quoting Frank performing a parody, reaching for Mr. Pacino's I'm in the dark! When doesn't he reach for Mr. Pacino, the suicidal and murderous Al reaching for Lear in an absurd movie, Frank reaching for Al reaching. Weep for what little things could make them glad. Quoting my father quoting Mr. Frost. My father said Mr. Frost. Quoting my father quoting. Quoting Frank quoting Al quoting. I'm also suffocating. He believes that his sinuses on the first night in Venice caused him to suffocate. He just wanted to write. Quoting is my sinus problem. I'll tell you a story. My father and my mother after the dishes, in the front room, without forewarning, without shoes, without music, in red union suits floating formally like trained dancers in a movie, in mutual appreciation. My brothers and my father, without forewarning, without backboard and hoop, without ball, so quietly miming in their loose briefs, driving to the basket, whirling and leaping, so elegant among furniture and doilies, impressive liftings in the groinal region. Jigglings. We cause ourselves to be entertained, says my bombastic father. Mr. Frost understood that we are children who create from shit. I can't breathe! Frank is truly desperate. Small dramatic pause. I'm in the nude! Frank has transcended his desperation. Is it clear to you that I have long given good audience? I believe that I grew up with Frank. I believe that we are having incest.

*   *   *

Bill called my husband moon. Hey, Moon! What a moon you got! Then he did this with his hands when he was saying those words. Have you ever seen this? This. Like this. I never saw anybody do this except Bill, my husband, and Robert De Niro. When Robert De Niro was going like this with his hands in that movie my son made us see on the

VCR, he said I'm going to open up his hole. That's the kind of language my son likes, who told me he watched that movie eight times. He told me the Irish girlfriend watches it even more than he does. She's off her rocker too. They call it *Insane Bulls*. By the way, that's what Bill was. My son and his father grinned the whole time during that movie. First Robert De Niro said I'm going to open up his hole, then after that he said, I don't know whether to fight him or fuck him. What words! They stick in your mind whether you like it or not. I wonder if Robert De Niro plays tennis? Does Mickey Mantle play tennis? I think I'll ask my son who was so crazy about him. Maybe they're all queer in sports, maybe they have to be in sports, what do I know. One time Joe Fiore said something bad about Mickey Mantle when he and his wife were having coffee with us when we lived on Mary Street and my son, who was fourteen, went nuts. My son was an angel when company came over, but when Joe Fiore said that bad thing about Mickey Mantle he became vicious. We were so embarrassed. If they love a sports player watch out, it's worse than if you attack their wife. You know what Robert De Niro said to his wife? He asked her if she sucked his brother's cock off! Before that he asked his own brother if he did it to his wife! My brother-in-laws are bad, but we never went that far in this family. I never got asked a question like that. But Robert De Niro's wife I heard fools around. My husband was called moon because he was lucky in cardplaying. Bill had a lot of language. Bill was saying my husband always wins in poker because of his big moon, but my husband's moon is not that big, it's just right and I like to look at it when he doesn't know I'm looking. According to Bill, my husband's hole was very big, that's why he was lucky. That's what this means, like this, your hole is big and it's open, like this. Isn't this a nice gesture? I think I'm the first woman to ever do it, unless my son taught it to the Irish girlfriend, which I wouldn't put it past him. Unless she already knew, which I could believe that too. I could believe anything about her. I don't know her well and maybe at my age I never will, but I know one thing about her. My son better stay in line because she'll open up his hole without thinking twice. I shouldn't say this because he's my son, but in my opinion it's about time a woman opened up his hole once in a while. When you do that to them once in a while they're easier to get along with and then after a while they like it, you have to shit on them once in a while, which they like even when they say they hate it. They like a lot of things they won't admit. We make them do things and they like everything we make them do. Can you figure any of this out? What the heck does luck have to do with your moon having a nice big hole? The only thing I can figure out is Bill was constipated a lot, which is true. He thought it was lucky to go easy every day, which is true about my husband, and which is definitely lucky. In other words, Bill was jealous about what went on inside my husband's beautiful moon. In that department my husband never had a problem in his life. I agree with Bill because I have that problem myself constantly. My husband is so lucky, it pours out every day. No strain. There's my husband playing poker like he's sitting on the toilet at the same time, so happy like he is every morning without fail and he's winning all the pots so smooth and so easy and Bill is saying *Madon'*, Hank, what an ass on you! Thank God he didn't refer to a piece of ass, I'm confused as it is by the way they talk in the Lentricchia family. People like Bill and me, we have to strain. Bill the big talker can't go. My husband says I talk too much and maybe if I keep my mouth shut more and stop worrying about moving my bowels I'll get over my bowels problem. I told him does he want me to get over it the way Bill got over it? You know how Bill got over it? I'll tell you how. He died, that's how. He died indirectly because of this problem, screaming and completely insane, he saw himself on television eating ice cream, and I saved my husband's life indirectly because of this problem because of what happened that New Year's Eve at Bill's house where the four of us were sitting around talking and all of a sudden the subject came up of hemorrhoids, which is another thing Bill and I had in common and my husband who is so mooney never had. Hemorrhoids are not lucky but Bill would have been lucky if it was hemorrhoids, even if he had the type where they have to operate. Imagine a sharp knife up there! I was saying to Bill, when you have our condition it's a good thing to look at the toilet paper every time you wipe, it's even good to look in the bowl to see the differences in there among your stools from day to day, they tell you about your state of health, when it comes to your state of health those things tell the truth about you, including your state of mind, don't kid yourself. Bill's wife was looking at me funny. My husband was looking irritated because he doesn't appreciate this type of discussion. He says to me, Why do we have to have on New Year's Eve a medical conversation? Lately, I said (I made believe I didn't hear my husband), I was seeing a little on my toilet paper. Suddenly my brother-in-law who always listened to me very seriously said in a loud voice: A little blood on the toilet paper? You think it's bad on the toilet paper? When I go you see it in the bowl! My toilet is so full of blood sometimes I can't see what I put in there! I said, Bill, that doesn't sound right to me. You better go to the doctor because that's not hemorrhoids. My husband looks at the wall and says, Dr. Lentricchia. Bill says, Why? So they can suck me dry? They say your hemorrhoids, Preparation H, fifty-five dollars. Don't make me laugh, he says, because after a certain age it's natural to bleed from your ass. My husband says, Don't harp on him, it's his internal affairs. Bill's wife gets up to make the coffee. All of a sudden Bill took my breath away, he doubles up and starts crying the way he did when Angie Bombace wouldn't take him back. We were frozen in our chairs watching him rolling on the floor crying and hollering. His wife from the kitchen said, Dear, did you say something? Two months later he told her off good, who wasn't hard of hearing. He told her her lousy American cooking which had no taste caused the cancer, it wasn't hemorrhoids and it was all over his liver and in his mind in the end. Bill was full of cancer on New Year's Eve. My husband and I got out of our chairs. My husband was crying. Bill said, Hank, I think I'm going bye-bye. I said, Don't talk that way, Bill, we all love you, even the one in the kitchen and the ones who used to be in the kitchen. Seven months later he was dead. The following April, Eckerd's was giving out those stool tests free. I made my husband take that test. I had to harp on him but finally he did it. He said, Why? There's no blood. I said, They have machines now they can see microscopic blood in your stool. I said, When it's microscopic they can cure you. You want to end up like your brother, up in Utica, under all that snow, just because he had a hard head? I had to help him take that test, I've done it a million times. He didn't know how, you're the expert he says like a wise guy, you put your hand in there. I put my hand in. It turned out to be microscopic. They claimed they got the tumor and he lived. Good thing

I harped. Now I can still look at my husband coming out of the shower. He lost his shape but so what? If that's what it takes, I'll put my hand in every day. Bill wasn't mooney, that sounds pretty snotty but it's true. The funny thing is, do you know what I remember best about Bill? Something crazy he used to do with his moon. It was something different. Years ago he was a moon artist. I don't mean what those kids do, anybody can do that, that's not an artist. Bill was an artist of the moon nobody ever heard of! He used to get a lot of gas and save it up somehow, nobody to this day knows how. Then he would go from chair to chair, first a wood chair, then a leather chair, then a cloth-covered one, then he went up against the plaster wall, against the door-knob, tight he went up against each thing with his moon, letting out a little in each place, first tight, then letting half his moon off a little bit each time because it was different material and different amounts of gas and different gaps of lifting, a different sound each place, high, low, deep and dark, how fast he ran around in our living room! and after a while it was just Bill, it was only Bill, dancing and playing his moon voice, I don't even think he knew we were there after a while, he was going around and around, he was gone. I saw this with my own eyes, he would have done it on the ceiling, he would have arisen if he could, and this is Bill, this is an artist, and now he is gone for good and I suddenly real-ize either I'm remembering or I'm exaggerating like my son, Mr. Exaggeration. I'm trying to have Bill on my mind, for sure I'm trying to have Bill on my mind, and that's not an exaggeration. I admit what my husband says is true. My son and I are a lot alike. But it would break my heart if after what I just told you you came to the conclusion that Bill was odd. I think Bill made that whole thing up about

Critelli, but that doesn't mean Bill was odd. That's just who Bill was. First he drove us crazy with a story that never happened, then we have to remember it even after he's dead, because this son of mine won't let us forget.

*　　　　*　　　　*

He is Al De Niro and I am Bobby Pacino. Then I'm Al and he's Bobby. Recently, visits from Marlon Keitel. Roles assumed daily. We move as rapidly as we can from imitation to parody to the grotesque, the monster versions, contortions, screaming the lines in the exhilarating ridiculosity of our everyday lives. Throw away the movies, do each other, go directly to the gargoyle faces emitting gargoyle voices. We depart, we return, we depart, we return. Eventually, nothing to depart from. Theater of theater, we've lost our shit. If I find out you're lying, Joey, I'm going to kill somebody. JOEY!! The next level, he says, is vocal vampirism, we must not hesitate to move to the next level. This, he says, is the true goal of our nightmares. To awake thinking his midnight voice is screaming out of my throat. We must not resist. Awake ripped from sleep, feeling him emerge. That is how you become my mother, you believe you're giving birth to my voice. You are you but your voice is me, which makes you even less you than you think. For two seconds this is what you feel, you feel me coming out of your mouth. The meaning of true love is you quote me from your wombvoice, Mommy. I leave you no room, then you vomit me vocally. You welcome my invasion, because it feels good to vomit me vocally. Nobody can hear you. They hear the woman in Florida. They hear me. You fuck my wife? YOU FUCK MY WIFE!? I don't want my brother coming out of that toilet with his dick in his hand. I'm in the nude! Can you breathe? Can you breathe? Or something of the sort he said. The next level, embrace it quick quick. Your turn. You do something for me I'll do something for you. Suck on my voice. Suck it to termination. Or something of the sort. One should not rush to conclusions. Much of it is light, if frenetic, comedy. Light, frenzied, and inflamed. Farce macabre. Quite pleasurable and benign, I think, much of it. Like sex at its finest. Nevertheless, my memories are different. May? Former Utican, professor at Duke, to deliver commencement address at Utica College. Phone calls the week before, trying out bits of the draft all over me. A college friend, with flaming red hair, killed in an automobile accident. Frank made it a musical motif, four citations in the space of a fifteen-minute address, his present to the graduating class, mixed in, blend until smooth with references to linguine in a red clam sauce. It's true. Large family party held in someone's honor, Frank can't remember whose honor. The faces of his ancient relatives collapsing all about him, skeletons asserting themselves. They're beginning to look alike, with strong resemblances to my dead father, he says, who never saw my father. Skeletons rising through the flesh, they come forward jumping at us. In Utica, a withering into the truth, like my father. Those who were living. Joe Flowers dead more than twenty years, Frank's father can't lose his grief. He drives up to the party, his father awaits him outside, look at me, son, a patch of sunlight flashing on the jaw of the father-in-profile, a patch of protruding jawbone, jumping at him. Looked for hard at the party thereafter, he could not find it again on his father's face, full and rounded, where is the hidden jawbone? He would see the jawbones of our fathers. He brings me gifts from Utica: dialogue from the party. "These false teeth, I can't get used to them. They make me sound like a drunk." "She won't wear her false teeth every day, so her cheeks are going in like this, like this, her lips are going in, and she was such a beautiful girl." Julio, the swarthy Sicilian uncle, called the African, bleaching out. "I can't wear these false teeth, they make me gag. I'm a gagger." "She says she's a gagger." June? There was no June. He didn't exist in June, he worked well in June. I have no June quotations. July? One item: in a restaurant he went by mistake into the women's room, he urinated not knowing where he was, in a toilet with the door wide open, where was the urinal? Woe to men, and when he caught a glimpse of a female emerging from an adjacent stall he hurried, he shook it off fast dripping on his shoes, because he needed to see her at the sink, he wanted a face-to-face with Roxanne. He said he felt she accepted him in the women's room and he can't possibly explain how good this made him feel. How honored. He said she was "genderous." He said, "The war is over." August. He looked as if he were dying in San Francisco. In the cool fog of an August twilight in Chinatown, he had to grip a wall outside a restaurant, white, cold sweat pouring off. He said inner ear disturbances, an old story, whirling going round and around. I said yes, an old story, the vampire's victims' revenge. They live in your inner ear. Afterward he apologized and ate the most expensive Chinese food I've ever heard of, in astonishing proportions, feeding the victims within. September in New York. He was working the death theme hard on a lovely autumn afternoon on the Upper East Side, as we strolled, he unaccountably—he of the swiveling head—gazing at the sidewalk. I say, Did you see that? "What? Where?" They just wheeled a body into that building. "A body! Where? When?" A body on a gurney, covered with a black sheet. "Was the sheet

86

made of rubber so it wouldn't lift off?" How could I know that at this distance? "I'll bet it was rubber so it wouldn't lift off in the breeze." We approach the building, a funeral chapel, door wide open. "Let's go in so I can see too, I want to see." We can't go in, that's preposterous. He says, I can smell the rubber sheet on my face. A month later he saw me on Fifth Avenue, wheeling a gigantic baby carriage, seven feet long, four feet wide. He was in the carriage, a corpse, with a black rubber sheet over him. I wheel racing along the park, stopping people along the way, whipping off the sheet. Look! See my baby! Later that same day, nighttime on the Lower East Side. A major cross street. Crowds. Suddenly the people evaporate. Twelve police cars come roaring to a stop on our side of the street, all in a row. Weapons. They focus about twenty yards ahead of us through deserted space. I say, Let's go back. "No." At least let's cross the street. "No. Let's keep walking." He wants to walk into the deserted space. "Let's see what happens. I want to see what happens next." False alarm. No shots ring out, no blood in the street. He feels robbed. He wanted to be in the middle of something. In person, "because I'm sick of television."

From May to September, he played with it. He fooled around, trying to scare himself. He believes it feeds the recurrent illness that he calls his writing. But when his beloved grandparents, Tommaso and Natalina Iacovella of Utica, New York, where was he when they died? On the moon? They raised him but he did not return to look at them. And Augusto and Paolina, beloved grandparents of Miami, Florida, Augusto the mythic father, the model of his discipline, where was the grateful grandson? Does he believe that he can make amends with himself and with the

dead by the homage of his so-called memories, his ridiculous sentences? I saw my father's death eek itself out. I saw
my brother's corpse. To see such things is hardly heroic.
There is nothing to be done, perhaps a wild ramming fuck,
if you can get it, then nothing and nothing. The wild ramming fuck works but once. Fifty-four years old and he has
yet to look upon the face of a dead familiar. He requires a
face-to-face. Frank, the phone is for you. Florida. Then we
shall see if he'd like to play a role, or write those offensive
sentences, or read a book, or choose a wild ramming fuck, if
he can get it. If he can get it up. The war is not over.

*   *   *

I remember the light on top of the ambulance in the dark
going around and around. This was in August of 1949.
Then the people on our block must have all come rushing
out of their houses the way they always did whenever an
ambulance or a police car stopped on our block. They were
standing in the driveway staring down at me. Eva the big
mouth next door was the head one as usual, in her house-
coat, which she was usually bare under that summer. I felt
drowsy and the funny thing was, this is what I remember
better than anything, I had no cares for my family. Isn't that
something? They were wheeling me down the driveway in
one of those stretchers with wheels on and I was on a cloud.
I didn't know where my daughter was. My mother-in-law
must have been taking care of her in the kitchen giving her
cookies, and I have to admit that it didn't matter one way or
the other where she was. My husband who was walking
beside me wasn't looking at me, he was looking at the
driveway in his T-shirt. I didn't want to say, Frank, look at
me, I'm your wife. He had finally filled out nice, his muscles

in his chest and arms were very beautiful. I don't have any idea to this day what he was going through because we never had a conversation concerning this, but I'm positive he wasn't playing tennis in his mind for a change, but who knows for sure. I heard my son's voice say somewhere in the dark what's wrong with my mother. My son was nine then, playing outside in the dark. He must have seen the light on top of the ambulance. I heard Eva say to him there was too much blood. That's all she said. There was too much blood. My husband kept looking at the driveway and walking and saying nothing. The crowd didn't talk and I couldn't see my son, who must have been in the crowd staring. I heard these things going down the driveway but I didn't belong to these things for a change. I was just going to sleep in August with all those blankets on me and that's all it was. They must have thought I was cold. I wasn't cold or hot. I wasn't anything for a change. Back then people were different with their kids. We didn't tell them I was pregnant. It was too embarrassing back then to talk like that. Besides, because of the risk we didn't want to disappoint them. I was told to stay in bed because Dr. Panzone said I might not keep it because of the spotting a little too much. That night I started to get terrible cramps and the spotting became a river. After I soaked the mattress they called an ambulance. I was just full of blood down there. Two children without trouble, now this. You know when I stopped wanting to have another one? The true answer is never. Through my fifties and sixties and even these days once in a blue moon I wish I had another one. They always say you should be grateful for what you have, but I keep thinking about the one who died inside me. I guess I became my baby's coffin, didn't I? My son was old enough to have been told about what happened, but he wasn't told until his late twenties. We didn't have the words to talk to a nine-year-old like that. My husband could have taken him with us in the ambulance, so what if I died right there? But then we would have been forced to say something to him in the ambulance. He would have seen them put that thing on my face. I don't think he needed to see that. Why didn't Eva at least lie? You don't tell a nine-year-old there's too much blood when in the dark his mother is going down a driveway into an ambulance out of the blue. I'm mad now, but I wasn't mad then. You should see my husband's face when I say I wouldn't mind having another one. I could use a cat or dog. This morning on "Donahue" I heard a woman professor say something that was very intelligent. She said what happened to me should be called a natural abortion. When she applied that word to me, I felt like slapping her face. I never had a picture of it in an album. I can't even have one in my mind. I've tried hard to make up a face in my mind. My son is so damn stubborn, I can't tell you, or I would ask him to do me a big favor. You wrote a Critelli. Now do this for me. I would like to ask my son if he has to write about us and make half of it up why can't you make me one in your mind, Frank, make me one in your mind and then put it in words in a book where I can read it every day. Make a picture of a face close up. Make it six months old, who cares whether a girl or boy, and let it be healthy, and say I nursed it until it was one year old. Knowing my son, he'll say I nursed it until it was ten. [She pauses.] I went to the toilet, and it fell out of me in pieces. [She pauses.] Write me a baby, Frank. Is that so hard to do if you're a writer?

*   *   *

90

My father once told of a man who ejaculated bloody semen every twenty-eight days. There's a theme for my friend, nicely confluent with the succulent ones he gives to the mother. Blood pouring from an anus, a vagina. Does he know the difference? Death holes. A plea to the son to conceive her a child, a baby born from wet words. I'm young enough for the real thing, but my time is running out. *Cunderwear?* I gave him that one in December while he inhaled a biography of the wife of James Joyce. Nora Barnacle, who wasn't one. Joyce called her Molly Bloom. Joyce, baby tuckoo himself, Mr. Joyce was the true barnacle. Why can't my friend give me a new name? I'm not a barnacle and we know who is. Listen to my friend: tell them about my summer and fall. I can't work it into my own voice. You take on the labor pains of chronology, I'm bored with chronology. Cut me a grapefruit, make me some hot cereal. And so forth. Yes, he said and so forth. He is the barnacle and I require a day off. That woman in Florida. Cast a woman of that vocal heft and the text goes straight to the toilet. Forget the play, because they will forget everything once she begins. How long have you known that we are rehearsing *Six Characters in Search of an Author*? It could not have been otherwise. The woman in Florida and I, and all the rest, we're human beings in the making, in flight from an author who wants to turn us into characters. Ignore his protestations to the contrary, this is his relentless intention, to make us textual puppets. He lies, the tongue wounds never fazed him. He reminds me of my father describing the last phase of his illness: I have a literary tumor in my brain. At the first rehearsal I told my actors that their central goal was to irradiate the consequences of Pirandello's description of The Father: alternately mellifluous and violent in his manner.

Because this is who you are, you're nothing but the irradiation of The Father's manner. Do as you wish, invent fantastic originality, do many things, entertain us, because we wish to be entertained, but above all ground your brilliance and your surprises in the energy of this unique irradiation. The Father's manner is your fate. Oh, you desire that I should specify an intention? You cannot play my meditation upon a stage direction? Very well. When all else fails, please me. I speak portentous nonsense. I intone redundancy. In other words, I give them what they need. I say, Do you wish to know why, truly why, Pirandello hath so described The Father? Yes, I say hath. They lean in, and I say, Because The Father is The Father. Our father who art in portentous nonsense, permit us to cling. My father was alternately elusive and elusive. A week after my brother, the first child, died, he wrote to me: You must become the first son, because my second, your putative brother, is disconnected. My second son displays no will to domestic self-immolation. The first, my first, has fled. Your mother is impervious, her guts are impervious to life and death, which is why we all need her. She spoke to me at the wake at stunning length of losing her hair. She fears baldness. I desire for myself a baldness of mind. This literary clutter, I need to be shut of it. I wish to be shut of my theatricality. Her sisters think her insane, but she is merely impervious and in all likelihood immortal. The onset of baldness means nothing. The other one was born disconnected. The scene of the First Son, nevertheless, must be played. Rehearsal time is short. Return. I offer you what no daughter has been offered. Forget Cordelia, Cordelia is weak. Return. I enter the last phase. Your mother and I love you very much. He signed it, Your desert father. He put father in quotations. Stories from the interior, they often cause us to react with memorable stupidity. We become remarkably worthless readers and listeners. We assume madness, extraordinary and hitherto unrecorded forms of deviancy. In the family, at the fortified interior, we make up words. We make crazy faces. We parade. The Father is permitted to prance. The family is where, if we are truly loved, we exorcise our extremity. The family is where we scream. You may assume my father was a bit cracked, if you like, because he spoke an absurdly and consistently distended rhetoric. He loved literature, that's all it was. He was an English major who earned his living as an accountant for the city of Detroit. My father's literaryspeak kept him lucid. Believe me, he was most amused by his own bombast. Three days before he died he said to me: Do parodies of me after my death. Recall me in extravagant parody and never hesitate to choose your material from the most disgusting episodes of my final illness. Drag your left leg, speak with a thick tongue. If you can, drool. Two days before he died, he said, I give you this, my sole purchase on wisdom. Always be present in your own voice to your loved ones. Speak to them in direct language. Never hide from the ones you love. On his last day he said, Bring me a copy of *Long Day's Yearning into Night*. When I told these tales of my father to my friend, he said: Your father is as intimate to me as my own most secret thoughts. Then he said, I miss your father. My friend never laid eyes on my father. On the first anniversary of his death, my mother mailed to me his living will:

To the alleged daughter, these directions for the achievement of presence. Cherish these aids to intimacy with the ones you love, in a tenuous light. Memorize this list. Play it with them, or die lonely.

With a stubborn, bitterly resentful look
Rebuffed and hurt, shrugs her shoulders
Kisses him—tenderly
Evading his Eyes
Forcing a laugh
Then dully
Wincing
Miserably
Then dully
She turns away. She attempts a light, Amused tone.
Sharply
Her casualness more forced
Staring in fear before her
Then dully
A tenuous light surrounds us, the breath of our fantastic
reality. —Dad

I'm quite a quoter. [*She pauses.*] I remember my friend best in Venice. Invaded by Tintoretto's force. How quickly he exchanged Bobby, Al, and Harvey for Jesus, Mary, and Joseph. He did the expected scenes, the crucifixion and so forth. But the Virgin in her Assumption? I was touched by the lightness and the modesty. Can you imagine his Annunciation? His shy reception of the angel? Roles assumed and discarded in seconds, one after the other in a makeshift loincloth, doing even those nameless bystanders of the Christian Theater at the edges of paintings. So many in an obscure light. He was shocked back by the agony and glow of transfigured flesh, so many burly bodies—his too—becoming balletic, dancing his awe, in Venice. [*She pauses.*] It's a beautiful sound and a summons. Critelli, the secret of Venice. He's chasing Critelli.

94

III

Augusto

$\mathcal{A}$ Sunday in July 1935, 11 A.M., and Augusto Lentricchia sits in a special chair, waiting for Johnny Critelli, who will arrive, according to custom, precisely at noon, in order to partake of Augusto's mind and best meal, a distinction that neither Lentricchia nor Critelli would have thought worth making. A two-course meal for Johnny, who seemed to Augusto to have come out of a book. *Che libro?* On the morning in question he was trying hard to see this book, even though he believed that it hadn't yet been written. *Perhaps I will write this book, because I have not written my sons, not even my eldest who thinks only of that thing always in his hand, swinging it always, even in the kitchen, let him masturbate that thing.* An hour ago, at ten, without belief, but with transfixed concentration, Critelli had attended high mass at St. Anthony's, faithful attendance (not belief) being the sole condition set forth by the Irish priest in this church on the Italian east side of Utica, for the continuance of their discussions, now two years in duration, eleven to eleven fifty-four each Sunday, of Christ the brooder. The one who detested saying all those didactic speeches and stories and clever little things that he had to say and that bored Jesus Christ himself into profound stupor. Who liked to think about his beloved twelve friends more than he needed to talk with them. That Christ. Eleven fifty-four sharp, because it required five and a half minutes at a brisk jog for the lithe and stinky Critelli to reach the second-floor Lentricchia apartment on Catherine Street—he, Critelli, having long understood and approved of Augusto's unforgiving rigor, who had whispered to Johnny, a week before their first Sunday, eight years ago, that failure to appear at noon *in punto*, even a second late, would result in banishment from the table. The door to the apartment would be locked to his sons as well, and even then, at ten years old, Critelli had been drawn to Lentricchia as the iron filing is seduced by the magnet, and had never been late.

Out of heavy crude wood Augusto had hacked his chair, and how he had enjoyed the hacking! extending the armrests disproportionately, because he needed to, a ridiculous thing to behold (though no one said so), so much the better to place across the gap between the long arms his short wide plank, as he had two hours ago, 9 A.M. sharp, this short wide plank of razor edges that permitted him to say aloud, on the rare occasion of a deserted apartment, or as the family slept, or when he no more could contain his rage, This chair is my desk. This is mine. Augusto the crack voiced, barely audible, who desires to stay inside, writing and meditating, and remembering his best friend, big Silverio Alteri, who he isn't seeing much anymore. He misses Silverio, who they now call Sam, who has become an American insurance man with a car. This chair was Silverio's idea. *My best friend gave me a better friend.* "My greatest poem," Silverio had said, "I dedicate this idea to you, Augu." Long ago, Alteri had encouraged Augusto to submit a poem to *Il Martello*, had harassed him daily for weeks, until his friend had relented. Upon its appearance in print, Augusto felt a wild rush, then immediately a coldness such as he had never before known. He told Silverio that he would no more mail his memories to these strangers in New York. His memories were for the eyes of Alteri and the ears of Paolina, his one-eyed wife, who could not read even when she had two eyes. In bed, especially, he liked to read to her, the spouse who was amused, particularly by the poems of rage directed against the rich capitalists, my dear Paolina, who late one night after love-making, and forty years before the fact, told her husband that he should not write about her final illness, that she knew for certain that he would not honor her wish, and that therefore she was forgiving him in advance, because you cannot help what you do with your pen on paper. And forty years later, he wrote, in ruthless detail, venting his love through the revolting final impressions—

> My wife's body eats her mind.
> When did we last make love?
> This poem is easy to write.

The absent Alteri spoke much in his mind, especially on the mornings and evenings when he sat in Alteri's chair. "In the tiny apartments of the poor, Augu, a writer needs protection. With these monkeys always jumping, you must put yourself inside this. And then Silverio had drawn a picture of it for Augusto in order to emphasize the crucial matter of the ridiculous-looking armrests. Put yourself inside this, only you in this, this is your private room, exactly like the rich have. This is where you belong as much as possible. I know a man who can help you, free, to make a cage around this. Let the monkeys climb the walls and eat the icebox itself. Let them yell all around you, but this they must not touch, and in this they must not sit. When you desire to kill them, take your big diary book and come here. Because it is better to write than to kill. [*Alteri smiles.*] And now? I am hungry! Do you have something in the icebox or have the monkeys destroyed everything? They eat the food and you eat the ice. If you ate as much as me, the seizures would not come. Why do they call it the small evil? Why is it small to fall on the floor like you are dead? [*Alteri laughs.*] You can break your head falling like that. [*Alteri laughs louder.*] The first time we thought you were dead. [*Alteri in tears of laughter.*] Now we put a blanket over you and wait for you to wake up and say that you are sorry, Where is my pencil? Dominick tickles your feet to see if you are alive. This is a subject to put in a memory, if you could have such a memory. But the tickling by Dominick is mine, which I give to you free, if you will only tell me where I can find something to eat in this barren place. After you die, your sons will find your big diary books full of thousands of poems, and they will read a few, and become interested in these things for eleven days. Why should your things be their things? They have their own things." The fanaticisms of cars and fucking and money and sports, and cars and fucking, these are the things of my sons. One will become Bluebeard, the sweet one will become Bluebeard, and another will become a famous gangster, working in a flower shop thinking thoughts that would frighten even Al Capone, and the other one, who is in the shadow even when he stands in the sun. Who is he?

As he brooded upon his first son, Frank, shrouded in shadow while standing in full sun, he was not trying to make a memory out of words. The memory he was creating this morning involved his dead father and other political matters ("A Brief Comparison of Mussolini and the Eternal Father"), and he desired to draft it before Critelli's arrival, he desired to make it cunning and insidious, because after the meal he wanted to spring this one on Critelli, he wanted to ambush Critelli with this thing of his, because Critelli, though he did not believe, displayed none of Augusto's corrosive wit toward the stories and characters of the Bible. Augusto had been hammering away for many months, but he could not subvert him. To Augusto's inevitable "The Bible is false," Critelli would reply, inevitably, in Italian, that the falseness of *La Bibbia*, with all due respect to you, Signor Augusto, is a thing of boredom to me, it is a triviality, this thing of falseness and truth, replies to which Augusto had no reply. Signor Lentricchia wanted to speak of reason and history and science and the shameful priests who steal from the poor, because in Italy these priests who disgust me love the big shots, the landowners, the Mafia, and the politicians, who are all the same. Sunday after Sunday, Augusto showed him essential pages in Thomas Paine, Marx, and Darwin, and Critelli in response would replay, Sunday after Sunday, the moment he had first sunk into in the presence of the clever Father Michael, though "replay" is hardly correct, the thing changing and filling out, the moment stretching out long and stretching Johnny too with each original replay, like an aria forever in process, of Christ walking on the water, on top of the water, Father Michael! a huge sun starting to sink blazing behind him, and the steady wind from behind too, it came whipping all that long filthy hair, the wind blasting and shooting it out to the east in the direction of his death, his greasy hair was like a big fat arrow shooting toward Golgotha, totally surrounded by the flashing water, how good this water feels on his crusty feet, how sucked in he is by the moving shadow bumping along, it looks so funny, Father, just ahead of him with those nice little waves rolling under and Christ looking completely black in the burning water too bright for his eyes, unless he concentrates on the fat arrow leading his shadow body to the east, which is what he does so easy, Christ is concentrating so easy and fearless out there in the sinking light as his toes—this is the best part, Father— the toes go under just a little bit with each step, so that the water can seep through the smelly hot tightness between the toes, which is why he permits the toes to go under, so the water can sneak through, because it's nice when the toes go under a little—he can float over it if he wants to but that would be flying, not walking on the water: he wants to give the water a chance to do what water can do, cool him off and suck him under, but the water can only do the first thing, how easy this is, all the way, if he wants, forever into the dark. Then they bothered him, said Critelli, at which point he, Critelli, like Christ, fell down out of his enthusiasm, back down into his stinky self.

Johnny Critelli's enthusiasm was a more powerful hammer and it was cracking, Sunday by Sunday, Augusto's skeptic armor, and the armor cracked, and it fell away leaving for anyone who cared to see, though only Critelli saw, the self of Augusto's own lyric ascent, which Augusto would not himself ever see, though it was plain to see all over his big diary books, even in the satires of his savage indignation. And what was Christ thinking? asked Father Michael, on that first occasion of Johnny's self-transcendence. And Johnny said, I don't know. And what are you thinking now? And Johnny said, I don't know. Yes, said Father Michael, and we do not care. And we cannot even remember if we were having thoughts, you and Christ and me, and we do not care, you and Christ and me, if we cannot even remember. There is no mystery here, Johnny. He walked on the water because it was his gift, because he loved his gift, because he enjoyed doing this, he just loved it, Johnny. He who will not drown. And this gift he cherished more than all his gifts of talking to crowds near lakes, and he walked on the water when the sun was going low . . . the picture he saw, Johnny, on the waves, he saw himself shimmering black on the bright waves, and the coolness, and most of all when he walked he thought of nothing just as you do when you remember him in your own words, when you make the picture for us in your words. You were happy when you made the picture, and I was happy too. Attempt, if you wish, to make this hardhead of a Lentricchia happy and you will succeed in making him almost happy. Can you guess, Johnny Critelli, why he walked into the twilight past those dopey apostles in the boat? And Johnny says, He did not do that on purpose. And Father Michael says, Yes, yes. He was happy. It was an accident arranged by the Eternal Arranger. Christ himself had no intention of walking by the boat. He wasn't trying to give signs. But they spotted him and called out to him. So why did he summon Peter from the boat? Why? Do you know why? And Johnny replied: Because he wished Peter had the gift of not thinking on the water in the wind. Did Peter have it, Johnny? Yes. Then why did the big dope begin to sink? Because he wanted Christ to save him, because he wanted to cry on Christ's chest like a baby. Because he missed Christ and he did not know why he missed Christ because Christ was right there, and he felt like a big baby. And Father Michael and Johnny agreed that

Peter saw nothing in the water, so how could Peter have been happy? Jesus Christ had a choice: keep on going and to hell with *them*, or get in the boat. He got in the boat, Johnny, he didn't have to, but he got in. Your friend Lentricchia will never get in. A choice for which I feel sympathy, and grief. When you speak of what he did on the water, Johnny Critelli, you are lifted high, but not by God, though God will forgive this in you with the greatest of ease. Because the Father himself enjoys forgiving this great sin.

Augusto was looking at his first son standing obscurely in the full sun. He was looking at an actual photograph that his son had given to him, taken two weeks before at Niagara Falls, where he had gone for a day trip with his future bride and her parents, Tommaso and Natalina Iacovella, the living legends of Mary Street. A five by seven lying on his chairdesk next to his work in progress on Mussolini and the Eternal Father. He studies the *innamorata* of excellent curves in a short-sleeved white dress, what animation comes forward to greet me, like a greeting from the excellent curves themselves. And he! Look how insane! In the heat of summer black suited with a black-banded white fedora throwing darkness over his face. My son's clothes love his body. May they protect him. Who took this picture with their arms around each other? Would they do this with their arms if the parents were watching? A stranger must hold the camera because the parents have gone to find a toilet, and still these children do not relax, what have these nervous lovers done? Nothing, and this is why the parents go without fear together to find the toilet. Let them make love like tigers until their bodies fall apart. His brothers have been doing the job since they were thirteen and he is the virgin who frightens everyone except me and this excellent daughter of Iacovella, the bawdy Tommaso who calls himself the King of Mary Street. I should record his obscene fables. I, Augusto Lentricchia, am sick of myself. I should repeat his stories, word for word. I could leave my family and move to Mary Street and become the King's secretary. Where has my father gone? Where is my husband? Is he dead? He has disappeared inside the flesh and blood of Tommaso Iacovella who tells me he will vote next time for Mussolini, because Mussolini deserves to live in *La Casa Bianca*, because he is the proper President of Dogshit. He says America is beautiful. He says America is fucked. Then he votes for the Republicans, who he says are fucked. He says if the socialist bastards like me take over this wonderful country, he will be forced to eat with the pigs, as in the old country, which is fucked. When I feel like suicide I go to his house because when he says who is fucked and I am a bastard he makes me feel like living, Tommaso, Tommaso, who says, Here they fuck me too but they give me benefits and time and a half, they pay me for receiving it in my center. The center of beautiful art is not Venice or Florence, it is the American asshole, because here they pay you for entering your center, Ah, thank you, Mr. Iacovella, you're a lovely man. Can I offer you a cup of tea and a Ritz cracker? In America, they give you a napkin to wipe yourself. My wife and I never use such language as the King uses, not even in private, but after we have seen him we have electricity in our blood and cannot sleep the whole night. He says people like me who criticize America should be hung by the balls. Then he wishes me a long and happy life and says he has neglected *la signora*, because it has been more than six hours since he last did the job and his sperm is backing up into his brain. He says people like me don't do it enough, and this is the problem of the socialist party and of England too, which, no matter what they say, still rules America, this beautiful country, which you don't deserve, Lentricchia, you son of a bitch.

And so this ingrate of an immigrant writer just sits there in his writing clothes, in a suit that looks as though its been expensively tailored to his form. But how could that be? The man is out of work. The man is always out of work. This pale man of small soft voice causes foremen to fire him in a second. Stiff white shirt, black bow tie, black vest. Cheap clothes, transubstantiated by the father of Niagara Falls Frank. And that handsome face, like a statue, eyes wide, high hair brushed back hard—the stare appears to register nothing of the human beings of his family who pay no attention, being of sound mind, who drift about the corpse as the hands press lightly the plank's razor edges (press harder!). Is it Iacovella? yes, it is always Iacovella lurking behind the eyes of the ingrate awaiting Critelli, ward of all East Utica wops, Critelli of rags and stinks. What had Iacovella (*Tommaso of my mind*) said a week after the braining of Johnny's mother? How did he receive Lentricchia's fulminations against the capitalist system? He said, You better see a doctor, you have an illness in your throat. Talk louder, I can't hear you. He said, Where does this Signor Capitalismo live? Is he a Spaniard? Tell me so that I can go to this house and place a big knife in his intestines, and twist it in there. I'll make linguine out of his intestines. We will rape his wife in all her holes. He said, Do you, or do you not wish to murder the Swedish guard, because I will help you to murder the Swedish guard, if this is your desire we can do this thing together now, said Tommaso, who grieved for fallen birds and run-over cats, and who wanted, he knew not why, this rough peasant, to pour all possible scorn on the abstractions of Lentricchia, Let us go to the home of the Swedish guard and eat the livers of his children and make him watch. Because you, Lentricchia, are a large turd! We can make our hands bloody with his blood. And what had Iacovella said when Augusto told him he had taken Johnny at seven to the insane asylum ("He is seven, he has rationality now"), in order to see his mother, the staring vegetable ("In order to look upon the fruits of capitalism"). He said, unable to hide his despair, They should have clubbed your brains to the sidewalk. He said, Write, read your books, suck on your books, and talk to adult people about those atheist bastards you read, but do not do human things with people, because in normal life you have less understanding than my ass. Augusto was delighted and almost swept away. No one had talked to him with such brutality of word and tone and such caressings of the eyes, Iacovella's hands lifting and falling, as if they were starting to die, trying to reach for the other man, the quiet one of courtesy, trusted, even by women, who nobody touches in the way Iacovella almost touched him, because nobody would think of doing it. To do so would be too embarrassing for both parties. Absorb him into your blood, Tommaso, this Augusto, this writer, this elegantly packaged chaos, whose children would hear no talk of the old country, whose children, questioned years later by a grandson, would not be able to remember their father's parents' names, and who himself, this Augusto, could not have memories of his parents, he tries hard to remember and retrieves images with partial faces in gray. And this Tommaso, who looks like a ruddy giant (five inches shy of six feet), the talking writer of clownish rage and humor (*Italia bella, Italia brutta*), whose parents' picture once hung in his dining room, and now hangs in mine. Tommaso, the pure Italian, who loves America. Augusto, the pure American, who despises all nations, and whose friendship with Tommaso was cemented when Iacovella had asked him about the whereabouts of Critelli's father, thinking he somehow knew, though never believing for a moment the evil tongues of the neighborhood that said Johnny was Lentricchia's illegitimate son, because it was clear to him that Lentricchia would not stray (the thought of it was a joke!), and Lentricchia had said to Iacovella with apparent sincerity that Johnny's father had gone to New York in order to find employment as a Shakespearean actor, and Tommaso Iacovella had replied, Augusto, your mind is so crooked I cannot wait until the next time I see you. My wife believes that you are the descendant of an Austrian sword-swallower.

"A Brief Comparison of Mussolini and the Eternal Father." He couldn't get beyond the title, he was beginning to think that he wouldn't get beyond the title, because the title was the thing itself. He would say it to the boy of rags when he passed through the door. Not even good morning. Ambush him with it, and then say, It is time to eat. During the meal, In the world of Father Michael, which you have yet to denounce, the dead may have joy, and the dead may suffer, but in my world the dead do not suffer, not even from joy, because death is perfect rest. His sons would show no reaction because they had heard this nonsense at table on Sunday ever since they were children and it was less than, much less than, I need more sauce, Ma, how come Dominick got the most sauce? And his wife would turn to him in such moments in three-quarters profile, showing the glass eye, which was blue. She might have chosen brown to go with the real one, a fact once indicated by her husband, to whom she had replied, with the nastiest language ever summoned by her, You have become a very large goof. Paolina would turn the glass eye toward him in three-quarters profile, and that was all she had to say about his nonsense. Critelli? He replied by telling Lentricchia a story that Lentricchia would take hidden pleasure in, in spite of the fact that Critelli had to say the name of Jesus Christ many times in order to tell the story of how the crowds gave Jesus Christ no room. They were choking him. The people were all over him all the time when they heard he was in town. Jesus Christ wanted to protect himself from their voices and their rantings and chantings of his name, which made him feel like he was disappearing into the sound of Jesus Christ when they chanted it. He was just too damn famous and they made him feel like nobody, he was coming out of their throats. He was becoming the crowd. Good thing they were near a lake and the boys had a boat, because naturally they had a boat, so he got in the boat but he wouldn't let the boys get in, and he rowed out a little ways, staring back at everybody, which only made it worse. They chanted Jesus Christ louder and louder. Then, in all the loudness, he started to talk and all they could see were the moving lips. They got the point in a hurry and shut up. But with the distance between them, and the coughing and whispering and farting and spitting, he knew they couldn't hear that much, and that was when he said some of his best stories ever, with ideas nobody wanted to hear or remember, and which almost caused the Eternal Father, who hears everything, to make his son go up on the cross a year in advance. While Jesus Christ was saying stories he never told or knew before this minute in the boat, he gave the crowd on purpose a sourpuss they couldn't miss, feeling better now making it up as he talked, and the only thing he lacked now was a little lunch which he wanted to eat looking at them from a distance, eating and dreaming up another twist on the story which he didn't want to finish. He needed to look from a distance. It was good for his story. But he didn't have anything to eat in the boat, and neither did the crowd, so he rowed back in and did the magic of the loaf of bread and one fish, and they all ate, and everyone, including Jesus Christ, forgot about the story. Later, when one of the boys asked him to tell the story he was telling in the boat, he couldn't remember it, not even in the dark when it was just him and the boys.

AUGUSTO: They will have to throw him out of the church, your Irish priest who created this fable.

JOHNNY: We created it together. The part about going out in the boat by himself is the only true part.

AUGUSTO: What is the moral of this story?

JOHNNY: What is a moral?

AUGUSTO: What we must remember in order to live badly.

JOHNNY: Throw away your memories after you write them. Maybe this is a moral.

AUGUSTO: Throw away your beautiful embroidery. Show nobody. Not even me. Maybe this is a moral for you.

JOHNNY: Never show what you love the most.

AUGUSTO: Yes, that is our moral for living like corpses. What part did you create? Please tell me quickly.

JOHNNY: I created the noises of the crowd. Then I created how he forgot everything in the dark. How he did not grieve that he forgot.

AUGUSTO: Throw away your beautiful embroidery after I touch it.

JOHNNY: Throw away your memories after you let me touch them. I want to touch them one more time.

AUGUSTO: Throwing away is not the same. I might not forget. I might grieve.

JOHNNY: You will grieve anyway. Take the path to self-forgetfulness.

AUGUSTO: What does that nonsense mean?

JOHNNY: I don't know.

AUGUSTO: Who told you to say those words that don't belong to you? Your sinful Irish priest?

JOHNNY: Yes.

AUGUSTO: What else?

JOHNNY: That you needed to be frightened into the present, but I do not. What does that mean, Signor Lentricchia?

AUGUSTO: It means you do not have to throw away your beautiful embroidery. It means you are here. I wish to touch your beautiful embroidery once more, but I will not. It means you have forgotten yourself.

Augusto was remembering that time with Johnny after dinner and coffee and fruit (pears and apples which Augusto had cut up for everyone), and his sons had gone out, where he did not care to know, and Paolina had gone to talk to Natalina Iacovella, perhaps to bring him back some bawdy saying of Tommaso that made her and Natalina blush and giggle concerning Mr. and Mrs. Roosevelt, and the trick that the President did with his cane, remembering how he had picked up a beautiful piece of cloth, scarlet and white, upon which Critelli had made one of his geometric renditions of the human form, and Augusto had draped this cloth over his head, covering his face completely, giggling all the time, sounding precisely like Paolina, and he said to Critelli, Perhaps you would like to do me the favor of sewing this beautiful work to my face, and Critelli had replied sincerely that the blood would drip onto Augusto's nice white shirt, and it would stain the white part of the cloth too, and, besides, the stitches will not hold or I would do it to please you, signore. But it would be a waste of time, the stitches will not hold. Then Augusto said, They will hold long enough. Then Johnny said, Are you making fun of somebody? Then Augusto said, Yes.

Again and again on those Sundays, these two monologuists. Always hearing but never intersecting. Arias of reason, arias of passion. Occasional dialogues of Lentricchia's exquisite self-torture and Critelli's naïveté, his beautiful literality, luring Lentricchia. Touching, that is what they mostly did, not talking: Lentricchia picking his way like a hungry raccoon through the box of embroidered and multicolored cloths of freakish sizes and shapes, lingering on one after the other, taking forever to go through the lot, bringing some up close, as if to smell and inhale the designs, but without commentary on Johnny's art. Never commentary. And Johnny the same: paging through the big diary books, not reading but entrapped by the handwriting, so fancy, so consistent, so clear, staring at the writing as if it were a delicious salami hanging in the window of Rosato's grocery store, running his fingers over it, as if he could feel the lettering. Augusto's memories were a kind of Braille. They felt each other's rigor, they lived each other's discipline. Augusto longing for Johnny's purity, his simplicity, his sheer presence. And Johnny longing for he knew not what in Augusto, the absence he could glimpse but not grasp, that was what it was. And by that much difference, the younger man of eighteen longing for something in the older man of forty-three, he did not even have a name for it, the longing for the unhappiness of the older man, that's what it was, though he never had a name for it, that's it—the pleasurable unhappiness of Augusto's privacy. Johnny in this ambience of Lentricchia became himself a little pleasurably unhappy, Johnny who could work anywhere, without distraction or anger, even as his friend teetered always at the edge of the unspeakable, Augusto's devotions constantly challenged and enhanced by the human barnyard of his Catherine Street apartment and his recurrent visions of mayhem—chain them to a tree in the public park, whip them. The racket, the awful visions, sending him always deeper into his art, making him safe, a good father in his way.

So there they are. Like this: together at table, but as if alone together. Or sitting in the little parlor, after dinner, the apartment deserted, on the little sofa (the Americans call it a love seat), where Augusto and Alteri used to read together. Or Augusto in his chairdesk, in a meditative stare, and Johnny in his crude and pleasant shed on Rutger Street, on the lot owned by several paesans (one of them Tommaso), the shed disappearing from view in the midst of the summer garden, overrun by richly flourishing vegetation, the fragrance and the tomatoes and the basil and so much more, and Johnny's constant companion, the burly German

113

shepherd, Lucy, lounging on the shed's dirt floor as Johnny worked. Johnny raises no questions. Augusto? Routinely bothered by thoughts of his own triviality. He says to himself routinely, but not that morbidly, I am not human. I am dead. And this boy is inhuman and dead too, but he does not know it. Not morbid, but with a small smile. We should stop, but we cannot stop. Tommaso says that the boy and myself are fortunate. It must be true.

And there was one other thing he knew to be true: that the postprandial time he would spend with Critelli today would be as nothing compared to what occurred on the previous Sunday afternoon, because no time could possibly again be like that time when the world could have come to an end, and he wouldn't have cared, and the world did, almost, come to an end that previous Sunday afternoon as he sat there with Critelli, reading to him from the episode in Dante of Paolo and Francesca, when first Alteri dropped by, who he had not seen in six weeks, then Henry DiSpirito, who Johnny thought might have been Augusto's twin brother, and then, as the four of them sat in the little parlor chatting under the gentle dominion of Alteri, who was explaining what a lovely death policy he could sell for fifteen cents per week, how an Italian could easily outlive Prudential's death plan for us and collect something when we can't work but still are forced to eat, son of a bitch, at that moment in came the ruddy Tommaso, in prime vocal estate, and tell me when he wasn't in prime vocal estate? glowing he entered, and immediately did he size up the scene: DiSpirito, Lentricchia, Critelli! Artists! Artists! And you, Alteri! the most idiotic, an insurance-man poet! And he? I am the boss of the groundskeepers at the Masonic Home, a Catholic gardener for those Protestants, and the number-one gravedigger, this is who I am, a transplanter of eighteen great elms, which even in the city of fucking New York they had to write about this amazement. I bury a Protestant once a week, and I am more familiar with the dead than you are with your wife's body! The first thing he does is spot the art books that DiSpirito had brought over of Michelangelo, Titian, and Tintoretto, and soon a comparison of these giants is underway and Tommaso is saying of Titian, whom he had never before seen, This one likes colors but there are no bodies underneath, this Tiziano thinks his shit doesn't stink, my dear Henry, where did you get the money to buy these books? Have you become a robber? Alteri is moving to the kitchen where he dons Paolina's frilliest apron in order to make the espresso in the proper manner, and Tommaso is saying to Augusto, where is your wife? and Augusto is answering, she has gone into the kitchen in order to make the espresso in the proper manner, and Tommaso is saying, this is the problem when you love these cunning artists, especially Michelangelo (whom he had seen in a book only once before), this Magnificent Faggot of Florence, they make you love what they love, like this David, look at this fucking David how beautiful he is! What am I supposed to do? Put it in his ear? Must we all become cocksuckers like Leonardo da Vinci, the Great Queer of Milan? Do you still desire your wife, DiSpirito? Or do I have to take care of her too, because of this Michelangelo? At which point DiSpirito turned to the page of the Christ in Judgment of the Sistine Chapel, and Lentricchia said, This is your God, Tommaso, this animal is the God of Flying Corpulence, this is the meat of God, Iacovella. And Alteri from the kitchen is saying, I am too modest for this animalistic conversation, I am going to pee in my pants, and Johnny says nothing because what

can Johnny say at this level? And DiSpirito tells Tommaso
that he, Henry DiSpirito, who has not yet become a homosexual, sculpts in order to assent to the desire of stone not to
be chiseled into life, I sculpt in order to fail, and Tommaso
says, You speak lunacy but I will tell you the truth: the
British bow to you, the French kiss your hand, but the Italians! Look at this Tintoretto! The Italians have it in the
balls! This bastard makes pictures more robust than my
wine! These pictures make me hungry! These pictures eat
me, I feel drained like I have just ejaculated. And so it went,
and soon there is no subject except the necessity to speak in
such leaping fashion, "I am most happy when I imagine
myself a stone," "The uninsured life is not worth living," "I
write, therefore I am," "I fuck, therefore I fuck," "Jesus
Christ is the Enrico Caruso of our meat!" "My cock has a
voice superior to Jesus Caruso!"

On it went in this fashion, but it could not have gone on
for very long, because this kind of thing would soon have
become boring to these imaginative men, and they would
have dropped, one by one, into a little snooze, in the small
warm space of this parlor, on Catherine Street, five vivid
bodies in there pouring it out, when somebody, it was no
doubt Augusto who found a common theme, he was troubled by a grievous fact, and he said, "Now Silverio, who has
lost his name, has purchased an automobile in order to do
his rounds, which he used to walk so easily." "A white automobile," said Johnny. "And he drives to Syracuse on Sundays, but why?" "To see the paesans of Syracuse, who do not
even give him coffee," said Johnny. "And the crooks of Prudential have changed his name to Sam," said DiSpirito.
"And he grows round and deep in the guts," said Tommaso.
"Because I am pregnant," said Alteri. "And he will give

birth to a death plan," said Tommaso. "He should drive his car under the grapevine in his backyard." "He should remove the engine and bury it in his garden." "I will dig the hole and shit in it." "He must remove the doors." "We can sit in it and eat the sausages your wife puts up in olive oil as we drink your wine as robust as Tintoretto himself." "Thank you, but my wine has less balls, though its balls are not to be despised." "And in the night the cats will go into Sam's car and fight and make love, leaving blood and semen on the seats." "And all day long the birds will shit on the white car with grape-colored flowing shit." "Yes, yes, and the grapes will fall and stain it in long streaks." "And the little demons of Mary Street will smash the windows." "Bluebeard and Al Capone will bring their women in there, even in the middle of the day." "Your son Frank will place a tennis ball in the shit and blood, then run away." "I will change my name to Uncle Sam." "Then we shall have to murder you, and put your body in the trunk." "I have seen such a thing in New York, the very thing we describe." "In New York?" "It is called, this thing, they call it modern art." "This thing of rust and stains and the semen of Italians and cats?" "Yes, we have created this thing in our minds which I have seen in New York." "Where did you get the money to go to New York, DiSpirito, did you become a robber?" "In New York the bastards pay to view such shit in a house of art?" "How many Protestants are there in New York?" "Four." "I will bury them." "Will you do this, Alteri, such as we describe?" "Alteri does not exist, bring me some coffee, Sam, pronto!" "What is wrong with Lentricchia?" "Why does he grin?" "He must be dying." "I will bury Lentricchia." "Lentricchia stinks already." "Yes, let's put Lentricchia in the car after the dogs and cats and birds and Bluebeard

117

and bury him in Alteri's garden, in the hole which we will all shit in with nobility." "In order to show our respect." "Because we love him." "Look how that bastard grins!" "I am tired." "Me too." "Yes, I must also go home now." "I am tired, I am dying of fatigue." "Good afternoon, Signor Augusto," said Johnny. Addio Addio Addio Addio. And there he sat, by himself again, in the chairdesk, tired, and a little glad that they were gone, though he missed them almost desperately, already needing to remember how they had lingered twenty minutes ago over Tintoretto's least-known *Last Supper*, the one hanging in the church of San Trovaso in Venice—DiSpirito telling them that this church was almost never open, and Alteri responding, "And it is a good thing too, because this *Last Supper* is a scandal," then adding without taking a breath, "This *Last Supper* is wonderful." An apostle passed out on the table, his hair in the food, another reaching for the jug of wine on the floor behind him and trying to look at Christ at the same time. What was that smear on the floor? *Gesu Cristo* in a saloon, with his eyes going up to the ceiling, drunk like the rest of those bums. Augusto, alone, wondering if he could write a memory of something that had happened only twenty minutes ago, but which felt very old, it felt like his oldest memory, this thing of twenty minutes past.

∗   ∗   ∗

It turned out it was his last Sunday with Johnny. It turned out he never saw Johnny again. And neither did his sons. Even in retrospect, a total surprise, because he could never say that he saw the signs. He couldn't see the signs because maybe there were no signs. Johnny got there as usual at twelve sharp, then everybody—Hank, Goody, Doom, Paolina, Augusto, and

118

Johnny—sat down together at the table too small for six people. The Lentricchias were poor, but there was ample pasta (thanks to Alteri), fourteen meatballs, a beautiful red sauce (enough for the week), a big salad, two loaves of bread, and a gallon of wine (thanks to Tommaso). Afterward, no fruit, for a change, but one homemade cannoli apiece (thanks to Natalina). Typically, no conversation, except for some coded brief chatter between Goody and Doom, good thing it was coded. On this Sunday Augusto decided to press his ascetic methods to another level, refusing meatballs and all but two tablespoons of sauce, and no bread, of course, since there would be no sauce left on his plate needing to be mopped up so perfectly it would look as though the plate had been washed clean. No one, naturally, took any notice of the patriarch's nonsense, unless, wait a minute, unless Johnny (maybe this is a sign), what's that tiny glance out of the corner of his eye when Augusto takes the two tablespoons of sauce? I wouldn't call that glance naïve. And that tiny thing with his mouth he does at the same time of the glance. A tiny smirk? Johnny Critelli? Too far out of character for this simpleton artist. Who would believe an embryonic irony, unless there is change going on, unless he's dying as we know him. He needs to move on. This would be Johnny's last afternoon as himself. And today, the brothers Lentricchia (as such) would be born.

They finish eating. According to custom, the three sons must now go their separate ways for the afternoon, Paolina must go to Natalina, Augusto and Johnny must retire to the little parlor for two hours of mostly silence, to be punc-tuated, here and there, by soliloquies that the speakers find a thrilling pleasure to deliver to a largely deaf audience of one. Augusto leads. He goes into the parlor and sits at the chairdesk. But Paolina decides to stay home today, for reasons unknown. She goes into the parlor too, without washing the dishes, and sits on the little sofa. Augusto immediately arises and goes back into the kitchen and does the dishes, which he does six days a week, but never on Sunday. He returns to the parlor. He opens his *Inferno*. Paolina says, Close your book. He closes his book. He smiles. She nods a little nod. They like each other, they've always liked each other. He once said to her that he wished that he could express greater warmth to people, especially to her. She replied, I couldn't bear it, your greater warmth, and for the first time in his life he experienced a belly laugh, and she turned red from embarrassment. This was a lucky marriage.

In the meanwhile, the sons have not gone their separate ways. They have instead retired to their bedroom. A room not that much bigger than a modern bathroom, with one bed for three advanced teenagers. Johnny followed and shut the door.

If Augusto and Paolina had not been so thoroughly and so pleasantly involved, they would have heard the muffled sounds of excited four-way conversation. They would have noted several stretches of dead silence. Conspiracy? They would have seen first one, then another, then a third, and finally a fourth note passed under the door. Eventually, Augusto read them, and then he read them to Paolina:

> *Dear Pa,*
> *I love you a lot.*
> *Love,*
> *Dominick*

*   *   *

Dear Pa,
I'm sorry for everything I did. Don't be mad at me, Pa.

           Your son,
           Frank

*   *   *

Pa,
Everybody in the world is a crook. Except Johnny. I am a
crook.

           Guerrino
PS: You and Ma aren't crooks either.

*   *   *

Signor Augusto,
You are wrong about everything.
      John Critelli

Late that afternoon, Augusto grew concerned, found the notes, then entered the boys' room. Empty, window open. They had taken the short jump to the first-floor porch roof, then had slid down the pillars. And off to Johnny's shed for the dress rehearsal.

Goody had arranged for a friend who would do anything for a dollar to puke at 8 P.M. sharp, in Donnely's Fine American Saloon. Goody had contacts. Johnny would take no money. Hank and Doom would earn a dollar apiece for their roles. Goody would take one for his role and another for the troubles he had to bear, because I am the boss and I have

121

rights. Johnny would do it eagerly, as if he were hungry, as if it were delicious, pronouncing it good, then speak briefly at the scene itself about The Gospel According to Mark, Chapter 7, on the cleanliness of all foods, which Johnny took to mean everything that can be eaten, and the filth that emerges from the heart, the evil intentions that alone make a person unclean. Goody said afterward that his friend, who would do anything for a dollar, would take a little less if we give him work three times a week. Hey, this is the fucking Depression. We all have our rights. Dominick said, I never ate a steak. I'll buy a steak six times a week. Hank said, Ma and Pa are broke. I'll give mine to Ma and Pa and maybe Pa will give me a little back, if I'm good. Then Johnny said, No more. Bill, you're the boss, you have a special job. You have to tell the story. Even our lives are good enough for a little story. The story is the wonderful place beyond all places. And then Johnny smiles big, and the corners of his mouth curl high in a great pumpkin grin, and his eyebrows jump, they jump again, the smile so big now he's squinting, and he's saying Goody Goody! Start the story! Do this in memory of us all.

The Knifemen

for
Jody McAuliffe

One doesn't own one's memories.
One is owned by them.

FEDERICO FELLINI

I

The Child

On the night in the spring of 1965, when he learned of his father's death, Richard Assisi slept soundly and dreamt of a child of three, or possibly four, 1943 or '44, all dressed up in the uniform of the United States Air Force. Such a brave little man was he, standing on the corner in knee pants, and with those rosy cheeks of olden times photography, wrapped tightly in a column of sunlight, and frozen in salute on a cold and rainy day in late autumn, when a rickety car pulled merrily to the curb. Toot! Toot!! Toot!!! The driver looked out at the child shyly, he smiled a little, and said: "I knew you were hungry, so I came." The child was happy now, because he was indeed hungry, he was starving, when suddenly there appeared another man, in a long coat with deep pockets, who approached the rickety old car stealthily, as the shy driver looked out at the child with such longing that he forgot himself and saw only the child and not the stealthy man standing at his door, leaning and peering in, reaching deep into his left-hand pocket, the two men in dark cold, the happy child saluting in sunlight, when with his right hand the man in the long coat returned the child's salute, while with his left he pulled from his pocket a long pistol and shot the driver through the head, blowing brains and blood everywhere. How the child clapped! And how he hopped up and down, as the stealthy man reached quickly into the merry car and stole a sandwich wrapped in bloody wax paper, then cunningly tossed it too high to the child, who leapt like Joe DiMaggio and snagged it, one-handed catch! "Bravo, American soldier boy! and hello," said the stealthy man, "I am proud to be at your service." But the child paid no attention because he was so eager to unfold the wax paper to find what he knew would be there: a luscious sandwich of little sausages and red peppers, his favorite of all good things to eat. And so he ate, quite greedily he ate, and when he finished, the man in the long coat wiped the child's bloodied mouth with his left hand and said: "Take this hand and come with me, or you'll be alone for your whole life." So the child took his hand, and off they went, as the child sang out, "Toot! Toot!! Toot!!!" merrily merrily down the street, into the cold and dark.

It comes in the summer of my obsession with the tribulations of Orenthal James Simpson. June 29, 1994. After thirty-two years of silence, a call from Victor Graziadei. Victor again, the man my father once told me had no life. I said, "You mean of his own?" "No," he says, "I mean no life." I say, "Like yourself?" My father ignores the snottiness. Without a trace of rancor, and almost without fail, he turns the other cheek.

My father told me he had such hope that I would stay away from Victor, as far as possible, even though it wasn't his place, he said, to say so. I have no idea what his place is. My father is blurry. Even though he knew I couldn't, he told me that I should make an effort. "Unless you need to eat yourself alive, Richard."

When the phone rings, I'm reaching into my stash of chocolate chip cookies, arranged before me on the coffee table, in geometric patterns with my reserve of Fig Newtons. Diane calls them "frigs," "your beloved frigs." Against my will, I find myself drawing ever nearer to Diane. Victor doesn't say, "Hello, this is Victor." He says, "How many hours with Orenthal today?" I reply, "Every minute, plus I taped. I thought you were dead." "No," he says, "you are." I say, "Tell me your opinion of our friend. I need to know." He says, "It looks bad for Orenthal, but she apparently did something." I say, "Of course, she's a cunt." He says, "Was. Was a cunt. And he's just a prisoner of love." I say, "We make no excuses." He says, "Orenthal and you." I say, "Orenthal and me and you, in our blood-smeared galoshes." "Ah," Victor says, "we converse." He pauses. Then he says, "I've kept track of you through Carmen, who's still alive, and who you abandoned. Notice that our man has a girl-friend of Italian background." I say, "Proves he's an ass-hole." Victor replies, "The meaning of this woman is that we have long been associated with affairs that enrapture this nation." I tell Victor, "Your stories about our ethnic back-ground always confused me." He says, "You desired involve-ment in the moods I was attempting to project. Don't kid yourself. Orenthal sandpapers his skin. And who can blame him with a name like that? He sucks on it. Behind the scenes, he sucks on it hard." I say, "Behind the scenes of his charisma and sweetness." "Yes," Victor says. "Rage like candy. Which reminds me. It dawns on me you're in love again. True or false?" I say, "Definitely. This time I'm going to extract satisfaction."

Toward the end of the conversation, I tell Victor that my air conditioner has broken down, "in this debilitating humidity." He says, "Good. You will embark upon a course. According to Carmen, you became the Chief Finger-Fucker. True or false?" I reply, "That's a way to put it." "Richard," he says, "tell me something. Is it possible for people of Italian background to eat properly where you live? Is the cannoli as we have always understood it, up here, possible in the Land of Cotton?" I say, "In exile, we suffer." A long silence. Then he says, "Someone created a spectacle in Los Angeles. Someone could have been somebody in my business, which you weren't. Tell me, Richard, hath fresh semen been descried in her vagina, and in her anus too? Was the loveliest of all our lassies gutted, skinned, and quartered?" He laughs. He says, "Happy Birthday!" He hangs up.

I'll try harder to stop talking about my father in the present tense.

It's the early fall of 1959, my first semester at Oneida County College, and I come into Carmen Caravaggio's Italian Pastries and Coffee Shop, corner of Bleecker and Mohawk, bearing my brown valise full of books, heavy enough to give me a hernia. Empty, except for Victor Graziadei and Carmen himself. Victor says, loud enough for me to hear, "I've been onto that kid from the start." Victor's voice is a deep hot bath. Carmen says, "Get over here, big fella, I have to introduce you to your destiny." I was a regular at Carmen's, but I had never seen Victor in there. In fact, I had never seen Victor in a stationary position. Carmen was eight years my senior, he was my next-door neighbor on Mary Street, and he was about to introduce me to a man who lived all his life across the street from us, and just a short block farther east. The cross street of Wetmore between us. Mary runs parallel to, and one block south of, Bleecker, Utica's Italian-American main drag, which Victor, who didn't own or drive a car, wore out, day in and day out, when he didn't take the bus at the corner of Wetmore and Bleecker. Don't worry about visualizing the tedious map. The map comes back. So does the bus. Bleecker runs west to the center of town, where it changes its name as it runs through the Polish west side. It was well known all along Bleecker that Victor, once a week, bearing a big black valise, bigger than mine, walked into Polish territory, sometimes detouring through a black neighborhood. To disappear for a few days. To perform a deed, as he told me much later.

Until that moment at Carmen's, I had never heard Victor's voice. With the exception of Carmen, I didn't know anyone who had ever talked to Victor. I didn't even know anyone who knew anyone who knew anyone.

Carmen gave me his chair. When he was out of earshot, Victor said, "The only man in Utica without malice." I said, "What?" Victor said, "We don't have a lot of time. Carmen has made an unusual success in this business. Carmen is a well of kindness. In other words, they hate him in this town." I said, "Who?" Victor said, "Forget it. They can't stomach him. We don't have a lot of time. You need to know about our first meeting, which I don't believe you recall. November 1941." I said, "In November of 1941 I was about six months old." He said, "That's one of my major points. This is not a story that leads into Pearl Harbor. I know something which you don't, which in later years may be helpful, when you wonder in your despair if you'll ever change. We are who we are. True or false?" Victor was in his late thirties. I was eighteen and a little embarrassed. He paused for a long time, his eyes still on me, mine trying to focus on the espresso. Then he said, "With men who enjoy each other's company, these awkward moments are traditional. After a point, you learn to accept the pain. You learn to love it." Victor said "men."

"Carmen," he said, "please, we need some now." Carmen came out of the backroom bearing a tray of three cannoli. Vic-

137

tor quickly seized two without a word. This slightly aggravated me. It slightly aggravates me even now to think about it. Victor read my mind. He said, "This is also one of my major points. You want what I have, from the beginning this is the case. Don't think I'm without the civilities. I'm attempting to dredge up a scene that lurks inside you, because you are who you are. Richard, I stand on the corner of Bleecker and Wetmore on a cold rainy day in November of '41, holding in my hand a pink cloud of cotton candy. I stand on the corner of the bus stop for those going east, but I am not waiting for the bus that goes east, because I never go east. I stand at that bus stop because on this lousy day there's a big splash of sunlight exactly there and nowhere else. I'm happy by myself in the sun. I'm eating and enjoying the beautiful leaves rotting on the sidewalk. Then a bus comes from the west. The driver thinks I'm waiting for him with my cotton candy, or maybe somebody wants to get off, regardless, and that's why he rolls to a stop. I never found out, because of what blossomed in front of me. A small boy comes flying on his bike down the little rise of Wetmore. He's flying toward me on the sidewalk. The bus is slowing to a stop, probably for me, though in retrospect I hope not. The boy puts on his brakes, like he must have done a thousand times. But this time he starts to skid on the wet leaves, and when he skids out into the sunlight he hits a section of dry sidewalk skidding too fast with his brakes on hard, and suddenly the bike flips, and over the handlebars he goes sailing in the sun in his blue jacket, the face still having fun. Richard, the face never caught up with the situation. The head makes a sound when it hits the curb. The bus is rolling to a stop while the body is sliding over the curb, and under the bus he goes, just as the bus stops, under the bus he goes, but not all the way under, which is what he needs to do. The timing couldn't have been better. He starts to go under headfirst in front of the back wheel, which rolls to a stop directly on top of the head. The head explodes. Blood all over me, including the cotton candy. First a little pool, then a stream flowing toward the curb. Flowing into the sewer. Brains, teeth, an eye. My mouth is screaming. It must have been my mouth, because it couldn't have been the siren of the ambulance yet, I had a sore throat after, and they come pouring out of their houses without their coats on before the siren, so many women, including your mother, pouring down the rise they come, including the mother and grandmother of the boy, who know before they get there. They all know before they get there. Except you. You in your mother's arms, with your face rooting relentlessly at her breast, which you're getting at through a special slit she made in her dress just for you. Richard, you were relentless. When your mother gets there, the screaming, not immediately, but pretty soon pulls you off the breast, and your head turns toward the carnage. At such a time, you could get completely out of hand, this would have been acceptable at that time, because you don't appreciate the transition, but you didn't get out of hand, because in the sunlight your eyes catch the blood and you are so fascinated by the colorfulness all before you. Your arm comes out and your hand points down at the crap. You smile, you make a sound that a parent likes to hear. Goo. Your mother, when you did that, definitely wanted to smile. Who could blame her? It wasn't you who had been destroyed on Bleecker Street, thank God it's not my son down there, with a head like a pancake, who they can't have a wake for unless they close the coffin. Then something else catches your eye. Your arm does the same thing. Then it's back and forth, with little turns of the head, between Bobby Zito's bright blood and my cotton candy. You're happy. Goo Goo Goo. Bobby Zito, who lived directly across the street from you. Like this your head, Richard. Like this. Goo Goo. Okay, Carmen, bring him another one now."

Carmen came out of the backroom with another cannoli. Carmen said, "We've been planning this for a long time. To give you perspective. Enjoy yourself, Richard." And so I enjoyed myself, because no one made a more beautiful cannoli than Carmen Caravaggio, not even my maternal grandmother, may she rest in peace.

In September of 1963, when I left Utica for good, Victor said: "Richard, may the life you take not be your own."

The cookie crumbs dirty the expensive oriental carpet beneath my coffee table. You know the coffee table I mean: the one between the couch and the TV. When the commercials come on, I go, whether I have to go or not. A few drops forced out and shook off from the sitting position, the utility and comfort of which I discovered at an age much younger than you'd expect. I've eliminated the splash effect universally associated with my gender. It takes me until the third day of the preliminary hearing to discover Court TV, and constant, commercial-free coverage: Orenthal full time. No appropriate time now to go, or to vacuum the cookie crumbs, or to observe the woodchuck who has moved into my yard. "The chuckster," as my friend across town, the redoubtable Diane, refers to him. She claims the chuckster is male. She says that I should be careful when I'm in the yard. That I should keep my wits about me, and my pants buckled tight, when in the yard I bend over. Because the chuckster wishes to perpetrate. Diane's colorful phrase is, "Fuck you up the ass." My heart leaps up! This kind of humor is typical of my friend, who is no cunt. Victor is wrong. They're probably not all cunts. I could give many examples, and probably will, of her delightful wit. I thought I was going to write, "many examples of noncunts." We improve. Victor said that Yeats said, "Men improve with the years."

Victor is a distorted human being. I have come to understand this, and Carmen, kind Carmen, is not far behind, that son of a bitch. I'm changing. In recent years, I've established proper psychic distance from the corrupters of my youth. Especially Victor. Not that I'm about to relent. "Let me in." "No." "Please." "I said no." "Why?" "Don't force me into specifics. You lack discipline. Don't force me to enumerate." "Give me specifics. Something to work on, as I grieve." "Don't break my balls, Diane." She folds her arms. So I say, "Crumbs. The bedspread. These are examples of a condition hostile to my happiness. The hostile condition is you. The kitchen counters. Don't force me to pile up the evidence. The blood on the toilet seat. Happy now? The blood on the toilet seat, and not just once. I'm pretty sure it wasn't butt blood, Diane." She cocks her head. She says, "You would know the difference."

He, my chuckster, has taken to living under the house, and is responsible, I'm convinced, for the broken air conditioner. My goal is to hand-feed him. The odors rise, heavy and moist, through the humidity, through my gleaming hardwood floors, from the roly-poly little cocksucker shitting under my house, who leavens my day during the interminable recesses, when they go off as a unit to the judge's chambers, leaving me to fend for myself, perchance to pee. And then off they go to eat their elegant Los Angeles sandwiches, delivered directly to an antiseptic room without windows, in the Criminal Courts Building, prosecution and defense teams together at last, in a semi-informal setting, sharing humorous anecdotes, planning further recesses, whining that they don't have time to go off to their respective bistros.

We, on the other hand, take everything personally. He in his two-thousand-dollar suits, me in my pajamas and red robe, the latter purchased three childless marriages ago. We eat alone. We do hundreds of sit-ups. We think. Of air fresheners, for example, and not only because of what he's doing under my house. There are many odors in my house that I cannot trace to the chuckster. And he, Orenthal, in his cell, thinking of similar needs, asleep in brutalizing proximity to his toilet, praying over his toilet. By the way, when she said "as I grieve," she was laughing, I believe. I could be mistaken. She was possibly crying. Fuck her, or don't fuck her, as the case may be.

Carmen's place met the sanitary standards of the operating room, which is how the Joint Chiefs of Surgery liked to refer to it. "A surgeon," Carmen says, "someone they pay and honor to knife people. Richard, we recommend you take it up in college. Major in surgery, because we need assistance in here. The workload is out of control." He says, "The kid is involved. He's perfect. The kid is fucking hopeless." Carmen laughs so fetchingly.

A day after our first meeting, I'm walking down Wetmore to the bus stop on the corner of Bleecker (to go west), Victor coming to me from the opposite direction. He starts talking when he's still fifteen feet away: "I understand through Carmen that already at your age you're involved in homicidal frustration. Carmen has seen you comport yourself with your father's car in a crazed manner. Carmen claims that humiliation in your high school period was constant. The skinniness, you're a string bean, Richard, the pimples, the ridiculous hair, etcetera. You tend to present yourself in a queerish manner. Boils in unlikely places. Carmen claims one in your anus. How does Carmen know? Most of all, the valise, Richard. In high school, with the roughnecks you went to high school with, a tender boy with a valise is an obvious asshole, which you were conscious of, you were a target, and yet you insisted on the valise, which convinces me you're well suited. Oh yes, you tower over me, and in your presence I verge on shyness and rage. You for your part are unusually sensitive concerning my forearms. You hunger for masculinity of the forearm. Look at my wrists, Richard. The thickness, behold the thickness and seethe. You're invited to my home tonight at eight. Honor me at eight, and leave your sullen face at home, because I'm not your father." These last words spoken as he walked away.

To this day, I consider it a sign of my normality that I listened to him without response; that I was scared; that I was eager for eight o'clock. I couldn't wait any longer. I wanted a girlfriend. I wanted to lash out. I wanted Victor to act as nuts as he talked. I wanted a physique. I wanted to attach my ugliness to his secret extremity, whatever his secret was, in secret consummation, no more masturbation, no more of that. I wanted to say to Victor: "We've had this date from the beginning."

In 1959, what I am is a six-one, 145-pound, dirty blond, the King of Acne, with glasses. Not that Victor was himself an amazing specimen, Utica's own Cary Grant he wasn't— though, speaking of Cary, there were these odd moments when I thought I could detect the faintest trace of a cultured English accent. When he said the word "humiliation," for example, or "cunt," especially "cunt." Victor with all that wiry carrot-colored hair, the paleness of the face, 170 pounds, five seven, no fat. The shocking carrot-top, unvalidated by genealogy or chemicals, is subject to tedious rumors. Victor Graziadei: president and sole proprietor of Utica Meat, Inc., a slaughterhouse.

When Carmen, Victor, and I occupied the pastry shop by ourselves, it was the House of Freaks, and Carmen's classic

Southern Italian aspect only enhanced the effect. The thick black hair, the swarthiness, the ample pouty mouth. Carmen is all passivity and enervation, despite his frenzied application to the business. Sloe-eyed Carmen, at five six, he oozes it, with just a hint of a fifties sweater girl, giving one considerable difficulty, so it was widely stated back then, whether one should fight him or fuck him. Even then, in spite of my vague reservations, my vaguer discomfort, I drew near to Carmen.

My father said he was a generous man, yet to be feared. So many times he had given me a box of his beautiful pastries to take home to my father. I said, "Generous, like you." My father said nothing. I said, "To be feared. Not like you in the least." He said, "Richard, stop stoning me with that song. Your mother had no qualms." "Meaning what?" I said. "That you didn't nauseate her?"

Carmen's place: I see it still. White ceramic floor tiles, framed in black grouting. Wrought-iron tables and chairs. The short back wall, brilliantly black-lacquered behind the stainless steel showcases. The long cool side walls in soft gray, accented by six huge black-and-white photos of Naples: street urchins, both sexes, various stages of undress. You could lick your gelato off the floor. Someone did. Someone had to. Glass of the showcases, cleaned thrice daily by Carmen himself, and no one else, with a vinegar-and-water solution.

One time, when it was just Carmen and me at the shop, Utica's Princeton-educated mayor, J. Kenneth Sherman, asked Carmen in the Princeton manner why he hadn't "worked more Italian colorfulness into the decorative scheme, you know, the Italian gaiety, Carmen." Carmen replied, "Your Honor appreciates Richard's perfect ass, doesn't he?" Mayor Sherman hugged himself. Carmen Caravaggio knew about the boil in my anus because I told him about it.

Diane has repaired my air conditioner, and he, the burly chuckster, has departed. I'm down to Diane, with whom I get on famously. I'll remedy that. Periodically, I smell my books, for the mildew level, which was awful this summer. I've read all the books. Let them rot. Luckily, my Orenthal hearings have taken a scientific turn. The dryness, the obscurity, and the jargon encourage me to focus where truth speaks plainly, in the faces and voices of the witnesses. I ignore the words. I concentrate on the complete bodies, including the blow-dried and spray-sculpted hair, and I believe in the vivid faces, the vibrant vocality, as Orenthal shoots them glances of disgust and hatred, so help them God. But when our racially balanced defense team finally gets its chance, the witnesses become quite shitty in their behavior. They touch themselves in odd places. They leak furtiveness. Why does the chief investigating detective need a seventy-five-dollar Los Angeles haircut? To offset the cascading potbelly? Orenthal is happy now, and with that killer smile he's exuding kindness and sympathy, even for the chief investigating detective. The evidence is a sham. The evidence is incontrovertible. I hit the power button on the remote, pull my mother's love over my head, the afghan that she made forty years ago, just for me, and in the dark assume the face of the accused.

The phone. He says, "This has been a wonderful day for our side." I say, "Today I was forced to go under cover." He says, "The orange-and-brown afghan?" I say, "Yes, the only true thing in life, a mother's love." He says, "And yet you gave so little to her, so much to the three wives, who Carmen claims were constantly underhanded. Now what do you have?" I say, "The afghan." He says, "Forget Orenthal's dead white wife in Los Angeles. We have a new pig on our hands. The white wife in South Carolina." I say, "She murders her two kids, then blames it on a Negro kidnapper." He says, "The two kids were driving her nuts. True or false, Richard?" I say, "They all took advantage of her, including the boyfriend who she loved deeply." Victor says, "These kids were a pain in the ass to this guy." I say, "He's fucking her and they're crying relentlessly in the next room banging on the locked door of the room where they're fucking in, screaming Mommy! Mommy! Mommy!" Victor says, "Yes, Richard, and all of a sudden the boyfriend has no cock. The screaming kids make it shrink." I say, "The estranged husband is banging some bimbo on the side, even before they were estranged." Victor says, "Yes, and when the boyfriend loses his cock he sees in his mind at the moment of humiliation, as the cock shrinks into a pitiful thing, he sees the husband's steel ramming the pig, in his mind he sees this quite clearly. So what does he do, Richard?" I say, "He attempts to turn the estranged cock in his brain to advantage, by imagining it as his very own, for the inspiration, Victor, as he attempts to fuck her, but the steel isn't coming back, even though he is at one with the husband. So he threatens to

148

leave her, because who wants a ready-made family?" Victor says, "Here's a hard one, no double meaning intended. Why doesn't she dump the kids on the estranged husband?" I say, "That's easy. She doesn't want to give him the satisfaction, even though she loves him, because she wants to ruin him for life. I saw the home movies on CNN. She loved those babies. Those little fuckers victimized her worse than those other two did. This is the story nobody wants to hear. Because when she looks at her babies she sees the man she lost and the man she's going to lose. Those little cocksuckers are destroying her. This is the truth that America can't face." He says, "Richard, I'm so proud." I say, "The constant shitting in their pants, the shit is spilling out onto the favorite chair, they're eating the cat food for Christ sakes, they're putting their shitty hands on the pristine walls. This woman is fastidious. The three-year-old pulls down the drapes. They're worse than high-strung dogs." He says, "Good, Richard. She had no choice." I say, "You're wrong, Victor. She chose to live." He replied, "Two more questions and you're done with your final exam. What is the estranged husband left with?" I say, "The cat." Victor says, "Excellent! And what does he do with the cat?" I say, "He eviscerates the cat with his bare hands." "Yes," Victor says. "Excellent! He tears out the ovaries. Because he needs to get it under his fingernails. He needs to smell his fingers the next day, for the satisfaction, Richard." I say, "Yes, *that,* most of all *that.*" Then I hang up, and pull my mother's love over me again. Cover my head. Pull my knees up.

At a minute and a half before eight, I leave home for Victor's, proceeding along the north, or poorer side of Mary Street, side of narrow two-family houses, then cross, at the appropriate point, to the south side of wide and much better kept two- and three-family structures, with porches on all floors sweeping along importantly across the entire front face. What I know, at this moment, as I'm about to knock for the first time on Victor's front door, is that Victor lives alone, in the home willed to him, only child, by parents who looked like Carmen's type of Italian. I know also that they willed him Utica Meat, Inc., where Victor rarely appears during business hours, preferring, according to persistent rumor, to work on the books starting around midnight, departing just before dawn.

Victor, as always, freshly scrubbed and freshly clothed, opens the door as I climb the steps. No greeting. We skirt the edges of the living room in order to avoid the leaning stacks of newspapers, magazines, and official-looking documents, and the sea of used envelopes, grocery bags, unopened personal mail and old bills, and the piles (neat, twine-bound) of what look to be manuscript pages of poems. Ancient heavy furniture, badly frayed rugs, walls darkish with strange stains. Several days' worth of unwashed dishes still in the dining room, leather-bound volumes of the master English and American poets strewn everywhere on the floor. Above all: the stench. I follow him to the back foyer, where we ascend the stairs to the second-floor apartment. As he opens the door, he says his first words. "But in here we resist," and the door gives upon an apartment fragrant with disinfectant: burnished hardwood floors, freshly painted white walls, ceiling removed, partitions knocked out, all space vaulting to the roof. A loft effect. Barren. Except at the dead center (Victor once called it "the death center"), a small unfinished wooden table: lamp, inkstand, legal-sized pad, black quill, sharp-edged wooden chair. On the floor, front of table, stacked in three neat rows, what looks to be a full *Encyclopaedia Britannica*. Victor says the letter *M* is missing, because "this is where I'm up to. It's in there," and he points to what I take to be a bedroom, but the door is closed. Victor says, "We'll never go in there. The letter *M,* for murder. Richard, I want to introduce you to Utica Meat, it would delight me. Plus Carmen tells me you need a part-time job to tide you over what the scholarship doesn't cover." I say, "In this town, to get part-time work you need pull. My good father has no pull." Victor says, "That's because your good father is good. But now you know somebody who is not good. I require a shackler between eight and midnight, weekends only. Let's take a walk and I'll show you the place. This," he says, indicating the ascetic space with arms outspread, "this is me." Arms still outspread. "When you're a little older, knock on wood, you'll have this too." Arms down. "Then you'll be me." He grins. "True or false, Richard?" I say, "Victor, I need to attempt to say something serious." He says, "With me you can feel free." I begin to weep heavily. My head on his shoulder. Victor is silent. I finish weeping. I've said nothing. He says, "I appreciate the confidence you show in me, Richard. Now let's go down to the slaughterhouse. I'll bet a kid like you doesn't even know what a shackler is. True or false?" I say, "True." He says, "Never mind. You'll love it."

I'm shrinking. I'm five eleven now with shoes on, and a tendency to curve inward, whereas Diane is a ramrod six-footer in bare feet, who loves thick-soled oxfords and cowboy boots. She tells me that she weighs in at 164. I believe her. The shoulders! Her hair is auburn, thick and long. To the waist when she lets it out, which is rare, because all that hair makes me nervous. She once told me, "Richard, if it comes down to it, you know, hand-to-hand combat, I could take you. Easy." (I still weigh in at a gaunt 145.) "True," I say, "but I'm not going into battle bare-handed, like before, with the first three."

My three wives are the type who, when you look at them sideways, they crumble, they cry. They won. They're still winning. "The paradox," I tell Diane, "is you're a dominatrix and I'm winning." She says, "Yes, it's obvious." I say, "Look at me. I'm a cultured whiner, respected in my field." She says, "You're a male of unique aspect, surprisingly dedicated to intimate health care." I say, "You're going to pay for the first three. Better get the fuck out." She laughs, how winsomely she laughs. Diane says, "I know what's good for me." Diane says, "You have a serious feminine dimension."

She advertises herself in the yellow pages: DIANE THE

HANDYMAN. I tell her that she can't fix me. I tell her, "I'm going to fix you good." She says, "Watch out, buddy." Diane is Diane Martello, my first Italian-American woman. I've decided to let her have her own key. What she doesn't know, what she'll never know, is that I have one to her place.

She comes in from work around six to discover me under the afghan. I announce from underneath that we're not watching Orenthal and the rest of the cast tonight while we eat dinner. Then I peek out. She's tucking one of my chocolate chip cookies inside her bra and saying, "For you, for later." I shower, shave, and change out of my pajamas, while Diane whips up one of her brilliant pasta sauces. I enter the kitchen fully dressed, with the exception of my dick (such as it is), hanging out of my fly, then go about my chores. I've been assigned the pasta itself, its cooking and draining, the setting of the table, the lighting of the candles. After dinner, on the customary walk, I take her arm, stooped over a little, a quarter step behind. Back home, the chocolate chip frozen yogurt, my portion triple the size of hers, then the cop shows, for which we provide surprising commentary. We believe that a neutral person would find us funny. It's just another Diane-Richard evening of lightheartedness, punctuated by frequent nonsexual touches. But then they start, they have to start: the motivated rubbings and squeezings, the finger and tongue probes. We sit close to each other on the couch during the eleven o'clock news, the afghan around our shoulders, windows open to the advancing chill of autumn: heading for familiar crisis.

I escape to the kitchen: to wash the dishes, to dry the dishes, to clean the stove, sweep the floor, deal with the kitchen counters. Then I just stand there with nothing to do, alone in the kitchen. Enter Diane, beaming.

154

"You want to do something?"

[*Silence.*]

"What do you want, Richard?"

"I think I want to read a little."

"You *think* you want?"

[*Removes chocolate chip cookie.*]

"I want to read a little."

"Make believe this is something else."

"No."

[*She eats.*]

"I've decided I'll read, Diane."

"I've decided I'll suck your cock."

"Unnecessary."

"What can I offer you?"

"Nothing."

"Richard, you're the first man I've known who could resist his own hard-ons. You've achieved manifest tumescence. I'm going to touch it."

I attempt to explain, for the millionth time, that sex ruins everything for me. I tell her to masturbate behind closed doors. "Go ahead, get it over with. Keep the door open, if you want. I don't mind that much." She says, "I'll tell you what ruins everything for me. I can't take you in my mouth and vagina at the same time. In my cunt, Richard."

In bed, we hold hands, as we lie facing in opposite directions. Diane is asleep. My free hand is clenched. I remember that I haven't yet put away the dishes. I get up to do that, because that's what I want to do.

It's located several blocks north of Bleecker, in the old industrial district, on a badly lit east-west thoroughfare of rough-house saloons, broken beer bottles, and occasional condoms, sagging with semen, from chain-link fences hung with care. I walk this street for thirty minutes in the dark, glancing frequently over my shoulder at Victor trailing some distance behind. "No offense," he says at the outset, "but I don't want people to think that in my late thirties fraternization is welcome." Suddenly, rounding a sharp bend, at last the slaughterhouse, a vast cinder-block affair. Atop four high poles, massive electrical fixtures—worthy of a small outdoor stadium—bathe the place and its adjoining areas in harsh light. Clustered all along one side, an array of covered holding pens; jutting far out from the other, the loading dock, where trucks a mile long take on hundreds of frozen carcasses for the trip to New York, and where the small, shabby trucks of obscure local entrepreneurs haul off profitable barrels of yesterday's guts, hooves, hides, and heads. Above the main entrance, surprisingly small, in red neon:

UTICA MEAT INC.

SINCE 1938

GRAZIADEI

"Everything here we use for something," Victor says, "except the blood, which is good in itself, like the fine arts of mankind. We just stare at it. You start with the fine arts, Richard, eventually you have a progression direct to blood, and vice versa. Which they don't teach in college. Don't forget the vice versa, and don't contradict me, because you know I'm right."

As we walk through the front gate, we're greeted by a scream, apparently from within, a sound of shattering size sustained on the night air, arching up and out over the city, then yielding, as if by virtuoso technique, to seamless diminuendo. Then nothing. Victor is saying, "The fat lady can sing," and he's ushering me past the loading dock, toward the back of the place, and I'm needing to assume an animal origin, saying, "What was that?" And he, deadpan, "Or *who* was that? All these years, Richard, I'm still not used to it, thank God. Are you thrilled?" At the back, a flight of exterior stairs leads to a tiny door just under the roof. We stoop through single file into an opaquely enclosed catwalk ending at another door, this one opening into Victor's glass-enclosed office, hanging high above the center of it all: a commanding view of the killing floor and the swing shift going full blast.

I think Victor wanted me to be seduced by what I saw. I think he wanted me to live in another world, his world, and I was eager. The two of us just standing there in his office, surveying the colorful scene beneath us, and then, after a long while, Victor says, "You're struggling not to smile, think I don't know? You're trying to keep your arm at your side, because you don't want to point. Your mind is remembering against your will. But let's face it, Richard, you're too mature now to say Goo, Mommy! Come on, Riccardo, let's go downstairs. Let's get involved. Later on, we'll go across the street and see Uncle Henry, who I believe you've never met." Victor was referring to the only family dwelling within blocks, a Victorian three-story structure, exceptionally maintained: Uncle Henry's, Utica's best-known whorehouse. As we approach the shackling room, Victor says, "Five bucks a pop, ten for half and half, twenty-five for around the world."

That night, this dream: In a deserted area reserved for the slaughter of large or unruly animals—cows, steers, adult pigs—there my good father hangs. Upside down. Naked. Feet shackled to a ceiling hook. Victor and I in attendance. Victor says, "Look, Richard, see shackle? Say shackle, Richard." My father's eyes roll up. His mouth opens. Light pours from his head. Victor says, "Your father is a woman. Your father stinks kindness." We walk around to his backside. I say, pointing to his ass, "She always turns the other cheek." Victor says, "Oh, oh, that's rich, Richard." I say, "I want my daddy to sing for me." Victor says, "Behold! A piano! Do you wish to accompany your father? Take this piano." He gives me a big knife. "Across the throat and deep," he says. "But if you cut the head off, your daddy won't sing for you. Play the piano, Richie." Victor waves his arms like a conductor. I approach the hanged man, who says, "Play the piano deep, but not too deep, my son." Victor says, "He wants to lave you all over richly with his voice." I slash my father deep across the throat, but not too deep. A voice of shattering size flows forth, tearing the roof off, sustaining itself over the city, and as his blood pours down, a ravishing diminuendo, as his blood pours all the way down to no more bloodvoice, good to the last drop. Sun from out of the night sky and from my father's head. His genitals are a floating flower. Victor says, "He's in heaven." I say, "The cunt escaped." Victor says, "Pick the flower, forget him not." Victor is holding high a broken beer bottle, opening and neck preserved. Victor is saying, "A kid your age without condom-knowledge. Behold! This is a condom! First we put our precious peckers in here, where we drink, and only then do we do our fucking. Doobydo. The jagged edge is your protection. This jagged edge goes into the woman, in order to prevent pregnancy. Now you have condom-knowledge! Repeat after me: Peter Pecker probed a peck of prickly pussy!" I'm hanging upside down, my genitals are a broken beer bottle. Victor dips a cannoli into my father's blood. He says, "Open wide, Richard." The blood sings gloriously. Victor says, "I said, Open up, Richard, or I'll lance your secret boil." Victor is holding up a volume of the *Encyclopaedia Britannica,* the letter *K.* He says, "*K* is for killing and for Keats. Richard, Richard, a thing of beauty is a joy forever." I open wide.

The shackler is a skinny black kid who is saying "Hello, Mr. G" and pulling a thing off a wall, a long chain with a hook on one end and an iron wheel on the other, and quickly around the calf's back legs he slips and wraps it snug in a second, hooking the chain onto itself, engaging the wheel end with a thing that ascends and descends constantly. The calf goes up. The wheel rolls onto an elevated rail. The calf sails quietly through an opening in the wall, dangling down, rolling toward the killing floor, toward the first station, where the bleeder, a lugubrious white guy, awaits his work, rubber-suited, iron-wristed. Victor says, "That thing with the wheel is called the shackle. That thing that goes up and down constantly is called the hoist. You are called the future shackler, who feeds my boys out there, who have constant hunger. The shackler doesn't feed steadily, the knifemen stand around with their knives. Next thing you know, they're thinking too much about the shackling room. Richard, the shackler is a relentless person, like Nelson here, my only Negro employee, who I give this sensitive job to because he's like you. Your build, no skill, and what woman looks at him twice?" The shackling room is tiny. We can't move. The calves can't move. "The purpose is to pack them in here like sardines. As the shackler, you move only with great difficulty. But you kick freely, or preferably you deploy the heavy wheel part of the shackle like a club, on the head, or preferably the fucking spine. Like Nelson's doing now. You induce paralysis, they don't break your balls anymore." The calf is sailing toward the lugubrious bleeder. "Pack them in without mercy, send them on their way, the room empties, etcetera. In four hours, Richard, which you work per Saturday and Sunday, three hundred closures, thanks to you. You know what you're doing here? You're reaching out to the people of New York City, think of it in those terms. Not to mention the rare opportunity for deep self-expression with impunity. Naturally, all you'll ever think about in here is the knifemen, a level you'll never reach, because that takes craft plus the union. Frustration alone will not get you through a shift as a knifeman. Richard, notice those three big ones over there in the corner in the 150-pound category. They go last. Always last, or else you create a jam in the line. More aggravation for my knifemen. Those bigger bastards watch you like a hawk while you do the small ones. In my opinion, they absorb the experience. They see the future. When their time comes, if you bend down behind them without caution, a kick in the face is likely. When Nelson gets to the 150-pounders, he assumes the worst. I'll put it this way: You and Nelson can't afford increased ugliness in the facial area. In other words, a heavy smash to the spine is immediately called for. I don't care, deploy your own technique when the time comes, because you have to appease yourself, after all, and I don't object to individual creativity as long as you don't get involved in a disembowelment attempt in my shackling room." Nelson's rhythm is good to look at. "These little bastards are stupid and stubborn to the point you feel they direct hostility toward you personally. The truth of this room is that the shackler wins. They always lose. Hang them up for the first station. Lift the heavy wheel easily overhead, smash it down on the spine. The pleasure of repetition. Forget emotion. Coldness is all. Your will is done, which from what Carmen tells me will be a new situation in your life."

"In other words, here I don't take shit."

"Richard, at this time you have it all over your faggot white bucks."

We move on, to the killing floor proper, to the first station, which we can't get to directly via the shackling room, unless we wish to climb into the opening through which the calves sail quietly toward the lugubrious bleeder, which we don't. We instead exit outside and come around through the main entrance, then through the coffee and pastry room supplied daily by Carmen, then onto the killing floor proper at last, into a space adjacent to the first station where the bleeder is reaching for the snout of the calf that comes sailing quietly toward him, and where the foreman, Dick Lentricchia, stands surveying the scene: "Dick, Richard Assisi, etcetera," the bleeder grasping the snout in his left hand, pulling up the head gently so that the back of the neck presents itself properly to the trajectory of the right hand descending already as the left is doing its job, the horizontal surface presenting itself properly to the bleeder precisely as the right hand makes deep vertical contact through soft butter, three quick little saws and the head is severed, the left hand flipping, gracefully tossing it into a barrel, and a waterfall of blood, so much of it in such a little animal pours down, and the left pushing the headless calf down to the second station, then reaching for another sailing snout. A two-and-a-half-second affair, if that.

Beneath the bleeder's feet, a rectangular reservoir, maybe twelve by fifteen, curb-enclosed, an eighteen-inch barrier against the blood, with a sewer in the center, invisible at the moment. Nelson feeds steadily. The reservoir fills to the brim. Dick the foreman in the high waders of a trout fisherman steps in with a rake which he works at the center. Reservoir recedes. Victor says, "We don't want my knifemen down the line slipping and sliding, though as far as that goes my insurance covers everything." Dick laughs and says, "Then, if that happens, we hang 'em up, finish the job, put 'em in the cooler. Those people in New York pay extra for a delicacy. They'll say it tastes just like chicken." Victor says, "It's not thicker than water, Richard. It's thicker than Jell-O. The sewer clogs. It becomes a lake in there. The fucking Red Sea." Dick says, "Is that the one where Christ walked across it?" Victor says, "I'll let you know when I get to the letter *R*. Come on, Richard, let's go down to the second station. Hey, Richard, you deaf all of a sudden?" Dick says, "He's in a trance. He's in heaven."

Three knifemen stand at the station of evisceration, another curb-enclosed area, each working a calf with a maximum longitudinal rip, a couple of quick moves, a yank, and the guts just can't wait to fall out. Ambience of shit stench. Victor says, "Strictly guts and assholes. When the shackler runs out of work he comes here and shovels the guts into those barrels. It gets deep in there. In the beginning, Nelson, who is quite sensitive, shoveled. Now he's acclimated, now he uses his hands. Quicker that way. They tend to slide off the shovel. No gloves, by the way. They just get soaked in a minute. You'll begin with the shovel, proceed to the gloves. Then you'll see the point of bare hands. You'll wash your hands a lot. After a week, you'll give them a fast rinse without soap and wipe them on your pants on the way to your coffee break. You'll eat your pastries with semi-disgusting hands, mark my words, as you inhale what's under your fingernails. You'll find a level of comfort in here."

We work ourselves on down the line to the last station, the washing and the scrubbing, the wheeling of the carcasses into the cooler. Victor says, "From Nelson to the cooler, maybe a minute and a half. Okay, Dick, we're ready." I follow them into a remote area, quiet, partitioned off. Dick disappears. Dick reappears leading a huge pig on a rope. Maybe 350 pounds. Dick gives the rope to Victor. Dick switches off the lights. Victor says, "Because pigs are the smartest of them all." A snort in the dark. Machinery engaged. Lights on. The pig is hanging from the ceiling. The pig urinates upon itself. Dick disappears again. Victor says, "Get ready." Dick appears with a dripping bleeder's knife. Dick holds the knife under the snout. The pig defecates massively upon itself. Victor says, "Dick, it's been years." Dick says, "Victor, I'd be honored to watch you work again." Victor slashes the pig's throat. Sound of shattering size. Victor grins. He says, "Behold! The fat lady sings! Come on, Richard, let's go across the street. I believe you're ready now for your first piece of ass."

"So! Were you ready or not for your first piece of ass? I fixed two kinds, by the way. You want the ham and cheese or the sausage and peppers?"

[*Silence.*]

"What do you have in your basket, killer?"

[*Silence.*]

"Pastries?"

[*Silence.*]

"So, okay, it was making a hole in your pants as you climbed the stairs to the second-floor bedrooms. To meet Uncle Henry's daughters. [*Pause.*] So you shot off as you took your pants off, and she suffered third-degree burns. [*Pause.*] She said, 'Sorry, kid, but it's way too big.' [*Pause.*] She said, 'I'm too young to die.' "

"She was my mother's age. Early thirties. I left her writhing in pain. Her, not my mother. My mother left me writhing in me."

"Heavy, killer. Did she look like your mother?"

"Of course. She said, 'With a thing like that, I think you made me pregnant.' "

"Stop hogging the blanket, Richard. And stop trying to

164

make me think you wanted to knock your mother up. I better put some more sunscreen on those legs. Look at those legs! Did he get laid too?"

"His focus was elsewhere."

"His focus? Is that how he referred to his cock? Did she make you happy like your mother was supposed to?"

"Even more so."

"Did she fuck you better than me?"

"No. [*Pause.*] Exactly like you."

"Exactly like me!"

"I have no memory of us. I try to remember, I come up with nothing."

[*Pause.*]

"Who's better than us, killer?"

"Do my feet, Diane. Make me feel like Jesus!"

"They were *washing* his feet, not massaging them, goofball."

"They were whores. There were two of them standing in the hall in front of their rooms. You had to pick. That made me feel bad. So I didn't pick."

"Having a choice made you feel bad?"

"I felt it would hurt the other girl's feelings. So I got picked. Victor stayed downstairs with the doorman, who was maybe four ten. Victor paid. He insisted. He said I had to let him express his fatherly instinct. Diane, there's the nurse I most respect."

"Which one?"

"The beautiful one playing with the little girl near the water."

"Oh?"

"Oh yeah."

"I thought you said the nurse you most respect wasn't beautiful?"

"She's not. That's in your mind. I was thinking through your mind. The first thing she does is take off her negligee."

"The nurse you most respect?"

"I'm undressing. She takes a little pan of warm soapy water and washes me."

"Your cock. She washes your cock, which was already rocklike before the washing."

"I was limp. She says, 'I'm going to give you a little half and half, handsome, even though you only paid for the main event, because you're so handsome.' She dries me off and puts me in her mouth."

"Your cock. She puts your cock in her mouth, which after the washing and sucking is an actual rod of steel."

"After the washing and sucking I was twenty-five percent steel-like. She goes down on the bed. Pulls her knees up. In retrospect, I realize she lubricated her vagina."

"Ah, her vagina."

"She forces me in. I start working her over. She says, 'Give it to me, big boy.' She says it sincerely. She says, 'Your cock is so hot.'"

"In other words, you fucked this cunt's brains out."

"Entry to orgasm, five, six seconds tops."

"How did you feel?"

"Like a man. Like a very great man. The best thing that ever happened to me. At the time, I mean. I felt tremendous. I was happy, more than I can describe. It crossed my mind to go down on her."

"You left out what she looked like. A movie star. Kim Novak, who you were crazy for at the time."

"Dumpy, I think. I can't remember. The first woman I'd ever seen naked in the flesh. I was grateful. That's it. No more story. Boring."

166

"That can't be it. Don't be ashamed to tell me you went down on Kim."

"That's it. I felt pretty tremendous, she was nice. That's it."

"You were pretty tremendous, she was nice. Just like us."

[*Pause.*]

"Dora wasn't a cunt."

"Dora!"

"Later, Victor asks me how was it. I told him nice."

"Give me your other foot, big boy. Give it to me quick. Then what did he say?"

"He said, 'At Uncle Henry's there are no cunts.' Here she comes."

"Dora?!"

"The nurse I respect the most and her daughter, you ball-buster. Stop with my feet! Nice to see you, Debbie."

"Doctor Assisi! What a nice surprise!"

"Debbie, Diane Martello."

"Hey, Diane."

"A pleasure, Debbie."

"Say hello to Doctor Assisi and the lady, honey."

[*Lengthy silence.*]

"She's at that age, Doctor Assisi."

"Mommy?"

"What is it, honey?"

[*Pause.*]

"He's got a funny name."

[*Pause.*]

"Lucy!"

"He's got a funny name."

"Kids are so surprising, Deb. She looks just like you. Already a knockout."

"He's got a ca-ca name."

"Lucy, now that's not nice."

"Doctor Sissy."

"Riccardo!"

"Excuse me, miss?"

"Martello. Which means 'the hammer' in Italian. I was just saying his name in Dago. Your daughter is amusing."

"You're making a remark concerning my daughter?"

"He's a girl."

"Lucy, you know he's a boy."

"That great big lady dresses like a man."

"Richard, the mouth of babes."

[*Awkward silence.*]

"Hey! What do you say, girls! How about some of this nice fruit salad I made? Huh?"

"Spell your funny name, you bad boy."

"A-S-S-I-S-I."

"Mommy, he said a bad word."

"Richard, she's definitely fallen for you, hard."

"Of course."

"Lucy too."

"I suffer the little children. 'Lucy *too*'?!"

"Say your funny name, Richard."

"Don't start, Diane."

"Bad boy, take me in the woods for ice cream! I want it now!"

Lucy fascinated, Debbie horrified, leave.

"Diane, I fucking depend on that woman."

[*Pause.*]

"You fucking depend on me. That's who you depend on. [*Pause.*] What did you say that foreman's name was?"

"Lentricchia."

"Sounds like a surgical procedure."

Richard massages his crotch.

168

Initiate contact with Victor? Victor the phoneless? Who refused to open, much less answer, personal mail? Call Carmen, arrange a time. During our first call, Victor and I, as in old times, had avoided asking after each other's health, but with cunning Carmen the civilities would be carefully observed, so much the better that he might violate them by telling me his personal truth. With Carmen, old times would be his current disease, and other intimate revelations, which at his age I'd have no interest in knowing. What was Victor insinuating? Carmen is still alive. "Hello, Richard, I've been informed that it's pancreatic cancer, two months I'm dead, three tops. I had such fatigue, but you know the hours I keep, and at my age who's not tired?" Then he'd tell me how he'd ignored the ever-deepening tinge of brown in his urine, "but when it went pure brown, like diarrhea, Richard, I went to the doctor to find out if it was possible my system was diverting shit through my dick. Twenty-four pounds in six weeks, no more appetite, no more hard-ons." What am I supposed to say to him who I haven't seen in thirty-two years? Call every day until the end? Every *other* day? Say I love you, Carmen, which I don't? I fly up there and appear at the bedside, gathering around with the loved ones, as Carmen moves into morphine vision, throwing off his sheet in his delirium, revealing his shriveled genitals to his kids and their spouses, calling me Fred, "bring me some gelato, Fred," with a stupid grin, both of us stupidly grinning.

This is what would happen: I'd fly up to Utica only to learn that Carmen had exaggerated. That he had a nasty summer cold. That the point was to get me to return, after thirty-two years, because Victor, at seventy-three, was past his prime, and he needed me to perform a deed. Because I am the "Chief Finger-Fucker." Because I am "surprisingly dedicated to intimate health care," as the senior obstetrician-gynecologist at County General. Lucy's deft deliverer, to whom all the mothers send gifts and cards: like knives in the heart. To Doctor Richard F. Assisi, a flood of invitations. And the doctor accepts them all. ("How many birthdays this month, killer?") How they love to send me the damaging evidence; how quick I am to preserve it in expensive photo albums: the ravaged cakes, the candles, the spilled Cokes; the ice-cream-smeared faces; the dense child-clusters, and I, the stunned magnetic center. The gangly man all clownish in a party hat. Then along came a spider, all clownish in a party hat, and sat down beside them. Thank you, Mrs. Gilbert, I had a very nice time, your pap smear has been interpreted as normal. Yes, Mrs. Gardner, reconstruction of the vaginal floor is possible. More than possible. No, Mrs. Turner, I am not a pediatrician too. A pimpled spider at the center, eating his turds and whey.

I don't want to talk to Victor anymore.

II

The Lover

Richard Assisi, villain manqué, stands in his boxer shorts, the pair imprinted with Goldilocks and the Three Bears. He's leaning far over the vanity in his bathroom, peering into the spotless mirror just two inches from his face. For this, the ritual with which he begins his mornings, Richard Assisi dons spectacles for the legally blind. As he raises his hands, from directly behind a distraction freezes him in the act. It's the female lead. She's turned off the shower. She's about to emerge when it occurs to Richard that this is the proper moment to ambush her again with his past. Do it now: "You know what Victor once said to me?" Words to be intoned portentously just as Diane Martello pulls back the shower curtain, as his hands go into action, his eyes fixed upon the disfiguring objects of his intention: the angry volcano adjacent to the nose, the incipient volcano under the lower lip, the stubborn blackheads—one high on the cheek, the other a spreading smudge in the middle of his forehead, reminding him of Ash Wednesday, and she emerges dripping and stepping and reaching for a towel, all that hair soaked and swept back, slick and gleaming the body Amazonian, like a goddess, how delicious the streaks all down her inner thighs. Against his will he would eat, against his will, because this is the moment to spring Victor upon her—fixed is Richard on the primary target, the looming ugliness adjacent to the nose, but the eyes have a will of their own, Richard's eyes are subverting Richard leaning far over the vanity, frozen still with those magnifiers hanging low and ridiculous, hands before the face, lips apart, eating greedily against his will from the body of the goddess, and she, lost in herself, toweling and gazing down upon her own glories, Diane Martello bends and reaches and stretches and bends, toweling between, above and below, and now here she comes, coming up slowly and spotting him in the mirror, she comes up spotting the transfixed and clueless lover, unwitting object of her wry gaze, lost in this woman who's dropping her towel at full height, so much Martello before him with the appropriate finger of her right hand rubbing now gently between, then dipping it down and under and up and in and out again, and the place again, and in again, oh Richard! this drifting doctor knows now where he is, he knows unresisting as fast as he can stripping off those colorful boxers, it may actually jump across the room, it's lurching! back buttocks thighs calves—a long, long lingering on the calves, sucking on her calves, licking her feet, Richard Assisi licks as Martello bends again to insert the happy finger glistening into his happy mouth and she's pulled to floor and under, a moving fullness within as she pulls high the legs that they may be licked and sucked and mouths like shy teenagers on a second date all smitten, this is the very best part of all, this is the part that makes Richard Assisi happier than he's ever been, this thing she taught that drives him deeper and bigger in long creamy strokes

174

oh Christ his cock! this heaving beneath him, this kissing at the edge of orgasm.

Diane Martello had taught him to kiss on the mouth while making love. He had never done that. No more the averted face buried in the mattress.

He should die. He stirs. He stands. He says: "You're dripping out." He means: "On my beautiful blue Mexican tiles it'll go into the grouting where I'll never get it all out." She knows exactly what he means. She replies: "Good. Then together we'll lick it out." He wipes it up with a tissue as she stands, as it flows down her thighs, and he says, in a tone that he does not will and cannot hear: "It's running down your thighs," drifting again he is, but this time the will wins, and he, as she sits to pee: "You know what Victor once said?" and she, tinkling, "No, I don't know what Victor once said." "He said, 'Richard, consider your pimples. Then consider the straight razor.' " Still peeing, she says, "What pimples? You don't have any pimples." Triumphant, naked Richard re-dons the reading specs for the legally blind, leans far over the vanity, and says, "What are you? Blind? These! I'm over fifty and I have to live with this loathsome skin condition." From numerous prior dealings with the big goof, Diane has learned not to reason. She does not say, "Nobody can see what you see with those Coke bottles and your nose against the mirror." Instead, she assumes the accent traditionally heard in the Jewish Alps: "You should see poor Robert Redford's complexion! *That* you should see! I saw him once in person in a store in New Mexico with those Levi pants on he always wears. Several terrific moles. What a size they had, Richard. Not to mention the face is full of cracks from that horrible type of sun they have out there in Utah, worse than the deserts of Israel."

RICHARD (humorlessly): How many moles?

DIANE: For the movies, they have to pour on the makeup by the gallon.

[*Pause.*]

RICHARD: Look at this hair. The hair is similar.

DIANE: The hair totally reminds me of Bob. [*Pause.*] I'm not even going to mention the weight, which is very similar.

RICHARD: Bob is big. Bob is very big.

DIANE: I saw him in a store! He's about 145, only you're a foot taller.

RICHARD (with relish): The guy we see in the movies is a lie?

DIANE: What is a lie? He doesn't think twice about his terrible complexion in the movies. He goes into a moment. When Mr. Redford goes into a moment, he doesn't have time to be disgusted with himself. [*Pause.*] Bob is a normal person.

RICHARD: Bob is not a normal person.

DIANE (in the Jewish Alps): Mr. Assisi, you weren't having disgusting thoughts about a complexion when you saw me come out of the shower. On the bathroom floor. On the kitchen floor. We've done it on every floor in this house including the cellar and the attic. What's wrong with a bed that we almost never do it in a bed?

RICHARD (giving in): We become invulved.

They laugh.

RICHARD (humorless again): Cut the crap, Diane. He's terrifically good-looking with or without the complexion, whereas I, look at me. My face cannot be said to be Redford-like in any sense. What do you think, I'm stupid?

DIANE: I prefer your face to Bob's. That's what I think.

[*Pause.*]

DIANE: Talk to me for real.

RICHARD: Forget it.

DIANE: Confide in me, my heart.

RICHARD: I'm standing here in the nude in my bathroom at six forty-five in the morning. You're sitting on the toilet in the nude. And I feel like it again.

Diane wipes. Arises. Something in the way she walks. Sinks beofre him to one knee. Takes the real thing in hand. Parts lips. He pulls back.

RICHARD: You want me to talk? Let's talk about our innermost secret secret. Okay? Let's talk about what we really think of the people closest to us. The so-called friends and lovers. The so-called family. Let's talk about what we never tell these people, the truth of what we really think about them. The brutal perceptions concerning the facts of who they are that never come out to their faces, because it would be too painful, and we're too nice. Let's talk about how everything we say to each other is beautiful bullshit—

DIANE: I've already read *Heart of Darkness.*

RICHARD: Let's talk about how you sweep everything under the carpet with your humor and your references, because you're a literature show-off. In your innermost secret secret you look at me and what do you say?

DIANE: Sweetheart.

RICHARD: You say, "I've seen Robert Redford, and he's no Robert Redford."

DIANE (in disbelief, laughing): Senator, I fucked Jack Kennedy, and you're no Jack Kennedy.

RICHARD: You think I'm funny? What's so fucking funny about my looks?

DIANE: I'm not the superficial asshole you think I am, asshole.

RICHARD: You want me to confide? Huh? If you said out loud your secret secret, you would say: "Richard, you are an ugly man."

[*Pause.*]

DIANE: Sometimes I say, He falls into assaholic behavior, because everybody has to sometimes. But then I say, There are compensations. Because, for one thing, he's my great lover and he has no interest in anyone but me, which I know because it's obvious. I say to myself, He has the sexiness of a tall and rangy and hard-bodied welterweight champion of the world. Richard, you want to be an asshole and focus on physical qualities, these are the comments I make to myself in secret. The fact is, when you love me, I feel totally loved.

RICHARD: You like it too much. You scare me.

DIANE: Did I mention sex? I said love.

RICHARD: In other words, in the sack I don't measure up.

DIANE: [*Pause.*] I need a gun.

Richard returns to mirror. Puts glasses on. Diane sitting on floor, dripping a little semen. Richard viciously pops a minuscule but pregnant pimple. White spots on mirror, of a sluggish viscosity.

Richard [*gesturing to mirror*]: Look! This is what I have to live with in my fifties. I had a case like you wouldn't believe when I was a teenager. Then I totally cleared up. Where is the dignity of the final phase? Where is the hard-won serenity of the golden years? (Giggles.) I meet you, and now this. Fifty plus and I'm back to Clearasil.

DIANE: That stuff on the mirror, what does it look like?

Richard is speechless.

DIANE: You don't have pimples, Richard. You generate secondary erections, because since you met me you can't get enough out through the traditional channel. Though we try. Richard, you're just full of come. Every morning your face needs to shoot off in the mirror.

[*Pause.*]

RICHARD: My face comes?

DIANE: You ejaculate the overload through the face.

[*Pause.*]

RICHARD: This is the function of Bob's moles?

DIANE: No.

[*Pause.*]

RICHARD: Bob doesn't shoot off through the face?

DIANE: He's undersexed. I thought everybody knew.

RICHARD: If Redford is told about my complexion, he experiences terrible inadequacy?

DIANE: He experiences terrible yearning to be somebody else.

RICHARD: Modesty forbids one to speak.

DIANE: Speak, my heart.

RICHARD: Redford desires to be Assisi-like in the face.

DIANE: Wrong. He wants to become you.

    Richard tries to suppress a grin.

RICHARD (crooning): It's too late for running, my heart . . .
    (Richard: full grin: full tumescence. Diane lies back. She says, "In your fifties!" Richard settles in. Kissing on the mouth. Clock radio on at six fifty-eight. Aretha Franklin letting loose with "Who's Zoomin' Who?")

Three days after the Lucy-Debbie debacle at Sylvan Lake. I'm on call, the usual thirty-six-hour stint, asleep in the attending physician's private quarters. A nice quiet night on Labor and Delivery. At 3 A.M., or thereabouts, I'm roused by heavy insistent knocking. Diane. Beside herself with fear. I do my best to keep a poker face, because I need to hide my pleasure. I ask her, "What's wrong? How did you get them to let you down here?" She tells me she's sorry. Almost came over to my place last night in the early morning hours. Actually packed the toiletries and a change of underthings. "But tonight I can't take it anymore." I tell her to calm down, Debbie is no competition. She says, "This is serious, you bastard." I'm delighted.

"Somebody has been in my house."

"Goldilocks?"

"I bought a gun this afternoon. I bought a goddamn gun, Richard."

"You were robbed?"

"Worse. Someone got in. I'm not sure how or when. They disturbed nothing. They made no noise. I never even knew they were in. I never even knew they left."

"Then how do you even know someone got in?"

"I found my bread knife, the long one, propped up against the TV."

I tell her that a bread knife, even a stainless steel one like hers, would make a disgusting mess. Had it been a scalpel, she'd know who it was. Calls me an asshole. I tell her that that's the one word she's not permitted to call me. She screams it out loud enough to be heard all the way down to the end of the hall, at the nurses' station. Another knock at the door. Debbie is also sorry, but she heard quite a noise. Debbie leaves as big Diane falls apart, looking weak and small, curled up on the bed. I lock the door and turn off the lights. I take off her blue jeans as she sobs. I take off her panties. Tongue into her vagina, deep. Nothing. I apply the KY. I'm harder than I've been in months. My orgasm causes me to rush out of myself, like the blast of semen itself.

In the dark, I pull the sheets over us. I'm on the verge of confession. Before I can speak she asks me what she should do. Without hesitation, I tell her to go to my place for the night.

Am I changing? *We are who we are.* This time I'll change.

I tell her, "Tomorrow we call home security people. We put in a sophisticated system, which I'll help you pay for. Door sensors. Glass breakers. Motion detectors. You punch in a code when you leave or go to bed. You give the code to no one, not even me." She manages a small smile. She says, "Especially you."

"Come on, Diane. This is serious."

"I couldn't do that to you. I'm not going to live that way."

"Okay. Me, but no one else."

All of a sudden she seems to grow back into herself. She's filling out. Wants it again, but I won't be pushed.

181

"Well, as long as you're giving me the code, it's best to tell me where you keep the handgun."

"It's not a handgun. That takes a few days. I bought a pump action 12-gauge shotgun. Under the bed, Richard. Loaded."

She puts her hand on my crotch. She says, "Speaking of pump action shotguns." She's herself again. I keep my voice small. I want my voice in the dark to be poker-faced. I tell her, "See you at home for breakfast." She says, "Obviously I didn't have my diaphragm in."

At 6 A.M., when my stint ends, I go directly to Diane's place. Unload the shotgun. Wipe it clean for prints. Put it back exactly where it was.

When I get back home, it's clear that she has not slept a wink, and that she's enraged. She says, "Why didn't you tell me you bought an answering machine?! On top of that, you turned the ringer off! I get into bed and I start to hear a voice at four-thirty in the morning! I finally figured out it was that other asshole. Stupid bastards, the two of you!" I say [*shoulders hunched, stooping*], "I don't want to talk to him directly anymore. I screen the calls now." She says, "*Directly?* Change your fucking number to unlisted. That'll end it. You *want* to listen, shithead." I say, "What do you expect? Overnight transformation? Eventually I'll change. Come on, let's listen together before breakfast."

*   *   *

"Imagine attempting to cunt-fuck that hippo! Who can blame him if he had to spousally abuse her? Another white woman, Richard, in case you didn't hear. She throws the two kids into what they're calling the storm-swollen Los Angeles River. She jumps in herself. One of the kids dies.

She doesn't. Orenthal knew they don't croak on their own volition, much less by natural or accidental forces. Our friend had the balls, Richard. We could say that in my time I had partial balls. We could say I did partial but lasting damage in my day. Concerning you, the jury is still out. [*Pause.*] So how many cuntlings did you deliver into this vale of tears last night? The *size* of that LA woman! She outweighs the theoretically abusive spouse by 150 pounds. When she hits the water, she displaces the entire river. Homes in the vicinity are said to be hopelessly flood-damaged. They had a storm out there last week so bad that a mountain runoff disengorged the coffins from a graveyard. Tore off the lids! Bodies in various states afloat in tract housing developments. I'm telling you facts. A long time ago, I chose to get involved. I formulated a response. You, you're still in a transitional state. A larval state. When does the butterfly emerge? [*Pause.*] There are female types where murder is deeply correct. Did you see her picture? When I see their pictures I need to do something. Their faces say give me sympathy. Their faces say don't hurt me. THEY CAN ALL JUST SUCK MY COCK! [*Long pause.*] She's claiming the husband went homosexual on her. Imagine this tall skinny guy with a woman like that! I speculate a mother complex. The letter *F.* Freud. After a series of sexual incidents with the mother image, he requires an enema. He gravitates toward faggary. I would myself! Wouldn't you? [*Extended laughter on the tape.*] Wouldn't you? So when are you going to send me a picture of this new love of your life? Ah, forget the picture, Richard. I said forget it. Because who gives a shit about the looks? Just send me the dimensions of what you're up against. [*Pause.*] Eventually, either you talk to me direct, or you go into total seclusion. With a woman like this Los Angeles pig, how would you ever know? Follow me? You'd have to constantly ask her: 'Is it in?' This has been my message after the beep."

✳   ✳   ✳

Diane is beside herself with laughter. When she calms down, she says: "Richard, what are the three words universally known to women? Give up? *Is it in?*'!" I say, "I have something serious to say to you. You said the shotgun's loaded." She sings, "I didn't knooooow the gun was loaded!" I say, "Keep it loaded. Don't unload it. Don't even touch it until we agree you're out of danger." She says, "I know that." Then she says, "Lately, you don't look at me when we talk." I gaze down at my fingernails. I say, "It's hard to look the woman you love in the eye."

"You love me?"

"Sure, why not?"

She has to leave: go home, pick up some things. The fear is back. I offer to accompany her. She can show me where the shotgun is. When we return, I tell her, I'll have to view the trial tapes for the last two days. She says, "You look sedated already."

"After the tapes, we'll make a call or two. Arrange to meet a security specialist. Some retired captain from the Air Force."

"What if I'm pregnant?"

"Impossible."

"How can you know?"

"Because I subscribe to an ancient rape theory. A woman can't conceive unless she's aroused."

"I was aroused."

"I greased you, Diane."

184

"After we talked, I felt aroused."

"And I declined to re-fuck you."

"Shut up, Richard. What if I'm pregnant?"

"The baby brings us closer, Victor becomes the godfather, and we live happily ever after."

A day later, while Diane is at work, another call on my machine: "I heard the cunt's head was practically severed off." The tape runs silently for many seconds. "I knew a boy once wanted to do a girl in. Any boy has to, needs to, once in a lifetime, do a girl in." Silence on the tape. "I have given you the wisdom of the letter *E,* after which there is none. No holes barred, Richard. *E* is for Eliot, T. S. Follow the logic, son."

Long ago, on the west side of Utica, there lived a tall Polish girl, a blonde of transcendent beauty, who died in childbirth, eighteen years before I was introduced to Victor. The beauty and the beast had secretly married. The child survived and was being raised close to Mary Street, perhaps even on Mary Street itself, with father and son in ignorance of their true relation, as they passed each other daily in the neighborhood—nodding as they passed, or as they sat across from one another on the bus.

And in a sad ghetto close to the center of town, there lived, and still lives, Victor's illegitimate son, black as coal, upon whom he took pity, and to whom he had given a job at Utica Meat, where not even the calves (so stated Dora) were safe from Victor, the insatiable pederast.

Victor's mother was infertile. No, she had had something on the side with an Irish redhead. The father was impotent from birth; the mother was a virgin, till death did them part.

As for the big black valise, which we said grew out of his left hand, it contained a large black-and-white photo of the heartbreaking teenage wife; or it contained hundreds of snapshots of the elegant coal-black son; or it contained a huge silver revolver in the style of Hopalong Cassidy.

Like Victor himself, the big black valise contained nothing, and the barren signora had been impregnated by the Infernal Prince, and Victor Graziadei was his only begotten son.

*   *   *

Through the last months of '59, through that winter and the following spring, summer, and fall, at our weekly meetings in the dead hours of the pastry shop on late Thursday afternoons, when it was just Carmen and me in rapt attendance of his cunning monologues, how abruptly they came, he called them "the natural facts of my life," personal revelations, if they are to be believed, out of nowhere, dispelling and confusing all speculations, anxieties, and yearnings: there were no redheads in the Sicilian backgrounds of his parents, "who went after each other, day and night, worse than rabbits. They made a regular fuckery out of our home. I was the bystander; I was the jerk-off in the fuckery." He confirmed that he was adopted from an orphanage in South Dakota, and brought by his loving immigrant parents to Elizabeth Street in New York's Little Italy at six weeks old. He said that they knew he'd grow up to be a gangster unless they moved immediately, and so they did, to Utica, where there were many paesans, and the gangsters were less plentiful, and the parents refused from day one to explain to their new friends the carrot-topped infant. And Victor confirmed, at last, that he had indeed been married, briefly, at twenty. A fruitless union, but she was still alive, because "this cunt is immortal."

The truth about the big black valise came out in the

middle of his story of Russ Columbo. Sooner or later Victor would have told the story. He told it that bright fall afternoon in 1960 because I triggered it by bringing to Carmen's my latest record purchase, Jerry Vale's new romantic album, *I Remember Russ*. Victor's first glimpse produced this: "Nobody will sing an album of homage to that foul ball Bing Crosby, who had everything to gain from what they did to Russ in the home of his best friend. What have you heard of Russ from your father, Richard? I happen to know your father loved Russ as I did." In response to his barked demand, I told Victor that my father had never mentioned Russ in my presence, and Victor replied, "Because there is too much anguish. We who go back to Russ grieve in secret. True or false, Carmen?" Carmen said, "What can I tell you, Victor? I wish I went back." I had trouble imagining my father in secret grief. I had never heard of Russ Columbo until I picked up Jerry Vale's latest. My recent purchase was all about Jerry's warm, liquid tenor of the forsaken lover:

> I'm all dressed up
> With a broken heart
> Pretending I'm with you . . .

Victor said, "I go back. Do we speak the truth and say what a remembrance is? I'm working on a new poem. The thought is, when we remember, we carry a tremendous grudge. There's no room for anything else in the mind. Memory is constant hatred. Richard, I remember Crosby. I'm saying the voice of Russ Columbo could not be resisted." Carmen says, "I have to say one word, Victor. Sinatra." Victor snaps back, "Sinatra is obvious. Russ Columbo poured it

188

in while you slept. You woke up with the voice in your body. Haunted, badly in love. Even today, twenty-five years later, I feel partially insane." Carmen says, "You meant 'madly,' right?" Victor says, "Carmen, you have a mind stuffed with clichés."

A customer comes in, Carmen excuses himself, and Victor falls silent. I'm studying the back of the record jacket. I feel courageous. I venture something: "It says here that Jerry modeled himself on Russ." Victor says, "We need our models. How else would we know how to die?" He laughs. He says, "Jerry's actual name is Genaro Vitaliano. Look it up! I'm told an irate husband beat the shit out of him last week in Las Vegas. Black and blue all over his face." He laughs. He says, "Jerry gets a lot of cunt." He says, "I hear nothing but good things about you from the boys at work. Hector says you've been baby-sitting for him on a regular basis. He says you have the touch when it comes to his babies." Victor puts on a detective's voice: "Mr. Assisi, did you at any point during the evening hear unusual sounds originating from the vicinity of the children's bedroom?" He says, "You know what Ronny told me? Ronny told me, 'Victor, good thing we have knives, and he doesn't. I feel it puts us on the same level.' I could pile up the quotes from my boys, but I don't want to give you a big head. I'm so proud, Richard, I'm not even going to mention the weekly reports from Uncle Henry, who says in the beginning you were a whoremaster's dream: you're in and out in five seconds. But now it's an hour and fifteen minutes before you come. You walk out of Dora's room stewed in your own sweat, reeling, and Dora needs to sleep for an hour after what you've done to her. True or false, Richard?" I say, "False, Victor." It's the first time I had ever said false. He starts to fade before my eyes. I decide to save him from certain death. I tell him the truth: "A little under an hour I fuck her, Victor." He returns. He's happy. He says, "You do come eventually?" I say, "Yes." He says, "I heard of a case where hardness occurs, where fucking of intensity occurs, but coming has ceased to occur. The case has gone into carnal retirement. Not even self-manipulation is attempted. I'm assured there is the beautiful pain of pre-coming, but there is no actual coming. This pain creates thoughts of self-slaughter."

Carmen is back. Carmen says, "You know who that was who didn't buy anything? Cocksucker!" We have no idea. Carmen says, "The mayor's brother. The mayor's daughter requires a favor." Victor acts as if Carmen doesn't exist. He's looking at me. He's saying, "What's in that brown valise of yours?" I say, "My books." He says, "No, the tools of your passion." I completely surprise myself: I say, "What's in your black valise?" Victor says, "The tools of *my* passion. I'll show you mine if you show me yours." I lay my books on the table. Victor selects one. *Major British Writers,* edited by G. B. Harrison. He says, "Harrison is a Shakespearean of international renown." He says, "Okay, Carmen." Carmen goes to the backroom and returns with the big black valise. He sets it down between Victor and me. Victor opens it. The first thing I see is a pair of matched meat skewers, long as the bag itself. Then a pair of scissors, the type used to trim chicken. Victor places the skewers and the scissors on the table. He says, "Don't touch anything." He pulls out a small grocery bag. He says, "Take a peek." I look inside. Full of dark-colored rags smelling of furniture polish and house-hold disinfectants. He pulls out a box of condoms. Takes one out of the box. He says, "You call this a condom; maybe you call it a rubber; I call it a sheath. Learn to call it a sheath. Go wash your hands and I'll let you touch these things. I'll let you pull things out of the bag." When I return, he says, "Go ahead." I pull out a nutcracker, three crochet hooks, four pairs of handcuffs, a hat pin, an elongated tubular device, and a small plunger. He says, "Carmen, how do we know for sure that our Richard is a person of uncommon taste?" Carmen replies, "Because he didn't ask, 'Where's the coat hanger?' "

We return our tools to their respective valises. Carmen carries Victor's to the backroom and returns with gelato for three. We consume it in silence. Victor says, "Ah, Carmen." He says, "Richard, 1930, 1931, the period of Russ's emergence, which is also the period of emergence for the foul ball, who is an embarrassment to the art. The two go neck 'n' neck for about a year for the heart of America. Then Russ starts to pull away. By the summer of '34, he's all by himself. Russ Columbo is going to dominate the era and Crosby knows this. Crosby stinks." Carmen says, "Who wants more coffee?" He goes to the backroom.

In a whisper, Victor says, "Carmen is not one of us. Carmen is one of them." He's pointing to the front cover of the album, his forefinger touching the pictures of Jerry and Russ. "The girls your age say Jerry is cute. They're in love. They're moist for him. When I was your age, they went nuts for Russ. But Russ wasn't cute. He was handsome. Remember: the mayor's daughter has a crush on Carmen, not on you, not in a million years. What is a remembrance? Follow me? Look at me, look at you. We're deep Italians, but we don't look like *them*. We're Italians, but we're not beautiful Italians. You know that song by Harry Belafonte? "Marry a Woman Uglier than You"? As far as Harry and Russ and Jerry and Carmen are concerned, no problem.

Anybody they marry has to be uglier than they are. Richard, it's going to be very hard for you to marry someone uglier than you, not to mention my own case. I tried, I failed. So I made her uglier. Sooner or later, you'll face the same crossroads. When Russ died, I cried for three days."

Carmen returns. He says, "The wife just called. She's going crazy. She tells me, 'I know you're doing something with the mayor's daughter, I just have to catch you at it.' I tell her, 'Andrea, stop, you're giving me a hard-on.' ".

Victor says, "Russ Columbo was born in San Francisco with that terrific hair they have in such abundance on the West Coast. The complexion is golden. The voice is Italian. My thought is, by September 1, 1934, Crosby is dead, because by this date Russ has his own dance orchestra. He has radio. He's releasing three or four vocals per month. He's even writing his own ballads.

> You call it madness
> Ah! But I call it love . . .

The movies. The women. His fan mail staggers the moguls. Russ is staggering the Jews. Russ is pulling down seven grand a week in the Depression. The Jews are in love. The Italians are raving. Even the Protestants are raving. The Negro, meanwhile, lives in his own musical realm, where he makes plans for our future. By September 1, 1934, Crosby is taking it seriously up the ass. By the early evening of September 2, 1934, the Romeo of song is dead and Crosby rises from the grave. Ever since, America goes on a date with the dope next door, boola boola, but America does not get romantically fucked in the Italian style. Richard, this is what Russ wrote, this is what he sang." Victor croons:

192

Alone from night to night you'll find me,
Too weak to break the chains that bind me,
I need no shackles to remind me,
I'm just a prisoner of love . . .

Carmen returns with three espressos, crooning in a soft high falsetto. Victor says, "The soprano always gets murdered by the baritone, who she won't fuck, and in this opera I am the baritone. They called it a freak mishap. The official accidental killer had the name Lansing Brown, Junior, of Los Angeles, portrait photographer for the stars." He goes into his wallet. Removes a much-folded, yellowed newspaper clipping. He says, "*New York Times,* September 3, 1934." He reads without affect:

" 'During my entire conversation with Russ,' Brown told detectives, 'I was absent-mindedly fooling with one of the guns. I was pulling back the trigger and clicking it, time after time. I had a match in my left hand and when I clicked, evidently the match caught in between the hammer and the firing pin. There was an explosion. Russ slid to the side of his chair. I thought he was clowning. It all happened mighty fast. I have had this collection of antique guns for seven years. I have never made an examination to see whether they were loaded, because they were so old. I had no idea at all they were loaded. I happened to have a match in my left hand.' "

"Lansing Brown, Junior. Ruggiero Columbo. The detectives say that the ball from a two-hundred-year-old French dueling pistol ricocheted off a mahogany dresser, then penetrated through the eye to the center of Russ's brain. A young woman they never identified was seen leaving the hospital weeping. After a brief interrogation, Lansing Brown was not held for this death. Crosby was said to be unavailable for comment." He pauses for a long time. "How soon does the mayor's daughter require closure?" Carmen says, "She's already four and a half months." Victor says, "Tell the brother that the presence of His Honor, J. Kenneth Sherman, is required tonight. Eleven o'clock. The father, J. Kenneth Sherman, and the best men, Victor Graziadei and Carmen Caravaggio, respectfully request the attendance of Mr. Richard Assisi, at ten forty-five. RSVP." I say, "I'll give you my answer now, Victor." Victor says, "Say no more. We are as one in spirit."

Carmen croons high, soft. Victor looks tired. He says, "The voice looked like Valentino." I check my watch. Four-seventeen.

A cocktail party. Orenthal with his hair in a ponytail, no one paying him attention. He's depressed. I approach: to console him. Vacancy of the eyes. He's dead. I say, "Strenuous is the work of slaughter. You are so tired. Victor was also tired, but Victor was tired *before*. Was there not great giddiness during? Be happy and sprightly, Orenthal. Recall thy giddiness." He replies, weakly: "You talk funny. You're some talker, big fella." I like it that he calls me "big fella." I decide to show him a picture of Diane. He smiles the smallest smile. He says, "She's an Italian." I say, "Yes! And so is your new girlfriend! So are you! Please show me your sadness. My name is Richard. Call me Richard."

Victor says, "In dreams begin responsibilities."

*　　*　　*

Morning. Her place. Her bed. In April, time of blooming azaleas in the Land of Cotton, time of woodchucks emerging from the burrows of their long winter sleep. "No, they actually boom down here," Diane insists, when I say to her you mean bloom. She says, "Last night, after you boomed me, killer, you promised to tell me the story. Tell me every-

195

thing, or I won't be able to give you absolution, or breakfast. Hey! Lover boy! That was a heck of a boom last night!"

"I got there at ten forty-five."

"What did you do between four-seventeen and ten forty-five, Mr. Assisi, on the night in question?"

"First I bought a pair of shoes in the exact style and size of Victor's. Black-and-white penny loafers. The tongue is the white part. Don't ask me how I know his size."

"Did you fill his shoes, Mr. Assisi?"

"My feet are two sizes longer. 'D' width. Victor is a seven and a half narrow."

"What size jock, Mr. Assisi?"

"Then I went home for supper. My father cooked beautifully, as always. I ate heartily, as always. My father was happy to see me. I was sullen, etcetera."

"You persisted in your asshole manner toward your good father, may he rest in peace. He turned the other cheek, et cetera."

"Then I studied until ten-thirty."

"You came into your own last night, big fella."

"At ten-thirty, I put on my new shoes and walked out into the rain."

"A Hemingway novel!"

"How would I know? Unlike you, I didn't major in English. I had an umbrella. Do they use umbrellas in Hemingway?"

"They 'utilize' them. What is the significance of the umbrella, killer? Phallic?"

"Have you no shame, Diane?"

"Killer, it's you who has the shame."

"The umbrella figures in. Bleecker Street is deserted. I go to the alley in the rear. I enter through the rear door. Victor and Carmen ask me to assist them. They're taping heavy black cloth over the front windows and the door. We work by the light of the street lamp. When we're finished, we're in total darkness until Carmen turns on a small lamp, a bedroom-type table lamp which he brought from home for the occasion. Victor and I carry out from the backroom a small squarish table. Carmen lies on the table. He pulls up his knees, heels at the corners, his arms in the position of crucifixion. Victor says to Carmen, 'She's a lot shorter than you. This is perfect. Now get off the table, because I don't want you coming in your pants on the table. It would be wrong.' They're relaxing. They're kidding around in the locker room before the big game."

"The crucifixion detail is much too heavy."

"You want a heavy detail, Diane? Let me tell you about the shape of the patient's table in the Labor and Delivery operating room. This is a true fact. The elements are a little wide to call it an actual crucifix. But it's a perfect cruciform. You need a tour of the L and D operating room. The cruciform allows us maximal clear access to the abdomen. We don't want arm spasms in the vicinity of the scalpel as we make our eight-inch incision just above the pubic bone. We create a sterile field. We erect an actual sterile barrier across the stomach area in order to protect the sterile field. Also, we don't believe it necessary for the patient to gaze down her body into the gore, which we have our professional hands involved in, which never troubles the professional."

"That night at Carmen's you were an amateur. You did it for love."

"Granted, we don't strap, handcuff, or nail in the patient awaiting her C-section."

"Eventually, your sense of humor gets you a ticket out of hell."

"You can't get out of hell."

"I'll graduate you to purgatory. Then the troubled teenager arrives with His Honor, the mayor of the Sin City of the East?"

"No. I notice the table is dirty."

"Ah, Richard!"

"I say to Carmen, who's more anal than me, 'I think I'll wash the table.' Carmen says, 'No you won't, Richie.' Then she arrives, who I have a secret crush on, with her father, His Honor. I had a terrific crush on Rosemary."

"She looks like Kim Novak?"

"That's also a true fact, Diane. She looks the same as Kim."

"Mind if I put my big leg over you, Papa? If memory serves me right, Dora looked like Kim Novak. Now Rosemary looks like Kim Novak."

"I never said Dora. That's your contribution."

"Did you make a contribution that night, or were you an innocent bystander?"

"I could use a cup of coffee."

"No coffee. Finish first or I'll crush you in my big legs. Good thing I don't look like Kim, Papa."

"You know who you really look like, Diane?"

"Shut up and tell me the story."

"It's very dark in there, with just that little lamp illuminating the squarish table. The mayor, Carmen, and Victor walk behind the showcases and talk quietly in the shadows. I look at Rosemary; she looks at the floor. She's very pretty. Suddenly Carmen says loud, 'We don't want your cocksucking money, cocksucker! Get over here.' They come over to us in the illuminated area. Carmen has a dish of gelato in his hand. He scrapes it off with his fingers onto the floor. He says to the mayor, 'That's how you pay me. No hands. Lick it up. You're good with your tongue. That's it. Very nice.' He looks at me and says, 'Now we pay Richard. Richie, take off her clothes.' "

"Did you?"

"I couldn't wait. I get her down to her panties and bra. Carmen says, 'Finish the job, Richie.' I take off her bra. Her breasts are small but full. I imagine almost getting a whole one in my mouth. I guide her to the table. I tell her to lie on it. She does, with her legs close together. I pull off her panties. I spread her legs somewhat. Carmen says, 'Your Honor, look at what I've been fucking. Richie, I can see even in this bad light the bulge in your crotch. Maybe later.' "

"You saw her in her illuminated nakedness. She was beautiful."

"Yes."

"You were scared?"

"Yes."

"You were dizzy. You thought you might faint."

"Yes."

"You were totally aroused."

"Yes."

"Getting aroused now?"

"A little."

"Feel evil?"

"Yes."

"Don't."

"Why?"

"It's natural, to a certain extent."

"At what point do I reach that extent?"

"Never. You will never reach it. Accept your banality. Did you participate in the killing?"

"There was no killing in that sense of the word. I was staring at her. She was staring at the wedding-cake ceiling. She didn't seem to give a shit. I always saw her as a shy person."

"*You* are a shy person. *She* was banging Carmen day and night. The wedding-cake ceiling is too obvious."

"That was the actual style of it."

"Life is too obvious."

"Then Carmen said, 'Now Victor gets paid.' Victor has not yet said a word. He pulls out the handcuffs. Carmen raises her knees. Spreads her legs maximally. Victor cuffs the ankles to the legs of the table. Carmen places the arms in the position of crucifixion. Victor cuffs one of the wrists to a table leg. One pair of handcuffs left. Victor gives them to me. I complete the job."

"Still aroused at that point?"

"No."

"Tell the truth, Richard. Lie to me now and you go straight to hell forever."

"I was not aroused."

"Good."

"Nor am I now."

"Bad."

"Who's sick, Diane?"

"Neither of us. We're nice and banal. Okay. She's handcuffed. Then what?"

"Victor takes out the bag of rags. Carmen stuffs one in her mouth and says, 'Ready, Victor?' Victor pulls my umbrella from under the table. Rips off two ribs. Carmen says, 'Now we're all set.' That was my contribution, Diane. That is the significance of the umbrella."

"No, killer. That was your umbrella's contribution. What we know, so far, is you took off her clothes. You did one wrist. To that extent you were an accessory. Your umbrella was utilized. You had a hard-on. So what you had a hard-on? An eighteen-year-old boy is a walking hard-on, a fuck machine with nothing to fuck. This is the story of an eighteen-year-old male of the 1950s, before the sex revolution. In your teens, fucking was only a word."

"Stop trying to make me feel better."

"Ah."

"I'm serious."

"Ah."

"What strikes me, after all the years, is the similarity. The cruelest of abortions; the difficult vaginal birth of a full-term baby. About six years later, I'm a med student doing his first rotation on ob-gyn, where I observe and assist in my first delivery, and the attending physician is one of the few women at that time in the Upstate Medical Center. She stepped out of Botticelli. Taciturn, intense, mythic."

"You're revealing too much, killer."

"The mother was ready. I had just completed the final cervix check: ten centimeters, fully effaced, the baby primed for uterine propulsion. I could feel the crown. Problem was the mother is exhausted from extended labor. She lacks the power to blast it through the final inches. The attending—Joanne? Corinne?—I can't remember her last name now—"

"Doctor Botticelli—"

"The attending slips her latex-gloved fingers deep in. She says, 'There's plenty of room,' and smiles just a little. What she's saying with her smile is, 'I'm not going to cut this woman open, because we don't need to do that to her.' The sterile gown, the sterile hair covering, the sterile booties of the physician; the sterile latex examination gloves with beaded cuffs. Victor is emerging from the backroom wearing Carmen's tall white chef's hat, the long white apron that descends well below the knees, and yellow galoshes."

"This is not a similarity."

"Joanne is using a new technique to help the weary mother. A little vacuum device, electrically powered. It fits easily into the birth canal, slipping nicely over the baby's crown. Joanne is tugging with steady strength. I remember her surprisingly athletic wrists and forearms. This baby is apparently big and the mother at this point is trying to push, but to no avail. Victor is attempting the insertion of a small unlubricated plunger, which is much larger than Corinne's vacuum device. He can't get it in. He takes the meat scissors and performs what I would come to know as an episiotomy. He's snipping away for some time at the vagina; Rosemary's thighs are awash, as are Victor's ungloved hands. The doctor reinserts the vacuum device; the motor hums, she's tugging. Suddenly the device slips off the crown and the doctor jerks back a little from the sudden slippage, the rapidly exiting device flings blood across the room to the opposite wall. The doctor's azure gown is red; she's at this point red up to the elbows. This is normal. The doctor performs the episiotomy skillfully. I can still hear the snipping. Later, she will sew it up with such skill that the mother and her mate are granted a new and tighter model, for which they shall be grateful. The mother's thighs are awash. All monitors indicate that the baby is doing splendidly in the home stretch. A nurse says, 'This is a very happy baby.'"

"This is not a similarity."

"Victor's white apron is red and he's barely begun. He forces the plunger in, working it the way you do with a plugged-up toilet. He yanks it out: blood flying all over

Carmen and his beautiful ceramic floor. Sudden polka dots on the tall white chef's hat. I'll tell you another similarity. They both have nurses; Carmen is the nurse. Victor says, 'Skewer.' The doctor says, 'Forceps.' In both events, I'm the spectator. The father in both events is weeping quietly. Don't tell me there are no similarities."

"The mayor was not the father in that sense."

"They were both called the father. They were both weeping quietly. Joanne or Corinne is perfectly focused. She will not be distracted by the weeping father. After all, she's a pro. Victor is also focused, undistracted, et cetera. The facts are these: weeping, flying blood, fascination, concentration, no screaming. Not even at the end is there screaming, when the mayor is smashing his head as hard as he can against the doorjamb."

"Smashing the head in order not to scream."

"Carmen says, 'Basically, we're looking for pieces of spaghetti squash. When we see the spaghetti squash in chunks, then we know we've achieved closure.' The skewer doesn't work, except for more blood flowing off the table. Rosemary is heaving, her hips rising and slamming down on the table with everything she's got. That is her only sound. The lubricated forceps fail and the doctor applies them again. Victor says, 'Crochet hook.' Victor says, 'Hat pin.' Victor says, 'Umbrella rib.' Again failure with the forceps."

"No parallel."

"You weren't there."

"That's a good point, but that's your only point. You were there. One of them was an angel, the other a butcher."

"Who am I?"

"You'd be surprised. You'll be the last to know who you are. Which is normal."

"Don't try to make me feel better."

"Ah. Your second point. Continue."

"The forceps fail for the third time. The doctor places her bloody gloved hands lightly on the abdomen. She's looking at the weary mother's face now. Victor is at it again with the scissors. The doctor says to the mother, 'I'm going to bring your baby out on the next try. I will make it happen.' Everybody is astonished. Except the baby. 'I'm going to bring your baby out on the next try. I will make it happen.' This statement is over the top. I have never said that to a mother, because you can't know in advance. She goes in again with the forceps and here comes the baby, and before even the nasal passages and mouth are suctioned the baby is screaming with a tremendous voice, smeared with blood and amniotic fluid, totally healthy. The doctor says, 'No wonder! Look at those shoulders!' This doctor puts not even the smallest bruise on that baby with her birthing instruments. She cuts the cord with a full smile. Two minutes later the baby is suckling like a pro. The father says, 'Thank you.' The mythic doctor says, 'You're welcome,' and leaves."

"In my nightgown, Richard, don't you think I look a little Botticellian? Call me Joanne."

"Victor is going in deep with his entire bare hand. He's crouched over her. He pulls out matter. He says, 'Ashtray.' He goes in. He pulls out matter. He goes in again. He's dropping the dripping matter into the ashtray held by the nurse. He says, 'Victory.' Carmen grins. Carmen says, 'The humor on this guy, I can't get over it.' They wipe up the floor with the rag which they remove from Rosemary's mouth, who's passed out. They wipe the rag on the mayor's pants and sport coat. Then Carmen goes outside with that rag and wipes the interior of the mayor's car.

When he comes back, he says to the mayor, 'Don't try to report this to Friggy. The blood implicates you.' Friggy is the deputy chief of police, who is on the take at Uncle Henry's, among other establishments. Carmen finishes cleaning the floor with a mop as I dress Rosemary, who's coming around. I use my clean handkerchief on her thighs. Carmen tells me to use one of Victor's 'special rags,' but I refuse. I use my sleeve. Victor is washing up in the backroom and when he emerges he's smelling the tips of his fingers. He's electric. After a month in the hospital, sixteen days of which I heard were in the mental ward, Rosemary comes back to Oneida County College looking destroyed, and more beautiful than ever. I wanted to ask her for a date. Tuna sandwiches and chocolate shakes at the Mello Shoppe. Then a nice stroll downtown on a sunny Sunday afternoon. At her doorstep, a little peck on the mouth. Thank you, Rosemary. I hope I'll see you again soon. Maybe you could help me with my solid geometry. You're terrific at math. Most girls aren't."

"It's supposed to be a peck on the *cheek*."

"About a week ago, I tried to get her number from Utica information. The entire family's gone."

"What did you do after?"

"After a while I went out and walked back home in the rain."

"Without your umbrella. I'm going to make you a big breakfast now."

"I don't want breakfast."

"Yes you do."

"We shouldn't eat now."

"Why?"

"It wouldn't be right."

"Ah."

205

"What the hell do you mean by that? That's the twelfth time you said 'ah.' "

"You know what I mean."

*　　　*　　　*

After breakfast, I tell her my obvious dream. Not the Orenthal one. With all my might I'm trying to keep a door closed. A great invisible force pulls against me. The force is irresistible. The door blows open, giving upon a darkened room. A bed. A woman naked on the bed. Knees up. Heels at foot of bed, spread-eagled. A man kneeling between her legs. The man's head turns toward me as the door blows open. Cheeks and mouth smeared with blood, not his own. Behind the head of the bed, brightness through a window. Luminous darkness. A painterly, a theatrical effect. I say to Diane, "Everything is obvious. The man is obviously Victor. Everything is always obvious in my dreams." She says, "You're wrong about that, too. You're wrong about everything. In our dreams, we are everything." I say, "That's ridiculous. I am the door? I'm the blood? The woman? Completely ridiculous." She says, "It's you, Richard, trying to keep the door closed, and you are the counterforce. Of course. Obviously you are the door, the bed, the man, the woman."

"Oh, yeah, the window, too."

"Oh, definitely. You are the window and the brightness. The brightness through the window, to be exact. The backlighting, Richard. You are the actors, the author, the set designer, the lighting designer, and the director. Most of all, you are the backlighting. How you love your theater! As that pathetic bastard said, and you never tire of repeating: 'We are who we are.' How many birthday parties this month, killer?"

[*Silence.*]

"I said how many, goddamn it!"

"Only four."

"Only four!!"

Diane is weeping; tough Diane is finally weeping, quietly.

*   *   *

About a month later, this from Utica:

May 12, 1995

Dear Richie,

After the game you played with me on the telephone, it must have been fifteen years ago, what's the point in me trying to call you now? I called fifteen years ago and said hello it's Carmen and you're making believe we have a telephone problem where you can't hear me but I can hear you. So I hang up and call again, and the telephone is busy for two hours then you answer and we play the same game. Victor you talk to, but I have a surprise. What I am trying to work up to eventually is Victor is dead. The coroner, some big Polack I never met is attempting to find out when and how, but who gives a shit anymore. It's a miracle I didn't throw up. I received your home address in case you are wondering from Mr. Carmen Caruso himself, the only one in Utica you kept in touch with who gave me the news over the years of your fame in the world of doctors who like to deal exclusively with women. I know you are reading this letter, so don't kid yourself. You hurt my feelings when you made believe you couldn't hear me on the telephone, I know you heard me because I heard a television in your house, I heard a car go by for Christ sake on the telephone. We gave you your head start that led to where you are now and I figure I deserve some respect from you since Victor is dead and now I am alone, after all I was good to you and your father, which you can't deny, and I am still alive. On my knees I went down and almost passed out but I didn't throw up as I previously said from the stink. My nose is still quite a problem a week later. Is it dangerous to attempt to disinfect the inner nose? How do I remove it from my nostrils? You're a doctor, at least answer me on this. If it's in my nose, if it's in my throat, if I taste it, is it in my system for good? Do you advise an enema? I took off my clothes in the backyard and threw them in the garbage, with the exception of my boxer shorts. I took a shower and I scrubbed until the hot water ran out. Andrea is saying that I smell like her father did when he had cancer. She says it's possible internal cancer, because it can't be Victor after a week, I say no, it's still Victor that I smell of. From such a smell can you get cancer of the inner nose? I sincerely doubt it but who am I to judge cancer? Advise me, Richie, please answer me soon. I saw him on a Thursday as usual every week ever since 1956 when I opened the business. Last Thursday for the first time in thirty-nine years all of a sudden no Victor. I go to his house after work. In other words, Fort Knox. After you left this town for good, Victor decided to insulate himself from that whore mother nature, which were his exact words. So he decided to keep the storm windows on all year long. He had them tinted. The storm window, then the regular window, then a shade pulled down over the regular window, then a drape over the shade, towels at the bottom of all the doors tucked into the gap. Aluminum siding, too. I broke down the back door and went down on my knees like a ton of bricks. He's on the floor in his boxer shorts. If I didn't know whose house it was, I would have said that this thing on the floor was some "Negro" who got in and died in the kitchen in his shorts. He blew up like a balloon worse than the fat freaks in the carnival. Plus the skin is cracked open everywhere and liquids that don't look like blood

are oozing out. Plus the maggots in the eyes and the mouth.
When I tell you he looked like a balloon you don't know what
I mean. The two legs were one swollen piece of meat and so forth.
Infested with white worms in his black skin is how I found this
man who meant so much to the two of us and now I feel
infested. As for myself I'm sixty-three on May 23 and Andrea
tells me once a month it's a shame I let myself go over the years,
I used to be such a good-looking guy. Richie, I'm pretty fat myself,
you might not even recognize me. When I stand at the urinal
at the shop I cannot see my you-know-what. There are times
when it is not easy for me to get to my you-know-what, when
I want to get at it for purposes in the privacy of my bathroom
not related to urination or washing. Andrea doesn't go to church
anymore, she doesn't talk anymore the way she used to except to
break my balls once a month about my appearance. She cooks.
The two kids live in San Francisco, the both of them ought to
hang themselves as far as I am concerned. Fuck my kids.
What I remember most about you is that you were always a good
kid unlike my very own. You studied, you got good grades, you
were polite, you never got into trouble, so why can't you be good
to me because I could use it. I told them to give the body to the
medical students for science purposes but they said a corpse like
this cannot be accepted by science for any purpose.
Your "old" (ha ha) friend,
Carmen

P.S. Speaking of laughs, I got the last laugh on our dear
friend. I arranged for a funereal mass at St. Anthony's. Send
me a birthday card, Richie. Is that such a hard thing to do?
I personally never thought you were a cold-blooded bastard,
no matter what anyone else says.

In the late fall of my initiation to Victor and the slaughterhouse, my father tells me that he's met a woman who's teaching him to play tennis. A week before Christmas, he informs me that he wants to throw a Christmas Eve dinner in my mother's style, and in her memory, and that he's going to invite the tennis teacher. He says, "You invite somebody too, Richard." I say, "Okay." He says, "Who? Victor?" "No," I say, "my best friend. She's a teacher of mine at the college."

"A teacher of yours at the college!"

"Oh yeah."

"What's this teacher's name?"

"I don't know."

For once, my father doesn't act like a saint. He says, "I've noticed your snotty remarks ever since your mother passed away, don't kid yourself, but I'm not going down into a pit just because that's where you are. You like it down there. Sit down, Richard, or I'll make you sit down. It's my turn now. In terms of your mother, maybe we both have something on our conscience, maybe we don't. You think life is complicated?" He goes to the refrigerator. He says, "This type of pie is complicated. I made it today. You want a piece? Christmas Eve, tell your professor, if that's who she is, which I doubt. Six o'clock. Christ! Lemon meringue! You want a piece or not?" I say, "I want a piece, but not of that pie."

*   *   *

We arrive at the front door at the same moment. She says, "You must be Richard." "Yes," I say, "I must be." She says, "I'm Elsie Barneveld." "Hello," I say. "This is my best friend, Dora."

As we walk in, my father's coming to greet us in an apron. For the first time, I see my father as a man that women would go for. I'm in a delicate position. I forgot to ask Dora her surname. I introduce her to my father, who has a look that I can't define. The look disturbs me. I say, "Professor Dora, meet my father, John."

"Hi, John, I'm Dora Brown."

"A pleasure to have you, Doctor Brown."

(I hear, thirty-six years later, "A pleasure to have had you, Doctor Brown." I see him, the dead father, making love to Elsie. The old man, age thirty-eight at the time, a journeyman plumber, causing her to scream out in passion. I thought Elsie was beautiful. They're all beautiful. To make love to Elsie. To say, "I'm fucking you," while fucking her. Force the old man to watch.)

My father says, "What subject do you teach at the college, Doctor Brown?"

Dora says, "Oh, I don't teach at the college, John. Your son was just pulling your big leg. I'm a medical doctor in the line of gynecology."

Wholesome Elsie's eyes flash steel. Then she says, sweetly:

211

"Golly, I don't think that John has such a huge leg. It's so fortunate to meet you, Dora. Lately I've been thinking that I require a female fing—, touch for my next pelvic."

(The conversation was playing directly into my plan for the evening, which is to make him pay. Vengeance before that night was out. They were definitely the right women, they were women, but they were tending too soon toward extreme behavior. I venture a spiritual theme.)

I say, "Let's not be monopolized by Doctor Brown's expertise. Let's not get sucked in. This is Christmas Eve and I feel we would be verging on sacrilege. Particularly in the doctor's case, who is a devout Catholic, if you don't mind me saying so, Dora."

My father, eagerly: "That's very true, concerning disrespect toward Our Holy Mother on the night of her labor problems. This is no time for making the doctor discuss inner pelvics."

Dora replies, "I've delivered for my customers on Christmas Eve. John, did you refer to the inner pelvis?"

(I say the word "patient" two or three times, in sentences that make things worse. I say, "When a doctor has a *patient* and religious duty comes, she sometimes has to make a hard choice.")

Dora says, "Don't kid yourself, big fella, it's rarely that hard."

(The key figures in my life: Victor, my father, Dora, Diane. They all say, "Don't kid yourself.")

ELSIE returns the ball to me: "It's darn refreshing, Richard, to hear a doctor refer to the patient as the customer. May I call you for an appointment after the holidays?"

DORA: "I'll have to check with the chief of staff, if he would permit this type of interaction, not to mention if I would have the gumption for it."

ELSIE, of rural New York, says: "Gosh, that's that wonderful Doctor Nathan, isn't it, the little Jew internist from Philadelphia?"

DORA: "No, it's Doctor Henry. You know, Ellen, Our Savior was quite a Jew in his own right, but I sense he was extremely tall and attractive for his times. Would you like an appointment with Doctor Henry?"

MY FATHER: "Hey! Time for the first course!"

(Homemade escarole soup, which my father and I pronounce according to the dialect of my grandparents: *'scarol'*: properly intoned, a bawdy figure of speech. As soon as my father says the magic word, I catch his eye, repeat it, and the two of us begin to giggle, at first a little cautious, a little wary of each other, then conspiratorially, while attempting to hold back. The two women forge artificial smiles. We go out of control. Me and my dad, on the same side, against them. The women feel ignorant. We know *'scarol'*. We know Dora. Their smiles harden.)

ELSIE: "Gosh, Dora, like twelve-year-old girls, if you ask me."

DORA: "I didn't ask you, did I?"

ELSIE: "Oh. Excuse me."

(Elsie, a wimp in my father's own image: I should have known. We calm down, the women thaw out, and we all sit down for the first course, in the tiny formal dining room between the kitchen and the parlor, where guests can't help but be taken by the huge photo, too big for the room, of an exceptionally sensuous young woman, hand on hip, baby on the other. Both of them robust and tranquil. She bears a strong resemblance to another mother, the one who sat for Raphael's most Italian *Madonna and Child,* the reproduction of which hangs in numerous kitchens of east Utica. The *Madonna and Child* of all things roly-poly. Approximately sixteen years after the photo was taken, and one year before her death, I will decide that my mother resembles a movie star, the voluptuous Kim Novak. I make sure that the guests are forced to take it in, all night long, by seating Dora and Elsie side by side, facing the wall of the looming photo. The women are having difficulty. Their heads keep bobbing up for the view, like puppet heads being pulled by an invisible string, the pull of the beautiful dead. I return to the kitchen for a refill.)

I hear my father say, "That's Antoinette Assisi you're staring at, and guess who, two months old. He grew up. They grow up fast."

I return. Raise my glass of wine: "To the chef and his various courses. To the Christ Child born of no intercourse."

MY FATHER: "This is what they teach in college. Disrespect toward the Catholic people."

DORA (finding her theme): "Our Holy Mother definitely put forth Our Lord without having to put out, but let's be honest, Richard. She had her experiences. Our Lord's Father in Heaven was attracted to a woman who knew the ropes, and even periodically liked the ropes, and who could teach the ropes to the son, though I doubt she taught certain special ropes to Our Lord. That so-called husband, who you hear almost nothing about in the Bible, or in those movies, he never got that

214

involved, just like the First Father in Heaven. Those intimate ropes I was referring to must have been taught by that other Mary—who can ever remember her last name?—who Our Lord did or didn't get extremely involved with, depending on who you talk to."

ELSIE: "That other Mary was Mary Madeline."

DORA (dead-faced): "I can't remember the last name, as I was just stating, in case you didn't hear." [*Picking up her thread*]: "Our Lord was endowed by his creator. His mother, and that other Mary, and even the husband were full people like ourselves. Can anybody tell me why they gave the two Marys the same name if they didn't want to put a certain message across between the lines, that either Mary could have been the other Mary? This is why there is such forgiveness in the Trinity and the Holy Family, and all their relatives, on our behalves. Those people don't throw stones down on this glass house of ours, with the exception of the Father of Our Lord, who was never a full person in the first place." (To Elsie): "Just like some other religions I heard of, which think their you-know-what doesn't stink, they forgive nobody."

Elsie the hayseed says, "Gosh, John, the Catholic people are so exciting. Antoinette looks so kind and so . . . I just don't know what the word for it is."

My father blurts out, "Exciting. I better check on the next course."

Dora, to the photo: "A person like that doesn't stab you in the back." Then to Elsie: "What line are you in?"

ELSIE: "I'm a traveling salesman for the Fuller Brush people."

DORA: "Ah, you know several ropes yourself. How long have you known John, if I'm not being too nosy?"

ELSIE: "Not nearly long enough, considering, you know, how far we've traveled."

I say, "Elsie, how far have you gone with my old man?"

ELSIE: "I'll help John in the kitchen."

I say, "Doctor Brown, I'd be honored if you'd perform a procedure in the parlor while they're washing the dishes, because the lovebirds will definitely wash the dishes, and this procedure requires only a little exposure."

Doctor Brown says, "While the lovebirds are washing the dishes? The first half of half and half!? Mr. Assisi, even if I were in the mood in this crazy situation, which I'm not, I would need my equipment. Listen, you're not as little as you think. Stop saying you're little."

Me, ignoring the reference to size, "What? A washcloth? A pan of warm soapy water? We could borrow some from the lovebirds when they're washing the dishes. We could say, 'We need this for the parlor. We'll bring it back in eight seconds.' "

DOCTOR BROWN: "I could care less, warm or cold. It's not my genital region that requires washing. But the soap is essential. How are you going to explain that we need it for the parlor?"

Me, preposterously: "We don't really need the equipment. I'm clean."

SHE: "Don't kid yourself." She pauses. "Especially with that uncircumscribed thing of yours. What if they walk in on us?"

ME: "Then I win."

(In east Utica fashion, we drink our wine from water glasses, and we're already semi-stoned. I'm more than semi. My father and Elsie enter with the second course):

The great-hearted Dora: "John, your wife is a gorgeous armful, who would be in terrific demand if she weren't
tied down by marriage at the time of that particular picture. Anybody would go for her, including, by the way,
considering how your son's mouth is hanging o—"
ELSIE (in the nick of time): "Speaking of an armful, John
wants me to put on a few, but I told him that I can't
compete with the past."
I'm looking for a fight: "Are you saying my mother was
fat?"
DORA: "People like your mother and me are quite similar,
we get blamed for that, because we're full-figured
women, which we can't help, just like she can't help
the condition of *her* chest region. Hey! Don't get mad
at me, Ellen. I'm not the one who brought up the
bust! We are who we are."
I say, "Hey! That's just what Victor always says."
DORA: "The day we find out who he is, that's the day I give
it away."
ELSIE: "Who's Victor?"
My nice father: "Homemade linguine with a calamari sauce!
I'm giving it away. *Mangia! Mangia!*
ME: "Dora, that means eat it heartily."
Smiling Dad telling the truth: "My son's Italian is no good."
ELSIE: "Oh, what the heck, John. I'm going to eat it heartily!"

(This, the second of five courses, consisted of two pounds of
linguine, a weight which doesn't include the red sauce or the
pound and a half of calamari. Elsie apparently believes that
we are to divide this course equally. Elsie serves herself one-
half pound of linguine, *not including* the weight of the red
sauce and the calamari that she scoops out, and she scoops

217

generously. Elsie apparently believes that it would be the crassest incivility, this slim and elegantly dressed lady, to leave even a trace on her plate. In the midst of her shocking assault on the second course, she asks this question):

"John, what is calamari?"

JOHN: "More or less a type of fish, if you want to consider the octopus, which calamari is a small version of, to be a type of fish, which I personally don't. To be exact, calamari is baby squid, Elsie."

ME: "To be exact, Elsie, an octopus has eight legs, whereas a squid has ten. A farm girl like you wouldn't know that. You are a farm girl, am I right?"

At which point, Dora distracts John's attention, and Elsie, as if waiting to get in a word with me in private, says quietly, while my father and Dora are chattering:

"Don't miscalculate me, asshole! I've been onto you from the start."

JOHN (catching her last words): "What about whose heart?"

I say, "Elsie was just saying as a farm girl you have to watch your step, because, you know, Elsie the cow, etcetera. Did you wipe your feet real good before you came in, Elsie? Or do I detect the faint smell of sewage?"

(Elsie reacts as if I have uttered a banality about Utica's lousy weather. Golly! But how much more snow they used to have when *she* was a girl. This clever gambit immediately unites the two women and John. They've had quite enough of Richard. John, Elsie, and Dora, who are about the same age, proceed to reminisce about the winters back in the Depression, which they doubt the asshole will ever experience, because Mother Nature is different now. Richard sees himself rise. He sees himself pick up his chair. He raises it

218

high overhead, and then with all possible force brings it smashing down upon the heads of the other three: one, two, three: splat, splat, splat. How like unto an orgasm! John says, "Pass me the wine, Richard." Richard goes to kitchen. Finds the big knife. They're still talking about the snow. Richard says, "Behold!" They're talking about John's '57 Chevy Bel Air. Dora says, "Did somebody mention a hole?" Richard severs his father's penis. They're talking baseball. The women love it. They love it more than any man has ever loved it. Mickey and Willy! Dora declares them both "greatly endowed by Our Lord." Elsie says, "Yes, how obvious! Even in those goshdarned loose uniforms! How greatly has the good Lord blessed those cute boys!" Richard says, "I've got a bat in my room. Who wants to suck it besides my father?" Elsie says, "I'll eat it heartily!" Elsie says, "Golly gee willikers, Richard, you're eating like a bird! If you don't watch out, I'm going to eat yours, too!" Much lewd guffawing all around, as Richard rages. Dora says, "Elsie, did you just say your tool?" The women squeeze their hands down the front of John's pants. See Richard-raging-ghost smile.)

JOHN: I spent the entire morning cleaning those baby squid. The guts filled up the sink. Elsie, you can't imagine the stink. Good thing you weren't around to see the facts of what you're putting away like there's no tomorrow.

ELSIE: Oh, God! I could tell you some stories about what we ate on the farm in the Depression days. I know some food smells.

JOHN: Listen, when I was a kid, we were so poor we cooked everything of the chicken. I used to use a toothpick

when it came out of the oven and got the eyes before
my big brothers beat me to it. I always got the delicious eyes!

DORA: Ah, we each have our own food smells to reflect on.
*Richard going green. Others vigorously into course number
three: the eel, the codfish, the shrimp, the broccoli. Much
wine. Richard rushes to toilet. When he returns, John is
describing the cleaning of baby squid: the spine, the ink bags,
the eyes, because they don't have the value of chicken eyes. You
chop the arms into small pieces, because people don't want to
see an arm in their plate. Richard flees to toilet. Powerful
sounds of evacuation: both ends.*

DORA: Ah, John, this dinner of yours! I should meet some-
one in the real world like you! Ah, Elsie! Forgive me!
What a tremendous pair you got on you!
Richard returns. Attempts third course.

ELSIE (to Richard): Have they taught you yet at Utica Meat
what a slinker is?
Puzzlement all around.

ELSIE: A slinker! Nobody knows a slinker!? Shucks!

(Richard rises: the chair, the big knife, etcetera, screaming:
"He killed my mother with spinal meningitis!" The gang of
three lifts a toast: "To Richard's secret boil! To John's big
leg! To Antoinette in heaven!")

JOHN: Richard slank away to the can, didn't you, son?
DORA: Is it slank or slunk?
ELSIE: A slinker, kids, is a Depression specialty of poor farm
people.

(Elsie takes her napkin and wipes cow shit from her shoes.
John says, "Give it to Richard, the college genius, he'll
know what to do with it!" Dora says, "He can use it for

Kotex, if you sense my drift, John." John says, "That's a little extreme to imply my son's bleeding from his vagina.")

ELSIE: Sometimes when my daddy slaughtered a cow, he'd find a baby inside her. Close to being born, but sometimes not that close. Well, my daddy would take that baby out, which is called a slinker—look it up, Mr. College!—and he would scrape it off, and then he would butcher it up, which he did in a jiffy, because it's only a baby thing, and then we kids got to have the slinker all for ourselves that night, and Ma and Daddy could have all the adult meat for *themselves!* Slinker tastes just like chicken, kids.

JOHN: We weren't so fussy back in those days.

DORA: We weren't so spoiled.

ELSIE: We didn't whine like this tall asshole.

[*Pause.*]

JOHN: Maybe we were a little fussy.

DORA: I got pampered on the holidays, sometimes.

[*Pause.*]

ELSIE: I was afraid to whine.

(Richard the whiner says, "I'll have more wine." Reaches over, half-getting out of his seat. Bam! Passes out, down onto table. Course number four: an epic salad, and the wine, all over table and floor.)

*   *   *

Richard's bedroom. Richard in bed. Dora sitting on chair next to him.

RICHARD: Who undressed me?

DORA: We all took part. We dragged you in here. In case you're wondering, we didn't take your shorts off.

RICHARD: How long have you known my father?

221

DORA: I knew him once. Last Christmas Eve.

RICHARD: Where's Elsie?

DORA: She's sleeping over. On the couch.

RICHARD: Where's my father?

DORA: Your father's still cleaning up. In a little while, I'll call a cab.

RICHARD: You missed Midnight Mass.

DORA: I did. I can't remember the last time I missed.

RICHARD: Last Christmas Eve, you knew my father less than a month after my mother. Then you went to Midnight Mass. You didn't miss.

DORA: He desired a miracle.

[Silence.]

DORA: He was in a state I never saw. [Pause.] I requested intimate details.

[Silence.]

DORA: I was the only one on tap that night. Good thing. Because I have an imaginative style. I believe that I achieved a semi-reincarnation.

[Silence.]

DORA: In my opinion. [Pause.] A good thing for everybody involved, including yourself, in my opinion. Including even myself. Then I went to Midnight Mass. Donny Daniels sang "O Holy Night." You should have heard him.

[Pause.]

RICHARD: Are you working New Year's Eve?

DORA: I'll be on tap.

[Pause.]

RICHARD: You sound different now.

DORA: This is how I talk in person. There'll come a time when even you will talk in person, God willing.

[She leaves.]

*   *   *

*Richard's room in darkness. Richard asleep. Father enters. Turns
on table lamp. Richard awakes. They stare at each other.*

JOHN: Richard.

[*Pause.*]

RICHARD: You're my worst enemy.

JOHN: I'm your father.

[*Pause.*]

RICHARD: You're nothing to me.

JOHN: That's what I said.

[*Pause.*]

RICHARD: Did you save any? You always save some for me.

[*Silence.*]

RICHARD: Did you save any for me?

JOHN: Let me help you up. [*Helps Richard out of bed.*] Feel
okay? Ready to go to the kitchen? [*Pause.*] You're too
big now for me to carry you.

RICHARD: I bet you saved some, Dad.

JOHN: Ready to knock off the rest of that rum cake?

RICHARD: I knew you did. I knew, Daddy.

III

The Monster

He drives up to her house. He steps out of his car and prepares himself there in the twilight. Then he rings her doorbell. She's greeted by a thing in full-body costume. It's not clear to her what this costume is a costume of. He's arrived early, much too early, to fetch her for the event. The thing in the doorway cuts a shapeless figure in royal blue shag of the heaviest, most thickly textured quality, cut from a remnant that he had purchased at Carpet World for a pretty penny. On a lonely country road he had finally located the legendary seamstress who agreed to watch "Sesame Street" for as long as it took. He told her he was not interested in duplication. The seamstress replied coldly, "I am an artist." He told her that he wanted her to watch so that she might absorb the aura of the thing. The seamstress replied, "There is no thing. There is only the aura."

The eyes are huge: two big white bulbs with subtly crossed pupils, attached to the top of the head. The mouth is that of an exceptionally broad-snouted alligator. The voice is a whiskey bass: guttural and gruff, yet somehow funny and childlike, though no one has ever heard a child speak in a whiskey bass, unless it was in a horror movie, where the kid requires exorcism, because the kid is spouting uniquely disgusting obscenities concerning his mother's various private parts, and how he intends to deal with them.

The voice is saying, "Me like you, Diane! Cookie! Me want cookie! You like me?" Under the costume, Richard wears a thermal red union suit, Arctic-proof, because his maternal grandfather had worn one, day and night, through the winter months. Over the union suit, an impenetrable Irish sweater, extra-large. For once, he would have a robust presence. Robust was a word he cherished. Diane was robust. In effect, Richard has encased himself in the skin and fur of a polar animal, on this unseasonably warm night in February. He does not understand that the professional full-body animal impersonator always installs a cooling system. He does not understand that he must drink gallons of water. Already he's drenched in sweat.

He says, "I thought briefly about Big Bird. I seriously considered Oscar the Grouch. It was almost Oscar. Then I realized: I am the Cookie Monster." She remembers now what a royal blue shag rug is a costume of. She says, "Obviously, killer. Because the Cookie Monster, like you, is a symbol of the Id. He's pure libidinal desire disguised as the child who demands sweets twenty-four hours per day. The child who drives every parent nuts at around age two or three, when we all become Cookie Monsters. Then we grow up. Then some of us grow up. Then the Cookie Monster focuses on sex. Cookie becomes totally horny."

Richard says, "He also focuses on murder, which is what we all need to repress. Maybe not all. Maybe not me."

Diane says, "As long as it's me, you don't have to repress s-e-x. The Cookie Monster is definitely you, killer."

Then he astounds her. He says, "I'm too early on purpose. Let's relax awhile. I need to confess. Everything's become more or less *pro forma.* I'm holding myself out. Diane, help Cookie to live in his skin."

She's embarrassed. She thinks he's referring to their relationship and it pains her to hear him judge himself so bluntly. It's not that it isn't true, what he said; it's that, to her, it doesn't matter. She tries a deferring tactic: "Since we've got a while, why not take that hot thing off?"

He tells her no, he could use the rehearsal time. He wants to stay in character, like DeNiro. He says, "Me not involved with small fiends. Me go to parties, but me not there. Me so thirsty, Diane." She brings him a glass of ice water. He says, "Me want cold milk." She returns with the milk, saying: "Counting the birthdays, the first communions, the first dance recitals—" He breaks in, in the voice of Richard: "Frenetic involvement is false." She continues: "The Little League debuts, the baptisms, the Bar and Bat Mitzvahs. Christ! You must average a party per week. At least. Over fifty per year!" He only says: "Frenetic involvement is not involvement." She says: "You spend whole afternoons at the malls seeking the uniquely appropriate gift, and you always find it!" He says: "Materialism." She says: "The money you spend, it would be cheaper to raise six kids of your own. I'm still young enough, you know." He says: "It's invincible. Don't argue with my guilt." She says: "Between these kids and that damn trial and your hours at the hospital, we're getting crowded out as a couple. Stop worrying about those kids. Worry about us for a change." Through a hole in the mouth, Richard drinks his milk with a straw.

Foolishly, she decides to lay out the evidence.

DIANE: Until tonight, I've only gone with you to two of these parties. But I'm onto you, killer. With the two-and-under group, you sit on the floor with them for hours, almost never speaking. You pick up the stuffed animals and you smell them. You bury your face in the stuffed animals and make muffled sounds in the fur. You're hardly looking at these kids. You inhale the stuffed animals. You crawl. One of them tries to nurse off your chest as you gnaw on the cardboard books. They start crawling all over you. One of them sticks a finger in your ear; another sticks one up your nose. You mime a grandiose sneeze. They go into hysteria. Then they offer you graham crackers and you eat off their hands, you're gumming graham crackers. With the five-year-olds you don't sit. You crouch and you squat. You give the appearance of being transfixed by the fire engines and dolls and seem to be capable of watching forever. Next thing you know one of the five-year-olds offers you his own piece of cake. In the history of the world, this has never happened. You eat it. You make a big growling sound when you eat, which makes one of the kids so happy that in an excess of energy she punches you in the stomach with all her might. They get you more cake and more cake. You accidentally on purpose smear some of it on your face and fingers. Pieces drop on your shirt.

RICHARD: Tell me how I seduce the twelve-year-olds. Quick!

DIANE: They should arrest you for molestation. You address the girls as "My Queen," the boys as "Big Guy." They levitate. The twelve-year-olds actually float up to the ceiling. When you finally decide to talk, it's the same trick with all age groups.

RICHARD: No trick. I have total respect for their minds.

DIANE: Deliberately you say words they don't understand. You use the voice of a college professor and they're mesmerized. Inevitably, someone will ask the meaning of a strange word and you offer a definition full of strange words, which leads to other definitions, etcetera. You're telling dictionary stories. In the meanwhile, the parents take it all in. Some begin to feel inadequate. Then they feel rage. Others think that this unmarried man could be called upon for baby-sitting duties. Some others, not that many, but enough, think that what they have in their midst is a total pervert. They're nervous the whole time trying to see both of your hands. What's he doing with that other hand I can't see? What's he doing? Isabel, did he just touch himself? Is that bulge in his crotch getting bigger?

RICHARD: That reminds me, Diane. Remember that famous pervert from Chicago?

DIANE: Which one?

RICHARD: The sex killer.

DIANE: Which one?

RICHARD: I'm referring to John Wayne Gacy, the guy who played a clown for kids' parties. A round, comical-looking guy.

DIANE: Ah, that one, who killed forty teenage boys. The serial pederast who buried them all in his backyard and proclaimed his innocence until the end.

RICHARD: Speaking of pederasty, until the end John Wayne also proclaimed his heterosexuality. He said he wasn't homosexual because he permitted nothing to be done to him *above the waist*. His words. He has the thesis that a homosexual is a man who sucks cock, and that, he suggests, he never did.

DIANE: In other words, having his cock sucked by those boys, and buggering those boys, which he obviously did, and maybe *getting* buggered, Richard, because his thesis does not rule it out—all those activities are in the category of heterosexuality.

RICHARD: John's very point. A man who will not suck cock is fundamentally straight, no matter what else he does. When asked in his final *New Yorker* interview about why he did it, he said: "Why would I want to kill those boys? I'm not their father."

DIANE: Oedipus Rex, killer. W-r-e-c-k-s.

RICHARD: Try this, Diane: Richard the Turd. And remember this: Reason is stupid.

DIANE: You and O.J. You and John Gacy. But you're the dope who got stung by a wasp once because you found it in your house and you wanted to give it its freedom. I know Richard Assisi, and Richard Assisi is no O.J. Simpson. I can't see you behind that costume, but I know that what I've just said causes you to be crestfallen. That bothers me.

RICHARD: Why would I want to kill you, Diane? You're not my wife.

(His hair is soaked. He's a little woozy. He requests a cup of coffee. Then he glances up at the clock on the mantel and says: "We don't have time for the coffee. They await; all my children.")

(Driving to the party in Diane's van: Richard is saying, "Please turn off the heat," and Diane is replying, "It's not on. What's wrong with your voice?")

RICHARD: I spent the afternoon on the telephone. In character.

DIANE: Who were you talking to?

RICHARD: First Gillian's mother. Then Gillian herself, whose birthday it is. Then Gillian's mother again, who gave me the numbers of the other thirteen kids who'll be there.

DIANE: So what's Gillian's mother's name, so I'm not embarrassed when we walk in?

RICHARD: I forgot. Gillian's mother.

DIANE: This afternoon you had fourteen telephone conversations with three-year-olds?

RICHARD: An average of six minutes per call. They believe they talked to Cookie. They await Cookie's arrival with the understanding he'll be very hungry. Which reminds me. Before we go in, help me to enlarge the mouth hole. You've got the tools, Diane.

DIANE: I've got what it takes; I'll open up your hole wide.

RICHARD: I wish I had a cup of coffee. I'm falling asleep.

DIANE: Gillian's mother will be happy to give you a cup.

RICHARD: What are you thinking, Diane? Cookie doesn't drink coffee in the presence of kids.

DIANE: This is not "Sesame Street."

RICHARD: This is definitely "Sesame Street."

DIANE: Is Lucy and what's her name going to be there?

RICHARD: Lucy's mother. Yes.

DIANE: Is she still drooling for you, killer?

RICHARD: Naturally, I'm to die for.

DIANE: We're here.

RICHARD: Already? I'm scared.

DIANE: Why?

RICHARD: I raised expectations too much. I was too good on the phone. The pressure. I think I'm hyperventilating, Diane.

233

DIANE: Your talent for self-dramatization is bottomless. Live in your skin.

RICHARD: Speaking of my bottom, I think I'm going to have a problem.

(He awakes in his bed the next morning and remembers being attended to in the Emergency Room, but not much more. He remembers the clock on the mantel at Diane's. The van. Jumping and whirling. He tries to get out of bed. He stops trying. Diane is asleep beside him. He nudges her. She opens her eyes and, after serious groaning, says: "You were right. Frenetic involvement is false. Last night you proved it was also dangerous, you big goof." He says, "It's starting to come back. Gillian's house was hot.")

DIANE: They keep it maybe ten degrees over what you keep this ice box. They're normal people. Toward the end you really lost it. You started yelling, "Turn off the heater, Martello. I surrender."

RICHARD: I remember it was crowded.

DIANE: Fourteen kids plus sixteen adults stationed along the walls of that small living room. I get cold easy, but in there I was sweating. My sinuses were driving me insane.

RICHARD: I remember the kids were frightened when they first saw me. There was crying and scurrying.

DIANE: You went straight into your act without missing a beat. You stuffed tons of cookies and cake down your hole. You went into perpetual motion. The kids were quickly sucked in. Later, when we opened up the costume, we found out that you actually ate everything. No crumbs visible. The puke was terrific, though.

RICHARD: I remember choking. I remember standing on a table and jumping up and down and whirling.

DIANE: That was near the end. When you came down from the table you collapsed. But we thought it was part of the act. The kids went into a frenzy. They piled on. They buried their faces in the fur. They poured lemonade on you. They smeared ice cream on the fur and licked it. They jumped up and down on you. Some tried to whirl. It was a sensational scene. Then I heard the choking and retching. When I got to you, you were out. Gillian's mother called County General while Lucy's mother attempted to cradle your head. She actually tried to elbow me out of the picture. I came close to decking the bitch.

RICHARD: I remember they treated me with dignity in the ER.

DIANE: Of course. They fear you. They know your stature in the field.

RICHARD: I'm a finger in my field.

DIANE: They told me privately that you came close to buying it from heat prostration.

RICHARD: Baloney.

DIANE: You were hooked up intravenously for six hours before they let me take you home.

RICHARD: In the ER they exaggerate everything.

DIANE: They want you to do nothing for three days. They said not even TV.

RICHARD: Oh yeah.

DIANE: They told me that the Simpson trial could prove fatal. [*Pause.*] You're still slurring your words a little.

RICHARD: I'm not slurring. Where's my coshtume?

DIANE: We left it at Gillian's mother's. One of the little ones did a number two on it.

RICHARD: As a sign of respect?
DIANE: No. Affection.
[*Pause.*]
RICHARD: How do you know?

Late on the afternoon of Carmen's letter. I drive to South Gate Mall with the intention of visiting a store I'd never before entered. In the parking lot, Debbie and Lucy. Lucy immediately hugs one of my legs with both arms and with all her might, looks straight up, smiles and stares. The normally nervous-around-me Debbie is composed. This cunt is casual. Not even, "What a coincidence, Doctor Assisi!" This marriage is putrescent. Debbie says that she's on her way to her haircut; Lucy says she doesn't want to, she wants to come with me; Debbie says, "Oh, Lucy," but it sounds like "Oh, Richard"; and I say, "Why not?" Lucy clings to the leg. I say, "Lucy and I will meet you at Francesca's in about an hour." Lucy hops up and down. Debbie says that Lucy eats too much ice cream already at her age and that she can't promise to be there in an hour. Then she makes a couple of halfhearted attempts to pry Lucy off the leg. I say, "Don't worry about it," thinking all the while, Why not? Because she'll obviously go for it, she's terrific-looking, and she has major plans for me—once a month with no strings attached, my carnal satisfaction the price of her assumption of intimacy. Then Lucy and I go off, hand in hand, as Debbie is saying, "You two sure make a nice picture." Off we go to Gary's House of Legendary Blades.

Gary does not recognize me, but I recognize him as the crew-cut fellow in his late twenties who does volunteer work at County General every Sunday morning. Chinos, white dress shirt, power tie. Gary approaches and says, "Your daughter is lovely, sir. Hi, I'm Gary." Lucy and I smile at one another and do not correct him. I begin my inspection of the locked showcases that line Gary's walls as Gary says, "We carry only the finest: Gerber's all the way." Lucy shouts: "That's what Mommy makes me eat: Gerbil's." Gary is beside himself. He says, "Why don't we adults ever think creatively?" I say, "Because we can't take the irony, Gary." Gary says, "The trapezoidal cleaver. Let it be a consideration, sir." I say, "The instrument is crude and thoughtless." He opens the showcase and removes a Bowie, sporting a coffin-shaped handle. "Coffin-shaped" is Gary's phrase. I say, "No, but let's have a look anyway." He tells me that the blade is nine and a half inches long; that the handle is made of "positive grip Kraton rubber for the comfortable and balanced feel"; that the "deluxe cordura sheath is on the house"; that the blade is constructed in the "full-tang style." I say, "Please don't spoil it by telling me what 'full-tang' means." He says, "The Patriot? The Gator Saw? The Skinher? The Guardian Angel? The Stallion? You want to hold The Stallion? Let me put it in your hand, it's simply tremendous. Or maybe something classic and truly big? Here it is. A complement to every kitchen: The Chef's Knife, an eleven-and-a-half-inch blade." Lucy says, "I want to go now, Daddy." I say, "Soon, sweetheart." Gary says, "It's like going to the supermarket for one item, you know? Only you're not sure what that item is, you're having consumer paralysis. Suddenly you want everything. The question that I, as a salesperson, have for you, as a customer, is this: What is your goal and/or goals? Half of my business is collectors. Another thirty to forty percent are hunters, fisherman, and other outdoor recreational-equipment types." I bite, I say: "So what is the other ten percent?" He says, "Miscellaneous. Housewives, as it were. Problematical teens. A few people with a private reason. You're either a collector or you have a secret. I'm trying to help you narrow the focus. So where do we stand?" I point and say, "That one. That's the one." He says, "Tremendous choice." Then he says, "Obviously you know the Gerber motto without actually knowing it: 'You must experience the need, to design the solution.' Sir, your need has selected the ultimate personal combat knife. Vietnam vintage and the first choice of our military professionals, often copied but never, never equaled. This is the Mark II. The high carbon stainless steel blade of surgical quality is here nicely united with the nonslip textured aircraft-quality aluminum handle, which guarantees us all an indestructible survival instrument, and a sigh of relief. This blade is our choice blackened double-edge nonglare and nonreflective honey, truly a proud legend, six and a half inches in length, fifteen sixteenths of an inch in width, point two five zero in thickness. Of course, the standard silvery blade is always an option, but it's also a bad joke in my opinion. And this is your elegant cordura sheath. This is the Mark II. There is nothing more to say. As you so well put it, sir: This is the one." I say, "I've never seen a blade like that." Gary says, "Hand-honed to razor-sharpness to serve you and me in the most extreme and hostile of environments." "No," I say, "I don't mean that. I'm familiar with razor-sharpness from my business."

Gary says, "Which is none of my concern, sir." I say, "I mean the serration that starts halfway back." "Ah," Gary says. "What we have here is the capability of both slashing and sawing when the need arises. We slash and we saw with the same instrument, and in alternate strokes. With the Mark II, you rough-cut rope, heavy vegetation, even wire." Lucy says, "I want ice cream now." I say, "Soon, darling." Then I say to Gary, "And tendons and bone, yes?" Gary only says, "This is the Mark II."

I have it in my hand. I look at Gary and say, "I feel guilty." Gary says, "Heh! Heh!" Lucy says, "What did you say?" "It's time for ice cream! That's what I said! Wrap it up, Gary." Gary says, "What about a Jap sword? Can I interest you in a sharpening system?"

We're sitting in Francesca's, we're on our third cone each, it's been twenty minutes, and still no Debbie. Strategy of a bitch. Lucy says, "You eat too fast. You're bad." I say, "Lucy, where does your father live?" She says, "Far away." "Where?" I say. She names a town about nine miles off. I say, "I bet you miss him."

"I hate my daddy."

"Why do you hate him? I love my daddy very much."

"He wants to steal me from my mommy."

"No he doesn't. You're a *big* liar, Lucy!"

"No I'm not a big liar, because my mommy told me he's going to steal me every Saturday morning. That's why I hide in the closet when he comes to get me. Mommy says he's a big shit! When I'm in the closet I shake."

"I'll bet he feels bad when you shake in the closet, Lucy."

"He cries and he cries!! Then I cry."

"Then your mommy cries."

"No she doesn't! *You're* a big liar!"

"I'll bet your daddy finds you in the closet."

"When he finds me I kick. Mommy says he deserves it."

"Then he cries again."

"I bled his nose when I kicked him. I bled him."

"Your daddy's a big shit."

"After he goes, Mommy and me have fun."

"Somebody ought to decapitate your mommy."

"What did you say?"

"Somebody ought to decapitate your mommy."

"Decapilate my mommy?"

"Yes, Lucy, because she deserves it."

"What does decapilate mean?"

"It means somebody ought to marry your mommy."

"Will you marry her?"

"I'm contemplating the deed."

"What?"

"I think I might decapilate her, Lucy."

"I want some of that over there."

"Too messy, dear."

"Tell me what is that, you big shit!"

"Honey, that's cotton candy."

A few hours later, after dinner at her place, Diane finally blurts it out: "He's not worthy of your interest, much less your passion. I want your passion. He's empty, he's a big nothing. With his kids sleeping in the house, this big shit kills her. How many feet away could they have been? What if one of them wakes up? I'm thirsty, Mommy, I want a glass of cold milk. He cuts her wide open on the doorstep, with the door wide open." I say, "Then he gets his kid the glass of milk. Fuck her." She says, "Fuck her?! What do you mean fuck her? She's dead! Fuck you! You refer to her as if she's alive." I say, "We go on the theory you eliminate the mother you save the child. Orenthal's kids are now guaranteed to survive the impact of motherhood. Above all, save the children. Diane, I heard a story this afternoon from my best nurse's kid, the one we met at the lake last fall. It'll make your hair stand on end." She says, "Good. Now that the sick fuck of Utica is dead, you're going to talk like him." I tell her about the shaking in the closet, I bled my daddy. She says, "So what does that prove? Your best nurse is a sick fuck, too. You want to descend into that hole? I want to know why you exonerate all the fathers in these cases, when you never exonerated yours, that's what gets me. What did your father ever do to deserve his son's anger even after he's gone? This is funny. What? Thirty years now? You never had kids, you want to save kids. Your mother was terrific, you express homicidal desire toward mothers. These fathers in the news these days are assholes, you stand up for them. Your father was a prince, you hate him. Richard: for a guy who's mainly normal and nice, you're totally fucked up. This trial you watch every day is boring." I say, "Like breathing in and breathing out." She says, "It cuts into our time together pretty deep." I say, "It's supposed to cut deep." She says, "How hilarious." I say, "You're jealous of my thing for Orenthal, who is absolutely, one hundred percent not guilty." She says, "You're hopeless. Make the decaf."

"By the way," she says, "why did you bring your valise here tonight? That's a first. What's in there? A surprise for your sweetheart?"

"You'll find out in the bedroom, good buddy, where I'm going to hide the surprise under the bed."

"Ah, Richard, I always hoped for a kinky development."

"Yes, Diane, I think you'll appreciate the tang, the full tang."

"Any relation to poontang, good buddy?"

"I could put it in there, if that's where you want it."

"You can put it anywhere you want. It's what *you* want. Look at you, killer. I can see it from here, your cock of steel."

"I'm going to fuck you deadly."

"Let's hold off until after coffee. We'll be totally wild by then."

During the coffee-ruse it becomes obvious that Diane has theories. She says, "You don't have any of the physical characteristics, but you're an old-fashioned wop, who never got over the fact that the Blessed Virgin Mary was fucking his father. Or that the BVM could get pissed off at the Divine Child, actually curse him out in foul language." I say, "This is psychiatrically deep." She says, "I'll tell you what I learned from my English major. Art is deep, life is obvious and crude. Real people are easy to figure out. Boys want to fuck their mothers, kill their fathers, etcetera. I'm not saying this is totally you." I say, "Thank you." She says, "Your old man was a good man, a nonviolent man, who could not do the right thing. Orenthal is the father who did the right thing. He saved the children. Orenthal is the father you wanted all along, or, since you wanted to etcetera your mother in order to father yourself, in your mind you are Orenthal the motherfucker. Victor is too obvious for discussion. It's logical: if only your father had murdered your mother before you were conceived, Richard would be a very happy man today. Big fella," we're laughing now, "what this is all about is your own failure of nerve to knock yourself off for having the desire to knock up your mother in order to give birth to yourself. Christ, Richard, they're both dead a long time. You want to hurt a woman?"

"Certainly."

"Who do you know who deserves it?"

"Nobody. Nicole is dead. The one in South Carolina is in custody. Lucy's mother."

"This would be good for Lucy?"

"The children cannot be saved."

"Good for who then?"

"Me."

"When you go to prison for the rest of your life?"

"Ripping the flesh off manually. Slicing in. That would be very good. This has nothing to do with my parents. You can't eliminate the mother. Or the father. The mother and the father are immortal."

"You want to kill a woman."

"I accept my nature."

"How about me? You want to kill me?"

"Let's go to bed."

"But I'm not the mother."

"There is no reason. Stop explaining or I'll kill you now."

"Your preposterous name! In St. Francis's prayer, I'm pretty sure it's: 'Lord, make me an instrument of thy peace.'"

"I'm God's hit man. 'Lord, make me an instrument of thy violence.' Let's go to bed. God hates reasons. He is mysterious. Tonight we honor God, in bed."

I am doing her from behind with my glasses on. This is not my favorite position, but I have a reason. No, not *in* her behind, *from* behind, like dogs. A mediocre erection, but we're getting the job done, her face buried in a pillow. Muffled moans. I pull out. Face still buried, she slurs, "What? Where are you going?" I say nothing. I need to go down on her. I have a reason. Her position unchanged. I'm on my knees at the side of the bed. My tongue in her *from* behind. My hand searching under the bed. Alongside the shotgun, I feel my surprise for Diane. I come up from my kneeling position, my tongue in reluctant exit, and reinsert a fabulous erection to the hilt, my right hand on her ass now, thumb in her ass now, to the hilt, left arm swinging and snapping like a whip as I sing out, "Ride 'em cowboy!" my left arm swinging my Mark II, which wants to be inserted to the hilt, but I intend to hold back my Mark II, because I haven't made up my mind yet, not as to where, though that is a legitimate question, but as to if at all. I'm here, that's all it is, and she is definitely here, coming, and I touch her in her coming with my Mark II on the small of her back as she's coming hard and I'm pulling out to watch myself come in surprising quantities all over her ass, and she's screaming and wrenching around, and there we are: Diane dripping sweat and semen and me still coming, my Mark II steady now before her eyes, I'm saying, "We're going to finally decide, Diane. Am I a leg man, or am I a tit man? You make the call." She rolls violently off the side of the bed, pulling in one motion her pump action shotgun from under the bed, and there we are, my Mark II held forward, saying, "It's time to settle the question, Diane." And she, the stone face, replying in a monotone: "I'm going to kill you now." I make a quick move toward her, a feint designed to draw the desired reaction. Click pump, click pump, click pump. Six clicks. I croon: "You thought you kneeeeew the gun was loaded! Look," I say, "I'm still coming a little! We are who we are. True or false?" She grabs the shotgun by the barrel. She's saying, "Hey! Hey! Hey!" backing me across the room, swinging it powerfully, and I'm stumbling backward going down hard on my back, as she smashes the stock of the shotgun against my knife hand. I'm defenseless and she's slamming down on me with that big body, the barrel across my throat. I'm trying to claw her big tits but she knees me in the balls and now I'm finished for sure. She speaks: "You ugly bastard." I croak out, "I wasn't really serious. I just wanted to see what it would be like. I wasn't going to do anything." She says, "I'm going to resist my nature and let you walk out of here. But if I ever see you again I'll kill you." Then she begins to press the barrel hard against my throat, and I begin to fade out, and she says, "I'll kill you. This is what it's like, asshole. You ought to live in a hole."

Later, at home, I wanted to call her and explain that it was only my idea of theater, that's all it was. I wanted to be totally honest. I wanted to say, "I just wanted to do something exciting a little bit, a little tang, not the full tang." But I never called, and I never saw her again.

When I left that night, she pointed at me and said, "That man used to love me."

IV

The Wake

ONE

On the morning after Richard dreamed of the man who said "Take this hand and come with me," and consumed by thoughts of the beautiful Marilyn Lake, who would become (within a month) the first of three nurses to be called Mrs. Richard Assisi, he drove east from the Upstate Medical Center in Syracuse, to Utica with a sustained and sustaining erection he drove directly to the empty house on Mary Street, where he took down the looming photo and turned it to the wall, took down his pants, masturbated vigorously, then slept like a baby until 6 P.M., when he arose, showered, retrieved Marilyn's image in the shower, masturbated again (in the shower, with vigor), shaved, and with the photo of Our Lady of Utica tucked safely away in the trunk of his car, to Rocco Ponte's Funeral Parlors he drove, trying (albeit sullenly) to retrieve his father, for the sake of his father's image trying to relinquish the image of Marilyn Lake and beginning to recall the scene at Memorial Hospital where John Assisi had admitted himself seven days previous to his death, worried about pains in his chest, because he couldn't remember if you could have gas feelings in your chest—pale, diagnosed as suffering from a mild coronary occlusion, this robustly built man of forty-two told that he must remain under observation for a week in the Cardiac Intensive Care Unit, his age being of special concern to the cardiologist, and John Assisi replying, "But I'm only forty-two. What do you mean my age?" And the cardiologist responding: "That's the point, Mr. Assisi: a coronary event in a man of your relative youth must be feared. I don't wish to alarm you, but we wouldn't want to get burned, would we?" And John coming back fast: "We?" When Richard arrived the following day, his father was tickled to relate the interchange he'd had with the caring cardiologist, because it covered up the extreme silliness he felt having to just lie there, hooked up to various monitors, feeling perfectly normal. With his son the medical student rushing back from Syracuse to see him in the hospital, shouldn't they at least be feeding him intravenously? How easily Richard and John (the father laughing, saying to the son who was trying not to laugh: "Are you too going to die out of sympathy?"), how easily they moved from John's little story to talk of baseball, how far they flew from the facts of why they were together in this awful place, father and son hiding themselves nicely in sports, almost relaxed. Four minutes later, the inevitable and sudden loss of words, not just for baseball, but for everything, and they become ashamed, each wanting to disappear in a puff of smoke, and the anger mounting because they couldn't disappear. They knew that they would have to look at one another eventually, because aversions of the eyes in silence can only go on for so long. Richard is smoldering, but so is John, who seven years after his wife's death was coming reluctantly to the

250

conclusion that Richard had gone too far, and that he, John, deserved a break after seven years, even saying in his mind "a fucking break," because hadn't he cut some slack for this son of his? Had he blamed him for her death?

"How could anyone know she would go to bed that night with a terrific headache, and a terrific pain in the neck, and never wake up? All of a sudden my wife is dead the next day."

"Plus a sudden high fever which she never complained about, don't leave that out. Classic symptoms of spinal meningitis, which you couldn't have been expected to notice. My mother never complained about anything."

"Classic symptoms? Classic symptoms my ass! Now that you're a medical man you can talk, but back then you knew nothing. Stop trying to make your mother into a saint. She complained about you and me both. Do I throw it into your face what you did the day before she died? I want an answer!"

"You're throwing it in my face now. Bravo. That's my answer. What about my question concerning what *you* did to her?"

"What story did you hear from that goddamn Victor? Your mother got it in her mind that some woman you and me know very well, but who I'm not revealing, because it doesn't matter who she is, this person supposedly made a pass at me, and I supposedly liked it. This is what your mother got in that mind of hers. The true story is that this person made a pass, but I never reacted to her visibly. Your mother went wild, she hollered, which was the racket you overheard when we got back late from bingo. What we know now is that she was already coming down with the spinal meningitis, and this must have aggravated her. [*Pause.*] She went to her grave jealous. [*Pause.*] The true story is I never had interest in that other party, who is still alive."

251

"Within a month you went to Dora Brown."

"What are you, anyway? I knew you knew because Dora confided in me for years, long after our involvement, if that's what you want to call it. I'm not ashamed that I went to Dora. This was not against your mother. I wanted your mother one more time. Is that a sin? You want to talk about what we're avoiding by attacking me for seven years? Your mother confided everything in me. I have a rough idea what you did. Richard, tell me the details. It'll be good for you."

"She was walking home up Wetmore with a heavy bag of groceries. I was driving by and I didn't stop to give her a ride. I don't know why I did that. For seven years I've gone over it. I can't understand why I did that."

"It was just one of those things. Forget about it."

"So I get home first, and in she walks a few minutes later, on the warpath. She says, 'How could you do that to your mother?' I had no answer. I had nothing to say. I can't remember if I had feelings one way or the other at the time."

"I can't tell from looking at you, Richard, I never could. That's why I have to ask you something. Do you have any feelings now? Look at it this way. You weren't mad at her when she went to her grave. My wife was beautiful even in her coffin."

"She was the one who was mad when she went to her grave."

"Did she holler? When she told me about it, she didn't mention if she hollered at you, too."

"She hollered at the top of her lungs, Dad. She said, 'You lousy bastard! You ungrateful bastard!' I said to her, 'You mean my father is not my father?' "

"You always had a tongue on you, Richard. Forget about it. She loved the both of us."

252

" 'You lousy bastard! You ungrateful bastard!' I never heard her talk like that. Then she wouldn't talk to me anymore. Then she was gone."

"Maybe you never heard her talk like that, but I did. Your mother blew her stack once in a while. She hollered at the both of us that day. She told me, 'I'm disgusted with the two of you.' Then she goes unconscious before it could be ironed out. Ever since, we have each other to take it out on. Let's try to be good to one another from now on. How about it?"

"You never took it out on me."

"I think I took it out a little."

"I said you didn't. You deaf? You're not the type. I'm the type. Be a little more like me for your own good. Strike back, get some revenge. Stop letting everybody shit all over you. Because who the fuck respects you? Who the fuck fears you?"

"Not you."

"When you grow up, try to become more like me."

"My wife wasn't afraid of me."

They fell silent. Then Richard said: "I happen to know who that unnamed party is that you referred to. I happen to know you enjoyed the attention, whether or not you fucked her. My mother saw what I saw. You fucked Carmen's wife." John Assisi said: "I'm getting desperate." Richard replied: "How many times did you fuck her?" John said: "I love you, Richard." Richard replied: "Scared you're going to die, old man?" Then he walked to the door and John picked up a butter knife from his lunch tray and threw it end over end, thudding harmlessly off Richard's back and clattering to the floor. Richard never bothered to turn around.

Six days later, John Assisi, who was afraid of dying, and

who loved his son, suffered a fatal heart attack in his sleep, still under observation at Memorial Hospital. Richard Assisi against his will remembered it all as he drove, including, "I love you, Richard," which he remembered exactly as his father had said it, the exact sound of the father's voice repeating itself in his mind, but it meant nothing to him, not then, not now, the voice repeating and repeating itself but meaning nothing, because it sounded so wooden and so fake. And it was wooden, but it wasn't fake. It was just the way John Assisi sounded, because it was a hard thing to say, even for John Assisi. Neither father nor son had ever heard an adult man say such a thing to another adult man. It was embarrassing and a little humiliating to hear such a thing. Probably between adult men who are not homosexuals, definitely between fathers and sons, such a thing should never be said in those words, out loud, or even between the lines. It's possibly okay to put it in a letter, but not ever in the form of an actual statement. Love, Your son. Love, Dad. That would be acceptable.

When Richard passed through the front entrance of Rocco Ponte's Funeral Parlors, without acknowledging Rocco's ritual presence, he did not turn abruptly right into the parlor of presentation, to kneel at the coffin, and to pray for the repose of the soul of John Assisi. He did not sit in the parlor of presentaton with his father's lone living sibling, the youngest sister with her antsy children and bored husband. He did not note the absence until much later of all other relatives except one from his mother's side. Nor did he greet the many who came that night to pay their respects, every one of them glad, as they passed through the front entrance, to have big Rocco lay his hands upon them. And too bad he didn't see the mother with her five-year-old son approach the coffin:

"Kneel and say your prayers, Angelo."

"Why, Mommy?"

"Because we're supposed to."

"Why, Mommy?"

"So God doesn't make him stay in purgatory too long."

"Where is purgatory?"

"Kneel right now or I'll make you see stars!"

So Angelo kneels and prays out loud, very loud: "Name of the Fodder, Sin, Holy Goes, Hey Men. Hail Mary, you are the Lord, pray for us skinners, who art dying in Hell. Hey Men."

No, Richard turned abruptly left and proceeded down a long hallway, at the end of which he could see Victor and Carmen, wearing black armbands, the only ones that night in black armbands, standing in one of two rooms that Rocco Ponte had dedicated to the affirmations of the living. Victor and Carmen in the parlor of consumption, whose door was always open, and whose table always groaned with food and drink supplied by mourners. As for the other room, the parlor of consummation, the door was at the moment closed: an act, or various acts, in progress. Or as the bookish Victor put it, just as Richard approached, and Andrea Caravaggio approached from the groaning board, one of Carmen's pastries in hand: "work in progress."

Andrea looks at her husband. Her husband averts his gaze. Andrea says, "Think I don't know which room you'd be in if I wasn't here? You bastard. But why should I care? The Prince of Mary Street is dead, and I have to look at you." Then to Victor: "And what are you looking at? I'm sick of your face, too." Then to Richard: "Why are you here? You're supposed to be with your father, not here. You turned out to be another worthless bastard!" Andrea Caravaggio walks away, cannoli in hand, to the parlor of presentation.

Victor offers Richard a black armband; Richard says "Thanks" and puts it in his pocket. Carmen removes his, puts it in his pocket. Victor looks at Carmen; Carmen puts it back on and says to Richard: "Victor says this is how we honor the old Italians who came over on the boat." Richard says, "Who?" Then Victor offers Richard a shot of Canadian Club. Richard takes it and knocks it back. Victor speaks: "The romantic poets tell us that in extreme times language is like a fading coal. In other words, it's almost useless. We can only assume that you grieve, which is impossible to tell from your face, I'm happy to say." Carmen says, "Yeah, Victor, with a face like that he could have been in the fucking Mafia." Then Victor ushers Richard, with Carmen trailing, back down the hall to the coffin. The kneeler is occupied. The three men stand there silently, gazing at the corpse. Richard whispers to Victor: "My father looks like a piece of furniture. Perfect for the Mafia." Carmen whispers to Victor: "What did he say?" Victor whispers in Carmen's ear, so Richard can't hear: "He says his father looks furious after joining the Mafia." Carmen whispers in Victor's ear, so Richard can't hear: "This poor kid is really nuts."

Victor touches Richard's hand and they walk back to the food room, where they can see that the door to the other room remains shut. Victor says, "Gentlemen, they've been in there an hour and forty minutes. Let us wait here and see who emerges from Rocco's fuckery on this solemn occasion. I happen to know who's in there. Because there is only one man in Utica who is that accomplished." Carmen grins and says, "I happen to know, too, Richie. I think Rocco better go in there with his embalming equipment, because this guy's going to fuck her to death, so help me God!" Victor says, "It would be a symbolical justice, Richard, and an honor to

256

your father, if it was you in there at this time, pumping her cunt."

A stream of mourners approaches Richard. Mostly strangers: friends of the sister, friends of the sister's husband, friends of the friends of the friends. Finally, a familiar face: "Honey, a good man like your father, Our First Father in Heaven is too stingy to share too long with this earth. Just like his only begotten son." Dora guides Richard back down the hall: "Your place is with your father. Those two don't count." Richard the walking coffin replies, "I don't think I'd care to lie in the coffin at this time." They sit in the coffin room next to the sister, receiving the mourners in the formal manner as Richard was supposed to, from the beginning. Dora says, "I notice you still haven't learned to talk in person."

"I'll show my humanity when I join him in the grave."

"You're trying to prove to me you're an asshole, and you're doing a good job, but you can't fool me."

"I don't want to fool you, Dora. I want to fuck you again."

"Why do you always use that awful word? Rocco has provided. We could go in next, even though it's not our turn, because after all it is your father, and you have rights tonight."

Then Richard's youngest male cousin: "Mommy, what does fuck mean? Can I fuck you again?" Richard is saved by another of the mourners, the one who made fun in high school of his name: Richard A Sissy. Richard Ass is I. After he moves on, Richard repeats the mocking names to Dora, who says: "Ass is I? That is not wrong." At last Richard smiles, but it's the wrong moment. And it's all that the next mourner needs to set her off, the only one from the mother's side to come to the wake. Three days later she will appear at the graveside, on Richard's left, Dora on his right, Elsie close behind him: three women supporting this collapsed

257

male body. Now she kneels with her rosary for fifteen minutes, creating a jam-up in the parlor of presentation. Muttering builds quickly to rage among those awaiting access to the body. Finally she arises and sits next to Dora. Still with rosary in hands, she starts, a whispered lament easily audible in the room: "What they did to my sister on her last day on this earth, God have mercy on these miserable people, she should have had a miscarriage, God have mercy on my soul, I never said an abortion, it should have been my nephew, not Bobby Zito, God deliver us all, now and forever, from my terrible nephew. Amen." Dora responds: "Who's Bobby Zito, if I may ask?" "Tell him Bobby Zito," the mourner says, "he knows." Dora leans into Richard's ear: "Who's Bobby Zito?" Richard leans into hers: "Somebody who long ago entertained me. A colorful kid."

The next one seeking to console, Richard can't quite place. He says to Richard, as he shakes his hand, "I'm sorry you lost your father. You don't remember me. I was his best man; I'm Joe Buono. Maybe you recall I married Dick Lentricchia's youngest sister. Please take this old picture of me and your dad. You worked for Dick, am I right?" Richard says, "I don't remember you." Joe Buono says, "I'm told Dick is here tonight." Dora, eagerly, "Oh, he's here, but he can't be seen or talked to at this time." Joe says, "I expect nothing less from my good brother-in-law." Dora says, "He's got a big heart," and suddenly she leans so that she can see all the way down the hall, and she delivers a crucial report: "The door is finally opening. Almost two hours in there!" Richard leans forward, and simultaneously so do the sister, the husband, and the kids, all seeing the door swing wide open at last to the parlor of consummation and out glides big-hearted Dick, electrical banana, dressed in a suit of midnight blue, various female heads snapping in his direction as he, the movie star, offers his hand to John Assisi's willowy girlfriend aflame, Elsie Barneveld, shattered by grief and eros, completely beautiful. Dora exclaims, "I believe they took each other around the world!" The sister of Antoinette Assisi answers, rosary still in hands: "She looks full of grace, God bless them both." Richard, responding to his mother's sister, "Dick filled her with grace, glory be to Dick Lentricchia in the highest." At which point John Assisi's sister's husband arouses himself from boredom and announces: "This has gone far enough, Conny. I don't want the kids to listen to any more of this." Conny, looking at Dick, says: "Sit down, Sebastian. You're blocking my view of Dick." Joe steps back as Dick and Elsie make their way to the kneeler together, pray briefly, make the sign of the cross, arise and approach Richard. Dick says, "It's a shame. I'll never get over it. Call me anytime of the day or night, except tonight if you can help it." Elsie, a little unsteady on her feet, "Your father was the love of my life." Dick and Joe are ready to catch her. She says, "I can stand." Then to Richard: "It would be a nice thing if we got to know each other a lot better." Then to Dick: "Take me someplace." Andrea sits quietly through it all, cannoli still in hand, untouched, staring, saying to the air: "I want to go someplace, too."

"Dora," Richard says in her ear, "my father really was crazy for my mother, wasn't he?"

"Oh, he was really crazy for her. He told me they couldn't get enough of each other. You're mature enough to hear that, aren't you? You should be so lucky, Richard. Come on, let's go down there now. We'll honor them both with an act of love."

"Let's wait a month."

"Ah, you want to be just like your father when he came to me. He waited twenty-eight days. How sweet you really are, after all is said and done. Which I knew all along."

"No. I couldn't get it up now."

"What's that got to do with it? Did I just hear what I thought I heard? What are you? Twenty-five now? I heard you're supposed to get married pretty soon. God forbid."

"Nobody's talking to Victor and Carmen. I'll see you later."

But he did not see her later. He saw Dora at the funeral. Then he never saw her again.

Two

Shortly before eleven o'clock on the evening of June 29, 1995, Richard's birthday, and he's just returned from County General's Annual Awards Banquet, stripping down quickly to his boxer shorts and donning the red robe, much too broad for him in the shoulders. He stretches out full-length on the couch. Parts the red robe. Inserts thumb and first two fingers of his right hand into the fly of his boxer shorts and commences, in long easy strokes, while with his left he picks up the remote-control device. Just in time: prosecution rests in the Simpson trial, glamor girl Lana Turner dead at seventy-five. These and more, right after this.

Richard would prefer not to. *And deliver me from ejaculation, ah men. Eleven years older than you, Dad. Who ejaculated once too often.* How had Victor said it? "Like the fine arts of mankind, Richard, an end unto itself. Stroke the flaccid thing, but seek not stiffness." Richard gazes down and says out loud in his empty house, "Flaccid thing, be thou me." A mother soothing her sleeping infant. Today in South Carolina, the judge in the Susan Smith case ruled that the formerly petite mother, who confessed to drowning her two toddler sons, is now a formidable porker at peace with her God. "I decided to commit suicide for the three of us, but then I realized at the last second, your onher, why should I let the shitters make me sink to their level?"

The hand would prefer a fuller flaccidity, but Richard would not. Richard fears the hand. Accordingly, he evacuates his mind of all erotic images. Richard is a narrow and bony ascetic of masturbation, purged except for this: *there was a young man from Nantucket, whose cock was so long he could suck it: Finest art: an end into himself. "Carmen, Send Richard the letter A in remembrance of me. Tell him look on page 837. Sincerely, VD."* A week after the funeral, it comes, volume one of the encyclopedia, and with it, Victor's last communication, Carmen's commentary beneath: "Dear Richard, Our friend lost his mind. He forgets his own initials, RIP." Richard opens to page 837. Neatly printed in the margin: "It should have been here. Your scarlet letter. Your genius. Insert here entry on autolingus." Richard thinks "autolingus." The hand is happier. He needs to defecate. He's remembering something strange said by Diane, a philosophical paradox, with pleasant pressure in his rectum, wonderful really. Bony Richard rises robeless, removes his boxer shorts, and walks naked to the toilet. As he squats, sudden and magnificent tumescence, cock big and alive, bobbing above the seat. Is it possible that he will come and defecate at the same time? Is this the promised end? "Richard, you love me. You just don't know you love me." But if he doesn't know, then just who is it that loves Diane? Is he not Richard? Several turds, how easily they slide, slip free, perfectly formed dropping down: little splashes on the balls. Shit water on the balls.

Since my fiftieth. Fifty years of gravity. He imagines himself at eighty, the balls breaking the surface, swimming with the shit *flush the balls, too.* He does not wipe, not yet, he does not flush, because he needs to look, he wants a clear view twisting and looking back down in there rising and *what was that in there?* *Me, myself, godlike in a wreath of turds* and memories of what he'd achieved frequently in the days before Dora inflame him huge approaching the blasting point, looking down the barrel, with his jaw hanging open, this nestling about to be fed. Beat off into a bowl of shit. Which will it be? His cock or the toilet lever? The hand strokes long and easy: once twice thrice on the verge of the verge of the verge with superhuman will he flushes in the nick of time and they swirl away, his dark-hued progeny, and detumescence is come again. Oh fie upon it! There at the very tip of his existence, he spies it. Oh fie! The pearl of his eye. With his forefinger he wipes off his failure. He licks it, relieved on his way to the kitchen with a toilet tissue tucked under his cock, fearing mixed drippage of urine and lurking semen, right hand of the bag of bones maintaining tissue under cock as left goes deep into the cookie jar, removing perhaps a dozen Fig Newtons in one fell plunge for the coffee table, the one between the couch and the TV, resuming prone position on the couch without drippage, fastidious rattling bones settling in again, *not young, not nearly limber enough, alas! Victor's utopia. Gymnasts luckiest among humankind. Suck their own selves at will. To fuck the self. And I myself am woman.*

Doctor Richard Assisi, tonight named County General's Physician of the Year, that and more, right after this message from our sponsors: he chews, he strokes, he takes in the segment on Lana Turner, waiting for the newscaster to say what she'll best be remembered for. Waiting for the name to ring out again after all these years. Johnny Stompanato. *One of us, Richard, but not one of us. A beautiful Italian.* Stormy romance with the husky, the handsome, the dark-haired gangster killed in Lana's bedroom by the daughter, a fourteen-year-old (*a fourteen-year-old!*), a skinny girl who ran him through, ramming Johnny Eager deep with ten inches of kitchen knife. But Victor! She was so skinny! A fucking girl! Unbelievable! And Victor laughing: "You're skinny and unbelievable, but not a girl, to the best of our knowledge. Are you a fucking girl, Richard? Our Johnny was said to be brutal. But in his work he's insulated from the alternative sex. Everything is relative. He's out of his depth, particularly when he's into theirs. True or false? My theory says he's fucking them both. They do threesomes. The Bad and the Beautiful. Lana and daughter: American females insatiable for the Italian sausage. They're fucking Johnny day and night. He begins to have trouble. Don't make me say the word. As a distraction he forces the daughter to eat the mother, or I'll bite the nipples off your tits. Johnny thinks of himself as a vicious person. Upon his command to suck her mother, the daughter's cunt flows. Richard, The Flame and the Flesh. Johnny says, Your mother gives better blow jobs. He figures, Now they'll throw me out for sure. In front of Lana he says this. Lana loves it. She says, Cheryl, honey, watch how I do it, and she unzips him gobblegobblegobble. This is the cue. The kid goes to the kitchen and waits a little, letting Lana work her art for a couple of minutes, because she knows Johnny's cock is loathe to rise again, the cock wants a day off, and then she hears him say Oh Christ and returns running at him as he's hitting the verge. He's Betrayed. The man is a tremendous romantic, By Love Possessed. He refuses to defend himself. Fuck it. I'll come first.

After, Cheryl says to Lana, Aw, Mommy, that's not fair. You swallowed it all. You were supposed to save some, you bitch. The blow job was planned. Okay. We take as a given he beat the shit out of them both. But the abuse, if that's what it is, does not set the plan into motion. Wake up and smell the coffee, Richard. The guy has the biggest heterosexual cock in Hollywood, and in the Land of Faggotry herein lies the rod to forgiveness. But after a point Johnny says, Hey, I am but a man. He can put out on a daily basis only for so long. You follow? *Ecce homo.* Richard, they will take any amount of physical abuse as long as we put out cock in corresponding proportions. You want a slave? Fuck them on a daily basis. Daily. You want to be murdered by one of them? Physical or psychical what's the difference? Start on a daily basis then stop. Unlike Johnny you are not strong, you are not beautiful, you are not animalistic, you are not vicious. But what am I saying? Neither was Johnny vicious. Our tragic flaw is we think we're vicious. You are not olive-skinned either, though for all I know you may be very well hung. This I know: You will not die a romantic death. And this too I know: You will live forever, and America won't get moist off your memory. On occasion you'll be remembered by your loved ones. Even if you are well hung, so what? Consider our Johnny. Consider the Stomp man."

The newscaster does not mention the name of the handsome gangster.

Richard rolls onto his right side. He lets go of his cock in order to rub his eye with the back of his right hand, gently working in the first knuckle. He pulls the afghan over his naked body. Right hand back to cock, still fattened after the bout with toilet tumescence. Left hand clenched loosely, tucked under chin. He's had enough of Fig Newtons. Thinks in despair: *the carpet.* Crumbs again. He will not vacuum until morning. This is a very difficult decision for him, but he makes it, and he's pleased with himself. He considers it a change in a healthy direction, an onset of latent humanity. He says out loud, "I have been inhuman." The thought does not displease greatly. He's half in love with the idea of his inhumanity. He's imagining the next morning already, his splendid vacuum cleaner, of "industrial strength," as Diane said, sucking up the crumbs, and the special set of brushes he uses for the toilet: a soft one, like a baby's ass, for the seat; a cruel-looking thing for under the rim; and for the bowl a standard job which Richard has dismantled and refitted with an extra-long and flexible handle, so much the better for reaching far down into the very hole itself. The fourth brush is a toothbrush (left by Diane) for the tiny crevice that had opened disturbingly at the front edge of the base, a conse-quence of constant flushing. Richard is the type who will flush just because he happens to be in the vicinity. *Might as well stop in and flush. Can't hurt.* He sees himself place two room deodorizers in each room of his house. A little wave of tranquillity washes over him as he plans his house-cleaning duties. New idea: disinfectant full strength for the closet floors, once a week. Back turned to TV, right hand still on cock. Our weekly review of the Simpson trial next. *Cheryl licking her mother while you're at it crawl back in. Walked in on her in the nude once and only once. Our Lady of Utica. Year she died. Covered herself not that quickly. I saw you a million times naked, sweetheart, all in the family.* He touches the tip of his cock for drippage. He's concerned about getting it on the afghan. First year in med school playing with it he couldn't stop and came hard into the afghan. He loved it in those days when he discovered that if he did it lying down, he could point it up

266

and watch it come on his abdomen: muzzle velocity and semen temperature experienced from another point of view with a lubricated finger shoved up his ass. Those were the days before Marilyn Lake, whose brains he could not fuck out. Those were the days. *Shit. Hard again. Shit.* He stops. He thinks of the woodchuck, spotted once again after nine months of absence. He would establish a bond. *Dora at Dad's grave.* Redness of his eyes, not grief but booze, his breath stinking. Obvious and offensive boredom. False *Pietà:* Three women supporting a hung-over male. Dora's last words, whispered fiercely in his ear: "You have no bonds. How could those two have created you?" His reply, grinning: "Like Mary and Joseph. The parents must not be blamed."

That night he'll dream happily of the woodchuck living in the house. The woodchuck in the kitchen, cooking in an apron. He decides to make a gesture. He goes in his naked-ness to the refrigerator for an economy-sized bag of carrots. Returns to TV room. Shuts down power. Returns to kitchen for a trash bag. Returns to TV room and fills trash bag with countless Orenthal tapes. Walks out naked into the night with carrot bag and trash bag. Dumps trash bag into barrel and then begins to lay a trail from his back door across the yard to where the lawn dips down to the woods' edge, where, a year ago, he located the burrow. Down on all fours. For a second, recalls Diane's warning that, unless he's on guard, "the chuckster" will "fuck you up the ass." Nose to ground. Yes. Urine. Scent of a woodchuck. Yes. Not enough carrots. Returns to kitchen, raids fridge for assorted vegeta-bles. Finishes job.

From a point high above scene, a certain ambiguity, not accessible to Richard, who believes he lays one-way tempta-tion from burrow to house.

Returns to house, at a loss. Stands there.

Antoinette, John, Victor. Dead and decomposed.

Dora, Elsie, Diane. Missing in action.

Imagines turds in toilet, moving with sluggish intention.

Drapes afghan over shoulders.

Today: Thursday. Richard's birthday.

Turdsday.

Standing.

Lights out.

Standing, TV room.

Glasses off.

Afghan off.

Afghan on.

Afghan off.

Left hand to penis; right to anus.

See Richard.

Stooping, open-jawed.

Curving inward.

Curved.

Eating himself alive.

See Richard eat.

See Richard.